A SEAL'S CONSENT

By Cora Seton

Author's Note

A SEAL's Consent is the fourth volume in the SEALs of Chance Creek series, set in the fictional town of Chance Creek, Montana. To find out more about Boone, Clay, Jericho and Walker, look for the rest of the books in the series, including:

A SEAL's Oath

A SEAL's Vow

A SEAL's Pledge

A SEAL's Purpose

A SEAL's Resolve

A SEAL's Devotion

A SEAL's Desire

A SEAL's Struggle

A SEAL's Triumph

Also, don't miss Cora Seton's other Chance Creek series, the Cowboys of Chance Creek, the Heroes of Chance Creek, and the Brides of Chance Creek

The Cowboys of Chance Creek Series:

The Cowboy Inherits a Bride (Volume 0)
The Cowboy's E-Mail Order Bride (Volume 1)
The Cowboy Wins a Bride (Volume 2)

The Cowboy Imports a Bride (Volume 3)
The Cowgirl Ropes a Billionaire (Volume 4)
The Sheriff Catches a Bride (Volume 5)
The Cowboy Lassos a Bride (Volume 6)
The Cowboy Rescues a Bride (Volume 7)
The Cowboy Earns a Bride (Volume 8)
The Cowboy's Christmas Bride (Volume 9)

The Heroes of Chance Creek Series:

The Navy SEAL's E-Mail Order Bride (Volume 1)
The Soldier's E-Mail Order Bride (Volume 2)
The Marine's E-Mail Order Bride (Volume 3)
The Navy SEAL's Christmas Bride (Volume 4)
The Airman's E-Mail Order Bride (Volume 5)

The Brides of Chance Creek Series:

Issued to the Bride One Navy SEAL
Issued to the Bride One Airman
Issued to the Bride One Marine
Issued to the Bride One Sniper
Issued to the Bride One Soldier

Visit Cora's website at www.coraseton.com
Find Cora on Facebook at facebook.com/CoraSeton
Sign up for my newsletter HERE.
www.coraseton.com/sign-up-for-my-newsletter

PROLOGUE

Three Months Ago

"I BET YOU'LL miss."

Navy SEAL Jericho Cook smiled at the beautiful woman bracing her hands on the table across from him, waiting to see if he could sink his quarter into the empty glass set halfway between them. Given the circumstances, he could have been at one of the dive bars he'd frequented throughout his military career, but he wasn't. He'd left the Navy twenty-four hours earlier, and now found himself back home in the town where he'd grown up—hiding in the kitchen at a formal dinner party given by an older couple who were by far the oddest people he'd ever met.

Barely twenty feet away in the Russells' immaculate, antique-filled parlor, the other guests chatted and entertained each other by taking turns playing an impressive grand piano, as if they'd stepped back in time two hundred years. Their host and hostess were dressed in perfect Regency attire—as they always were. James and Maud had informed Jericho earlier they'd decided years ago to live a Jane Austen–style life, and their clothes, their house and the horse-drawn carriages they used to get around Chance Creek all fit the early 1800s time period.

Many of the female guests were in Regency dress, too, including Savannah Edwards, the blonde egging him on from across the table. She had taken her turn at the piano just minutes ago, and had impressed him with her considerable talent before slipping away with him to the kitchen. She'd come to Montana with her friends Riley Eaton, Avery Lightfoot and Nora Ridgeway to spend six months at Westfield, the ranch that had been in Riley's family for well over a century. They planned to concentrate on the artistic and musical pursuits they'd given up since their college days—donning Regency outfits to remind themselves daily of their pledge to forgo anything that distracted them from their goals. When they'd arrived, they hadn't known Riley's uncle had already sold the ranch to an eccentric billionaire named Martin Fulsom—or that Fulsom had given it to Jericho and his buddies as a place to build Base Camp, their sustainable community.

They did now.

What they didn't realize was that Jericho and the others had to pass a series of difficult requirements, or lose Westfield to a developer. One of those requirements was that all four men had to marry.

Jericho figured he'd just found his bride.

Savannah leaned closer, and Jericho stopped thinking about pianos, the Russells or the sustainable community he was supposed to help build. He stopped thinking of Boone Rudman, Clay Pickett and Walker Norton—the three other Navy SEALs he'd joined to launch this endeavor. He stopped thinking about Fulsom and all his ridiculous demands—and the reality TV show they'd all soon be a part of, although the women didn't know that, either.

Instead, he focused solely on Savannah. The way she was trying to distract him.

Framed by her deep blue gown, plumped up by some old-fashioned corset contraption, her breasts were something to behold. When she leaned against the table, it was hard to look anywhere else.

"I won't miss," he assured her, even as his pulse beat a little faster. It had been a long time since he'd been with a woman, and Savannah was stunning.

Funny.

Smart.

Amazing.

Perfect wife material—now that he had to have one.

When they'd met, her lively conversation had drawn him in as she'd alternately enthused about Westfield, poked fun at her deadly dull job back in California and hinted about her aspirations to become a renowned concert pianist. Everything about her had intrigued him; especially her excitement about living in Chance Creek.

Which is why he needed to make this shot. Savannah had promised him a kiss if he did.

And he wanted that kiss.

"Big talk, sailor. Let's see what you've got."

Her trash talk didn't bother him. His prowess at quarters was legendary. His father had taught him to play the game—minus the alcohol—when he was nine, and Jericho had taken to it like a fish to water. He had a steady hand and good aim, and practice makes perfect, as they say. He rarely lost.

Savannah bent a little lower. She *was* trying to distract him. Jericho bit back the grin attempting to spread across his face. He was enjoying himself. And so was she. Savannah had already tipped back two shots of tequila after he'd sunk his first two quarters. He had a feeling she was celebrating her new life at Westfield as much as he was. He needed to focus.

She needed to stand up.

Time to turn the tables on her. "What does your family think about your career choice?" No one could flirt while they answered that.

Savannah made a face and straightened. "They don't even know where I am."

Jericho bounced the quarter off the table as soon as she began to talk.

Sunk it.

"Drink up," he told her. But her words stuck with him. "Why doesn't your family know where you are?" Why would a woman so intelligent and determined hide from her parents? Everything he'd seen so far—except this drinking game, which was all his fault—had shown her to be a responsible, caring individual.

Savannah knocked back the shot, wiped her mouth with the back of her hand and pursed her lips when she'd swallowed the fiery liquid. "We'd probably better get back before the others notice we're gone... and that we've raided the liquor cabinet."

"The Russells won't mind."

"The help might." She nodded toward the gleaming dishes piled high with food on the far end of the table, covered and ready to be carried out as soon as the party sat down to dinner. The Russells had hired a local woman to prepare and serve the meal. Mrs. Wood, who wore a Regency-inspired cook's uniform, had bustled out of the kitchen to serve drinks a few minutes ago, but she'd be back any time.

"First I want that kiss." Jericho drank his own shot, placed it back on the table, screwed the cap on the tequila bottle and tucked it back into the cabinet where they'd found it. He threaded an arm around Savannah's waist, tugged her out of the large kitchen and into a side hall where they wouldn't be seen. He leaned her against the wall, prepared for her to push him away and escape back into the parlor, but Savannah smiled up at him as if she didn't mind in the slightest.

"Why are you hiding from your family?" He braced his feet to either side of her and placed his palms on the wall, caging her in. He couldn't wait for that kiss much longer. Now that he'd let himself think about a woman, his body had unleashed all its pent-up desire for physical companionship.

"Not just my family. From my ex-fiancé. I don't love him. I never loved him. My parents do, though. They have this idea about me." She smiled again but this time it didn't reach her eyes. "That I can be the cement to hold our two families together. Just like in an old-fashioned novel." She lifted the skirts of her gown and smoothed them back into place. "My family is new money. His family is old money. A match made in heaven."

Jericho swallowed and pulled back. He was unprepared for the jealousy that surged through him. She had a fiancé? Even an ex-fiancé was a complication he hadn't looked for, and he found he didn't like the idea of another man hanging around Savannah.

Savannah leaned toward him. "I finally came to my senses and left that all behind. I'm free—for the first time in years." She put her hands on his chest. Jericho's libido ratcheted up a notch. The alcohol had warmed him—made him feel a little reckless. "I didn't want any part of the life they were building for me," she went on. "I can't think why I didn't act sooner. It was like I was under a spell. But now I'm here—in Chance Creek. Everything's changed. I'm going to do it. By this time next year I'll be a concert pianist. No one can stop me." She leaned up on her tiptoes and kissed him.

Jericho's instincts took over. There was a soft, warm, lovely woman in his arms. A woman who was kissing him.

A woman he intended to marry, ex-fiancé or no ex-fiancé.

He kissed her back and tried to shut off the worries that had plagued him these past few months. In three short weeks a reality TV film crew would descend on them to capture every moment of the process of building this community. He couldn't screw up.

As his body responded to Savannah's closeness, he suppressed a chuckle. He'd thought the need to marry would be the hardest goal to reach.

But maybe it would be the easiest.

Savannah shifted in his arms, and those wonderful breasts of hers pressed against his chest.

Jericho savored the touch of her mouth on his. Her lips were soft, and when they parted to let him in, his body fired up with a quick, hot desire.

He wanted her. Whatever the future might hold. And this hallway wasn't nearly private enough. He spotted an open door, linked his arm around Savannah's waist again and whisked her inside a large, spotless bathroom. The marble counter was impeccable. The throw rugs lush and soft. Savannah deserved better, but short of sweeping her off to a motel, where her old-fashioned clothing would garner a lot of interest, he had nowhere else to take her. Back at Westfield, he and his friends were camping in tents near the old bunkhouse. Savannah and her friends had claimed the old stone home at the top of the hill for their own. Would she invite him to the *manor*, as they called it?

He didn't know.

And he wasn't willing to wait and find out.

He caught sight of himself in the mirror, the shine of desire in his eyes. This was reckless. Savannah did deserve more. He should stop now, bring her back out to the party and pursue this another time, when he could do it right.

"That all you got in you, sailor? Just one little kiss?" Savannah taunted him. She ran her hands down his chest, around to his back and down again to rest on his ass, before giving him a hard squeeze.

Hell. Jericho tossed his qualms away. He had a lot more than that. And if she was willing, so was he. Sometimes it was best not to question things too carefully. He had a hunch Savannah didn't flirt with strange men all that often. She was too well bred. Too beautiful. Too confident. She was the kind of woman you got your ducks in a line to impress. The kind of woman you wined and dined and went to museums and art gallery openings with, even if you could care less about any of those things.

He pushed Savannah up against the bathroom door and boxed her in with his body again, still continuing the kiss. She wanted to see what he had to give her? He'd play along. He braced his hands on her hips, covered her mouth with his own and went to town. Soon they were both breathing hard, as he let his tongue enjoy the depths of her mouth. She tasted so sweet he wanted more. Much more. But surely Savannah would stop him soon.

When he pulled back, however, she laced her arms around his neck and came after him.

She must really want to erase that engagement from her mind, he thought as he tightened his hold on her. Whoever had put his ring on her finger had nearly stifled the life out of her. Now she wanted to put him in the past. Just for a moment, jealousy burned again at the base of Jericho's throat. He didn't want to be a palate cleanser between other men as far as Savannah was concerned.

He wanted her.

And he wanted her to want *him*.

So far, all he'd told her about himself was that he'd served in the Navy, he was interested in green energy sources and he was interested in her. Now she needed to know he was a man to reckon with.

But before he could make a move, Savannah began to unbutton his shirt.

It threw him off, but only for a second. Jericho chuckled. "You're playing with fire, you know."

"Oh, you haven't seen anything yet."

He forced himself to wait as she undid button after button, wanting nothing more than to rip off the shirt and toss it away. When she smoothed the fabric back and placed her palms on his chest, he sucked in a breath.

Hell. If she wasn't prepared to follow through, he was going to have a hard time heading back to that dinner party.

"Jericho, we don't have much time." Savannah pressed her lips to the hollow at the base of his throat and he bit back a groan.

"I know, sweetheart. But we can meet later—"

"No. Not later. Now." She looked up at him, her expression serious.

Jericho pulled back. It was what he wanted, of course, but he hadn't really thought she'd go through with it. "Now—?"

"Right now." She nodded at him. Bit her lip.

Jericho fought for restraint. "Right now?"

"I've never done anything like this. But I want to. I want—I want you. Because I just want you—for no other reason. I want to feel an impulse and carry it through. Do you understand that?"

Two years ago Jericho would have said, "Hell, yeah." He wasn't uptight about his body, or sex, or any of it. But after the disaster in Yemen he'd wanted something… more. And given that now he had to find a wife, it seemed like Fate wanted that for him, too.

So how ironic to find himself with a beautiful, willing woman and actually consider saying no.

"Honey, are you—"

"Have you ever been so thoroughly misunderstood you nearly lost yourself?" she blurted.

He swallowed hard. Oh, yeah. He knew that feeling.

"Have you ever found yourself living a life and you couldn't understand how you got there?"

"Yeah," he managed to say.

"Then, please—please. Make love to me. Because I want you to. No strings attached. No future. No— nothing. Just… fun," Savannah begged him. "Please. It's important."

He was only a man, Jericho reminded himself as he gave in.

A man half enthralled by the bewitching woman who'd lifted onto her tiptoes to kiss the underside of his chin. What if he wanted strings attached, he asked himself as Savannah tugged his shirt right off him.

What if he wanted a future—with her?

Then he'd better make her happy, he decided and spun her around to try to get her gown off her. Confronted with a complicated set of ties and fastenings, he wasn't sure where to begin.

"We don't have time for that," Savannah said. She fiddled with the neckline of her dress, still turned away from him, then pulled his arms around her and lifted his hands to cover her now-exposed breasts. Jericho groaned out loud as his palms covered them. They were heavy in his hands, her nipples hard. Jericho lifted and squeezed them gently and Savannah's breathing hitched. She braced herself against the door. "Oh, that feels good."

Jericho edged up against her, no longer working to hide how much she'd turned him on. Pressing his body against hers, he knew she could feel his hardness through his jeans and her skirts. He decided not to question this gift Fate had given him. Savannah wanted to erase her past.

She wanted him to erase it.

He'd play along—and enjoy the hell out of the journey.

And do his damnedest to convince her along the way she wanted much, much more than a one-night stand.

THIS WAS WHAT she wanted.

Passion.

Desire.

Hot, racy encounters with a man who wanted her as much as she wanted him.

Not the cold, calm, calculated wooing of the man her parents had chosen for her—a man who liked her well enough, but not any more than he would have cared for half a dozen other wealthy Silicon Valley socialites.

She didn't want calm or calculated or safe. She didn't want to be tucked into a cocoon and protected from the ups and downs of the world—a pretty toy to hang on a man's arm while he furthered the empire their two families wanted to build.

She wanted raw lust. Overpowering desire. Sex so hot and heavy it melted all her defenses.

Someday she wanted love, marriage—all that entailed. But only with a man who set her heart racing and pulse beating and made her hungry for life.

A man like Jericho.

She couldn't believe how bold she was being. How she'd lured him into drinking too much, how she'd bet on the quarters game, lost on purpose and now was begging him to make love to her.

She didn't know what she'd do if he said no.

But Jericho was never going to say no. Not to her. He wanted what she had to offer—a no-strings-attached encounter was right up the SEAL's alley. She'd heard his friends joking about the way his good looks attracted all kinds of women. She bet he had a string of girlfriends.

She didn't care.

All she wanted was this once. Or maybe a few times; Jericho looked like a lot of fun. Whatever it took to get Charles Scott out of her mind once and for all. She was done with him, done with California, done with her family and their machinations.

She was Savannah Edwards. Pianist. Prepared to take on the world. With an audition in just under four months with the world famous virtuoso Alfred Redding. She would dazzle him—make him take her under his wing—let him introduce her to the world and start her brilliant career, at last.

But first she was going to make passionate love to Jericho Cook, Navy SEAL, in the Russells' mauve bathroom. She'd blow his mind.

And then she'd take the world by storm.

But when Jericho cupped her breasts and squeezed, she lost all thought of the world, her debut, her audition and music in general.

"Oh—"

He seemed to take her indrawn breath as an invitation, scooped her breasts higher and ran his thumbs over her sensitive nipples until Savannah thought her knees would give out. He pressed closer to her and she could feel the length of him hard against her. Soon he'd be inside her. The thought of it turned her muscles molten.

"How do I get this dress off?" he whispered into her ear, his want—and need—all too evident in the roughness of his voice.

"You don't. We don't have time." Regency gowns,

not to mention the stays she wore under hers, were far too complicated for that.

She reached down and began to lift her skirts. It was the only way.

Jericho palmed and squeezed her breasts, pressing kisses up and down her neck and shoulders. She was so hot—so aching at the thought of taking him inside, she didn't need any foreplay. Sex had never seemed so simple before. Charles had always had to coax her.

But with Jericho it was different—maybe because she had chosen him, culled him from the herd, made her play for him—

Won him.

Jericho pulled back and looked down as she lifted her skirts around her waist, and she swore she could feel the heat of his gaze on her bottom. "Oh, sweetheart—" His tone was reverent and she could guess why. She wore old-fashioned garters and stockings with her stays—and nothing else.

She'd come to dinner knowing exactly what she wanted.

He moved a hand from one of her breasts and slid it between her legs, his palm pressing hard against the part of her that wanted him the most. As he teased and touched her, she grew even more turned on. He had to know it. Savannah felt shameless, unafraid to show this man exactly how much she wanted him.

"You are so hot," he murmured against her neck, and without her asking him to, he kicked off his shoes, unzipped his jeans and tugged everything down until he was naked behind her. He placed his hands on her hips and positioned himself.

So she wasn't going to have to beg the SEAL.

Why did she feel disappointed?

A flash of herself kneeling before Jericho, taking him into her mouth, flushed her hot with wanting him. He bumped up against her and she closed her eyes, wanting to feel him inside.

Jericho groaned again. "Baby, I don't have a condom."

"I'm on the Pill. I'm safe." If he stopped now, she'd scream and bring everyone running.

"Me, too—just had a checkup." He nudged against her again. "But are you sure? There are other things we can do—"

"Jericho!" She braced her hands against the door, and pushed back against him.

Jericho didn't protest. Instead he braced a hand on the door above hers, clamped the other one on her hip and pushed inside.

Savannah let out a rough sigh.

He paused, just for a moment, before easing out and into her again. Savannah hung her head, her eyes closed, lost in the sensation of him.

"All right?" he gasped.

"Wonderful."

His masculine chuckle nearly undid her. He was pleased.

He should be.

He was amazing. Everything she wanted from a

fling—

Everything she wanted—

As Jericho moved again, his slow slide out and in nearly brought her to her knees, distracting her from that last disturbing thought.

She didn't want a man in her life. Not in a serious way. A permanent way.

Fun, yes—that was fine.

She had time for nothing more.

But as Jericho made love to her, Savannah felt her control of the situation slipping fast. She had been the one to hunt him down, she reminded herself. This was her fling.

But he was the one spinning her into a dizzy tumble of pure desire. She wanted what he was doing to her. Would never get enough. Wanted him to touch her. Wanted him to make her scream.

She was moaning, she realized. Making sounds she'd never made before as Jericho did wonderful things to her, filling her, drawing away and pushing back inside again. When he lowered his hand from the door back to her breasts, teasing and caressing her nipples, driving deeper into her, faster—harder, she braced herself firmly, panting with need, and slipped ever further under his command.

No man had made love to her like this. No man had made her forget everything else. She was pure emotion—pure heat.

Pure passion.

And she couldn't get enough.

Savannah braced harder against the door. Jericho filled her further, moving fast inside her. He caught both her breasts in one hand. Squeezed—

And she crashed over the edge with a cry she buried against her arm. Jericho came with her in a series of thrusts so hard they lifted her off her feet as her orgasm washed through her. Lost in ecstasy, tossed in the waves of her release, she didn't come back to earth until Jericho hugged her close, holding her until her tremors stopped. He pulled out carefully, but her legs didn't want to support her and she sagged against the door until he turned her around and held her in his arms.

"Hell," he breathed. "That was… something."

Savannah laughed. "Yes, it was." How long had they taken? She didn't know if they'd been gone from the party for minutes or hours. "Guess we'd better get back."

But when she moved, Jericho held her in place. "I want more," he said simply. "Got that, Savannah Edwards? I'm not satisfied. Not by a long shot."

She shivered. *Because of the cool air*, she told herself. Not because of a trace of premonition that whispered down her spine. Jericho was hot. He was amazing. He was the perfect partner for her fling.

But a fling was all this was.

She didn't have room in her life for anything else.

Even if Jericho was bending down to kiss her again.

Even if she was going up on tiptoe to kiss him back.

CHAPTER ONE

Present Day

"SINCE WE'RE ALL gathered anyway, might as well draw straws for the next victim," Boone said. Jericho, standing near the doorway of the old bunkhouse that formed the headquarters for Base Camp, the sustainable community they'd been building these past few months at Westfield, hesitated as he put his arm into the coat of his old-fashioned Revolutionary War uniform, then finished the task, yanking it all the way on. Harris Wentworth was marrying Samantha Smith in a matter of hours, and it had become customary for the men to don the old-fashioned uniforms to match the women's Regency gowns.

A lot had changed since he'd arrived in Chance Creek in May. Now it was August. More men had joined Base Camp—including Harris. The tenure of the reality television show had jumped from six months to a year. With two couples married, and another wedding happening today, it was time to figure out who would come next. After all, according to Fulsom's demands, they had to televise a wedding every forty days.

There was an uncomfortable shuffling as the yet-to-be-married men contemplated their future. Cameramen, grouped tightly around them as usual to gather footage for the next episode, honed in on the straws Boone had produced in his hand. *Base Camp* always had high ratings, but the wedding episodes garnered the most attention.

"Walker, Jericho, Curtis, Kai, Angus, Greg and Anders, come on down. Let's see who's up next." Boone wasn't going to let anyone off the hook. Jericho caught Harris grinning, and guessed the man was glad his future was secure.

Jericho's wasn't.

When he'd had his way with Savannah in the Russells' bathroom—or when Savannah had had her way with him; he still wasn't exactly sure who had been in charge of that encounter—he'd thought it was the start of something fun and satisfying. The start of something permanent.

He'd been wrong.

For a couple of weeks it was simply time and circumstances that had worked against them. They'd teased and flirted with each other, but didn't get the chance to be together again. He and his friends had worked on their community. She and hers were starting their Jane Austen experiment. He'd been okay with being patient.

But when Boone confessed to Riley about the reality television show and the crazy goals the men had to meet to keep Westfield, all of the women became furious. Including Savannah. She'd backed right off and refused to be more than civil to him ever since.

He couldn't blame her; he and the others should have told them all of it from the start. After all, the women wanted to keep Westfield as much as the men did. Months had passed since that fight, though—an entire summer through which Jericho had waited for Savannah to relent. Riley hadn't just forgiven Boone for his part in the deception; she'd married him. Nora had married Clay. Today Harris and Samantha would get hitched, but they didn't count; Sam had known from day one the nature of the arrangement when she came to Chance Creek, unlike Savannah.

Still, Savannah held back. She'd softened a little in the last few weeks. He'd managed to sit with her at a meal or two, engage her in pleasant conversation, even flirt a tiny bit.

None of that satisfied him, however.

He wanted her to be his wife.

Jericho swallowed as Angus drew first. The straw was long and Angus frowned. Maybe he was ready to get on with marrying Win Lisle; the two had been an item for months. Kai Green and Greg Devon drew next. Theirs were both long, too. Curtis Lloyd drew a long straw, and exhaled visibly. Anders Olsen drew another one.

"It's down to Walker and Jericho," Boone said. "And rightly so. One of the founders should marry next."

"Don't know about that," Jericho said, wiping his damp palms down the homespun fabric of his breeches. "Seems we're all in this together."

"And everyone drew their straw, fair and square." Boone thrust his fist in front of Walker's face. "Don't think keeping quiet is going to make me forget you," he said. "Isn't it time to put Avery out of her misery?"

Walker shot Boone a long, brooding look, but reached out and grasped one of the straws. Everyone knew Avery liked Walker. It was a lot harder to guess Walker's intentions.

He hesitated, and Jericho held his breath. When Walker finally tugged a straw out of Boone's grasp, he held it up so everyone could see it was long.

"Well, hell." Jericho flushed hot, then cold as Boone handed him the remaining straw. Half the length of the others, it was dry and brittle in Jericho's hand. He swallowed again. "Guess it was bound to happen sooner or later. Would've liked it to be later, though," he managed to say. His feet propelled him out the door before he knew that he had moved. Once going, he couldn't seem to stop.

He'd drawn the short straw. He had to marry next.

What if Savannah wouldn't have him?

He marched blindly up the hill toward the manor, where the wedding was to be held, his long strides eating up the ground as his mind swirled with conflicting thoughts. On the one hand, maybe it was time to grab the bull by the horns and find out what was going on with Savannah. On the other hand, if he couldn't convince her to give him a chance, he didn't know what he'd do.

At least Base Camp and the manor were in shape for the wedding. Only a few weeks ago, there'd been a riot here. The old greenhouse had burned down and the gardens had been destroyed. Thank goodness they'd had help to put it all to rights. They were all proud of the brand-new greenhouse, and you could barely tell the gardens had been replanted with donations from one of the local shops.

"Good—I'm glad you're here. I need some help." Mia Matheson blocked his way, scuttling backward when Jericho nearly railroaded right over her. "Jericho?"

"Sorry. Wasn't watching where I was going." He looked around in a daze, realized he'd reached the manor already and tried to focus on the wedding planner in front of him. Mia was petite, with long, dark hair pulled back into a ponytail high on her head.

"The tables are all in place, but I need the chairs set up. Can you help?"

"Sure." He had to get a grip. No matter what he faced in the next month and a half, it was Harris's wedding day today, and he meant to make sure it went well for his friend.

Mia pointed to the chairs. "Six per table. Thanks."

Jericho got to work. He couldn't slow his thoughts, however. Where was Savannah now? What would she do when she found out?

"Jericho?"

Jericho groaned aloud as Renata Ludlow stalked up,

a camera crew not far behind.

Of course she'd come to find him. The reality television show director had a nose for ferreting out trouble wherever it sprung up, and liked nothing better than to document it—especially if she could humiliate one of them in the process.

"Back off, Renata—I've got work to do." Her interference was the last thing Jericho needed right now. Maybe the wedding would make Savannah receptive to hearing him out for once. He'd have to try. He had very little time to get her on his side now.

"Not when I just heard the news. You drew the short straw. Your life's about to change! Marriage and children."

Jericho forced himself to grab another chair. Marriage—sure. Children?

Never.

As if she'd heard his thoughts, Savannah stepped out of the manor, followed by Regan Hall, who lived on one of the nearby ranches. Savannah was cradling Regan's infant son, Hugh.

"Babies," Renata mused in her sharp, East Coast accent, following his glance. "You could say they define your life, couldn't you?"

Jericho jerked his attention back to her and shook his head in disbelief. Babies define his life? She had to be kidding.

He did whatever he could to avoid babies—and children. Always had—

Well, not quite always.

Ignoring Renata, he unfolded another chair and pushed it into place.

"Your split with your family. Your trauma from your time in Yemen. Both of those have to do with children." Renata ticked them off her fingers.

Jericho worked faster. "How do you know about any of that?" He'd borne the brunt of Renata's inquisitions before, but not like this. He supposed he'd have to be prepared to be the center of attention on the next few episodes. Renata liked to see what made people tick. She liked to expose their deepest fears to the world. That got ratings up and lots of comments on the show's website. She always focused on the couple who would marry next. Interspersing their story among the rest of the happenings on the show.

"I have my sources. You're going to have to marry soon, and then everyone will expect you and your wife to try for a child," she pointed out.

She was right. Fulsom's demand that they all marry was outrageous enough. His demand that at least three of the women be pregnant by the time the show ended went far beyond the pale, as far as Jericho was concerned.

And yet Boone and Riley were trying for a child. So were Clay and Nora. Harris and Sam hadn't hidden their desire for kids, either.

Jericho wasn't like them. He'd marry Savannah—because he wanted to, not because he had to. But he counted on her obsession with her career to make her just as resistant to children as he was.

"Have anyone in mind?" Renata asked archly, following his gaze.

"No."

Renata wasn't one to back down, so he was surprised when she said, "All right. Why don't we talk about your cousin, Donovan, instead?"

"Fuck that." Jericho shouldered past the dark-haired woman and set up another chair. He'd never discuss Donovan on television. His cousin was off-limits.

"Then let's talk about Savannah." Renata kept up with him somehow in her ridiculous heels. She always dressed for a New York boardroom, even though she was directing the filming on a Montana ranch. The way she tottered around on her high heels, sooner or later she'd turn an ankle, or worse, Jericho thought.

"What about me?" Savannah turned their way, Hugh still cradled in her arms.

"Are you aware Jericho drew the short straw and has to marry next?" Renata asked her.

Jericho wished he could decipher the emotions chasing each other across Savannah's face as the cameras focused on her. Surprise, concern, wariness—and something else. Something like... fear?

His stomach sank. How could she turn her back on him so easily when their encounter in the Russells' bathroom had been so—

Jericho wrenched his mind from the memory. If he thought about it now, Renata would read the truth of it on his face, and so far they'd managed to keep their secret.

Savannah opened her mouth, but she couldn't seem to find anything to say.

"How could she know?" Jericho asked to cover her confusion. "It just happened." And trust Renata to stir the pot and make this harder for him.

"Congratulations," Savannah managed finally. "I'm sure you and your bride will be very happy."

"Don't you think you'll be that bride?" Renata pushed.

Jericho stifled the urge to punch her. He'd never hit a woman in his life, but he'd never known someone as obnoxious as Renata. Even his sister, Kara, wasn't this bad.

Savannah swallowed. "I... I..."

Regan came to her rescue. "Savannah, could you do me a favor?" she interrupted.

"Sure, anything," Savannah said, a little wildly. "I can't resist you as long as I'm holding this little man, you know. Because you're just the most darling baby," she cooed at Hugh.

If she was trying to redirect Renata's attention, it worked. The cameramen now focused on the baby. Hugh was all smiles and pudgy cheeks. Maybe six months old, Jericho estimated. Taking care of Donovan had given him the experience of judging a baby's age—

He pushed the memory from his mind. That had been years ago. Donovan was as grown as he was.

Although who knew what kind of life the man was leading.

Swallowing the old, bitter taste of guilt, Jericho tried

to keep his attention on the present.

"Would you watch the kids when we fetch Ella and Isaac home from the hospital tomorrow?" Regan asked Savannah. "You've always been so comfortable with the kids when you've stopped by. I hope you don't mind my asking."

"Ella's coming home? Oh, that's terrific." Savannah smiled for the first time.

Jericho knew Ella Hall had been in the hospital for several days after a rough time with the birth of her son. Born with the cord wrapped around his neck, the baby had to spend some time in the NICU before he was allowed home. It had been touch and go there for a little while, and he knew everyone was thrilled that both mother and baby were all right.

"We all want to be there to pick her up, but we can't bring so many babies and toddlers to the hospital at once. It won't be for long. Do you think you could manage it?"

"Of course! I'd love to," Savannah said.

Jericho thought of the last time he'd visited Crescent Hall—the tumble and cries of children all through the large house. The four Hall brothers and their wives lived together on their ranch, three of the couples in the main house and one in a converted bunkhouse.

"That's a lot of kids for one person to watch," he said.

"You're right; I think Savannah could use an extra pair of hands," Regan said brightly. "You could come, too, if you like, Jericho."

Savannah turned to him, eyes wide. Hugh watched him from her arms, his somber expression tugging at some paternal instinct Jericho hadn't known he had. What if that was *his* baby—

No.

Never.

"Jericho? Do you want to come tomorrow and help Savannah?" Regan prompted.

Hell, no, he wanted to say. But maybe he should. It would give him a chance to talk to Savannah alone about the fact he'd drawn the short straw. He needed to propose to Savannah.

Hell, first he needed to have a full conversation with her.

"Uh... yeah. Sure," he heard himself say.

And wondered if he'd just made the biggest mistake of his life.

JERICHO HAD DRAWN the short straw? And he was coming to babysit the Hall kids tomorrow?

Savannah fought down her rising panic. She knew what this meant; he was going to propose to her, and she wasn't ready to answer him.

Why did this have to happen now? She needed three more weeks to prepare for her audition. Then, when Alfred Redding accepted her as a protégé, she'd be in a much stronger position when she approached Jericho with her news. Her career had to be on rails before she confessed her secret—so far underway he couldn't tell her she had to quit.

She'd waited for this chance to grasp her dream for so long—to prove to her family they were wrong about her—

She couldn't stop now.

Even if she was pregnant.

She wanted this baby. Wanted it more than almost anything.

Couldn't she have both?

She could. She knew she could.

But only if Jericho was willing to be the best of fathers. If she couldn't be with her child every minute of the day—Jericho needed to be. The SEAL was honorable. He had integrity. And he desired her—she knew that.

But did he ache to be a father? Enough to throw over conventions and take on the role of primary caregiver while she pursued her career—at least for a while?

Every fiber of her longed to break the news to him. Keeping this secret from Jericho and almost everyone else had been one of the hardest things she'd ever done. She kept having to invent excuses to sneak off to the doctors—and to Two Willows, where Alice Reed had already loosened the seams of her Regency gowns twice. At least she wasn't due for another appointment for several weeks.

Still, she couldn't wait to see the look on the SEAL's face when she told him he was going to be a daddy. When she pictured the moment, he held her tenderly. Kissed her.

Told her he loved her.

She could see it all so clearly in her mind, but when she pictured asking him to put his own plans on hold to spend his days with their baby, the vision ended and she was left wondering what would happen next. He had goals, too—and everyone at Westfield depended on him to reach them. What would she do if he asked the obvious question? Why couldn't she put off her dreams—

Again.

"There's only one problem," Jericho said to Regan, breaking into Savannah's thoughts. She had to remember she was still being filmed. Still standing outside the manor with baby Hugh in her arms. "You know wherever we go, the cameras follow. I doubt you'll want your children to appear on TV."

Savannah held her breath. Just as she thought; he was trying to get her alone—away from the cameras.

Was it her imagination, or was Jericho giving Riley a significant look?

Don't fall for it, Savannah urged her friend silently. *Say the cameras have to be there.*

"Wait a minute—" Renata stepped forward to intervene. "Don't think you can get rid of my cameramen—"

But Regan had obviously decided to help Jericho out. "Sorry. I can't have strangers filming the babies while we're away. But," she added, forestalling Renata. "How's this for a workaround? Come fifteen minutes early and you can film Jericho and Savannah with our children while we're there. When we leave for the hospital, you and your film crews leave, too."

Jericho looked like he wanted to kiss her. Savannah had to admit Regan had played it perfectly. Which meant she'd be alone with Jericho for more than an hour at Crescent Hall—no cameras on the premises.

She was so screwed.

"Half an hour," Renata demanded.

"Deal." Regan reached out a hand and pumped Renata's. She scooped Hugh from Savannah's arms and, to Savannah's surprise, handed him to Jericho. "There. You can get a little footage right now."

Savannah sucked in a breath, unprepared for the impact of the visual. She didn't think she'd ever seen anything so... good... as the image of baby Hugh in Jericho's arms. The SEAL cradled the baby expertly, even though he was obviously taken aback by this abrupt turn of events. He stared down at the little boy, who stared back up at him just as intently.

"Hey," Jericho said softly. "Hey, Hugh. What's up?"

The baby smiled at him, a big, sunny smile that made Savannah's eyes sting. She had no idea what Jericho felt about fatherhood, but she was going to find out soon enough.

As soon as she got Redding to take her on.

Watching Jericho cradle tiny Hugh in his arms made her long to hold her own baby. It would be so hard to leave her child while she traveled to concerts—

But it would be worth it, she reminded herself. Worth it to prove to her family she had what it took. They'd never taken her seriously. Had undercut her at every turn. She couldn't turn her back on the piano again—even if Fate had thrown her this curve ball.

It was all about timing. First she had to know if Redding wanted her to be his protégé. If the answer was yes—it had to be yes—then she could tell Jericho about their baby, and let him know at the same time how much help she'd need in the coming years. Then, if he still wanted to propose to her, she'd agree to marry him.

She had no idea what she'd do if he backed off.

Jericho looked up, as if he'd heard her thoughts. His expression was strange—half wonder, half consternation—and she felt as if he was asking her a question.

Was it okay for him to hold a baby?

Did she think he was father material?

Could this be their future?

Of course she had no idea what was really running through his mind. He might simply be afraid he was about to get stuck babysitting a bunch of crying kids.

Which he was.

When she didn't say anything, he turned back to Regan. "We'll be there when you need us," he assured her. "And we're okay with being filmed for half an hour."

Savannah bent to move the nearest chair to cover her reaction to his statement. For some strange reason tears pricked her eyes, and relief washed over her. She realized she'd expected him to try to get out of babysitting—and she'd assumed that would mean he'd refuse to take responsibility as their baby's father, too.

But he hadn't. He'd made a point of saying he'd be

there.

Jericho was a good man. She wanted him as much as she wanted this baby. Over the months they'd both lived at Westfield, she'd grown to admire him for his dedication to his work, his single-minded pursuit of powering their community with renewable resources and the way he always had a smile ready for her, despite everything else that was going on.

Despite the way she'd built a wall between them without any explanation.

She couldn't wait to knock that wall down.

"We'd better get back to work setting up," she said before her desire for Jericho got the better of her and she spilled all her secrets to him right now. "You'll be over later for the ceremony, right?" she asked Regan.

"Of course. See you then!" Regan beamed at her, as if she thought she'd done something clever by inviting Jericho to come along the following day. If only she knew, Savannah thought.

But that was the thing. No one knew about her audition. No one knew how important it was.

And no one but her dressmaker knew she was pregnant, either. Except maybe Sam—and she'd leave for her honeymoon in Mexico in just a few hours.

Jericho carefully transferred Hugh into Regan's arms. "There you go, big guy. See you later. Be good for your mama."

As Regan and Hugh headed off, Jericho stepped closer to Savannah. "Save me a dance later?"

She nodded, feeling like she'd stepped on a roller

coaster that was doomed to go off the rails. Might as well dance with him while she could.

Her life was about to get pretty complicated.

"FORTY DAYS GOES fast," Harris Wentworth said a number of hours later as he and Jericho stood outside the manor watching Sam's parents' band, *Deader Than Ever*, prepare to play. Jericho had heard from Harris the band would stray from its normal hippie repertoire to play more classic wedding fare, and he was sure they'd all have a good time tonight. The ceremony had been simple but moving, and Harris was about as giddy as Jericho had ever seen the ex-sniper. He'd been a man of few words before he met Samantha. Sam had brought out the best in him, and now Harris was far more likely than before to join in group events and relax his constant vigilance. Even now, Harris's gaze rested on his new bride where she stood among a knot of well-wishers near the house.

"I know." Jericho didn't want to think about how little time he had to convince Savannah to marry him. He didn't want to think of the alternative, either. Failure wasn't an option. Savannah was the only woman who stirred his blood this way. He'd thought of little else in the months he'd been at Base Camp, and he decided he was glad he'd drawn the short straw. Time to settle this matter between them once and for all.

"Do you have a plan?"

Jericho nodded. "I'm going to ask her to dance as soon as the band gets going. And I'm helping her babysit at Crescent Hall tomorrow." He still couldn't believe he'd gotten roped into that.

"That's your plan?" Harris looked skeptical. "Might take more than that."

"It might." Jericho decided he was ready for the challenge. He would pursue her day and night if that's what it took. Today's wedding was the perfect place to start. Weddings were romantic. Savannah would be thinking about her own future. She'd softened up a little lately, so maybe he wouldn't get the usual brush-off. "Gotta start somewhere, though, right?"

"That you do."

"I'm happy for you." Jericho was. Harris and Sam had taken a bumpy journey to this wedding. But today both of them were positively glowing. Jericho wanted to feel like that.

"Thanks. Hey, you'd better go ask Savannah before someone else does." Harris nudged him and nodded toward where Savannah stood near Sam with several of her friends. Harris was right; the music had started, and one of the local cowboys was making his way toward Savannah already, his nervousness plain to see as he mustered up his courage to ask her to dance.

Jericho sprang into motion. No way he'd let another man pull Savannah close tonight—or ever. He pushed his way through the crowd, apologizing as he went, and beat the cowboy by mere seconds to Savannah's side.

"Let's dance," he said and took Savannah's arm just as the other man reached them.

"Hey," the cowboy said, but Jericho ignored him.

"Just a dance, that's all," he assured Savannah as he led her to the makeshift dance floor. He wouldn't give her the chance to say no.

A glance back told him the cowboy was fuming. Jericho gave him an ironic salute, caught Savannah watching him and cleared his throat.

"Old friend," he told her.

"Right."

As he took her into his arms, she kept a distance between them, and Jericho's heart sunk. She wasn't going to make this easy. This was more like dancing with your cousin than the woman you hoped to make your wife. He was glad the gathering was so big. The camera crews were far too busy to focus on them.

"Nice wedding, huh?" As he guided her around the floor, he refused to be cowed by her lack of cooperation. He'd known this would take some effort.

Meanwhile, he appreciated the low-cut neckline of Savannah's gown. Jericho was a modern man, and he knew he wasn't supposed to objectify women, but Savannah's breasts were nothing short of miraculous and it was hard to keep his gaze from hovering there too long. They were full and enticing, and he couldn't help remembering the feel of them in his hands, even if it had been months.

"You've been avoiding me," he said.

She shook her head, but Jericho wasn't going to let her get away with that.

"Yes, you have." He pulled her closer and leaned down to speak in her ear. "Ever since we were together." Deciding to shatter the polite distance between them, he added, "Was it really so bad?"

She tilted up her chin to look at him and he saw all the desire he felt echoed in her eyes. "Of course not." A faint flush traced over her cheeks. Was she thinking about their encounter in the Russells' bathroom? How they could have gotten caught?

"I think about it all the time," he told her. Her flush deepened and she looked away, but Jericho pressed the matter. "How about you? Do you think about it?"

After a long pause, in which he thought she wouldn't answer, she finally nodded.

Jericho pulled her closer. Smelled the delicate fragrance of her hair as she rested her head against his chest. She felt so right here. He needed her to know that, too.

He wanted to tell her how much he wanted her right now. Hell, he wanted to propose, to make sure she was his forever—but that wasn't the way to play this. Savannah had been spooked when Boone went after Riley—and finally won her heart. She hated the way she and the other women had been strong-armed into participating in Fulsom's reality television show. But if Boone and Riley, and Clay and Nora, had been able to work things out, couldn't he find a way to do so with Savannah?

She needed to know he wanted her because of who she was—not because he was under some deadline. Try as he might, he hadn't made that clear enough.

That would change tonight.

"How's the practicing coming?" He had to stop himself from kissing her. This close she was irresistible.

"Pretty well." The tension in her shoulders told him something was wrong, though.

"Are you getting enough time?"

She shrugged.

He had an inspiration. "I can talk to Boone. Tell him I don't need you to work with me anymore. Then you'd have more time to practice."

She tilted up her head to look at him again. "You'd do that? Let me practice instead of work with you on the energy grid?"

He hadn't really thought that through, had he? He didn't want to give up those hours with her, but he needed to show her he took her dreams seriously. "Of course. Your career takes precedence over everything else."

He read her surprise in her upraised brows.

"What about the deadlines you have to meet to keep the ranch? I'd have thought you'd want me working with you more, not less."

Jericho knew why she'd think that. Boone had made a heck of a fuss when he decreed the women each had to work at Base Camp for two hours a day. The women hadn't figured out yet he'd done so to make them spend time with the men who were trying to woo them. It hadn't worked for him and Savannah, though. She had a goal. Helping her reach it was the way to be a hero in her eyes.

"I'll meet my deadlines. Don't get me wrong; I love

it when you work with me. Makes the time fly by. But I know you've got things you want to accomplish. If I have to work double-time to cover for you, I'll do it. I want to see you up on that stage."

"You do?"

She pulled back a little. Jericho kept her firmly in place. He supposed he should have told her this a long time ago. Of course he supported her musical career. Life was short; you needed to do what you loved. If he could be here at Base Camp working on the green power grid and she could be playing concerts and wowing audiences, theirs would definitely be a happy marriage.

"I'd do anything to help you reach your dreams," he murmured against her temple as he drew her close again. "I just want to see you happy, Savannah."

If he'd thought she'd melt in his arms when she heard that declaration, he was wrong. Instead, she grew rigid.

"Does that surprise you? Did you think I'd stand in your way?" he asked.

"Everyone else has."

He had to strain to hear her words over the music, and he contemplated taking her somewhere they could be alone together to talk more intimately. He decided against it. He didn't want to risk losing this moment.

"Like who?"

"My family. My parents never supported my piano playing," she said, putting her lips near his ear to be heard. "They got me lessons to make me well-rounded.

They never thought I'd go off the deep end, as they put it, and consider a career in music. I had to fight them all the way about studying it in college. Luckily, I got a scholarship."

Jericho maneuvered her farther away from the band.

"So you always loved music?"

She hesitated. "Yes—but... what really fired me up was the applause." She shrugged. "I'll never forget my first recital. The way everyone clapped when I was done. I felt... good... in a way I'd never felt before. I was always messing up as far as my family was concerned."

Jericho's gut twisted in sympathy. His family understood nothing about him, either. "Even when you were a kid? What did they want you to do?"

"Programming," she admitted. "Right from the beginning. They sent me to computer camp. Tried to get me into website design, at least, when it became clear I was no programmer. When I refused point-blank, they demanded I stay in the tech field in some position. I ended up as a headhunter for some of the biggest Silicon Valley firms after college. That was moderately acceptable."

"You were brave to walk away from them and be true to your real calling." Jericho knew a bit about that. Although he wasn't sure if he was being brave or stupid when he'd joined his friends to build Base Camp. He wasn't making money presently, and while he had savings to tide him over, they would diminish fast if he kept up his payments to Donovan.

What would happen if Base Camp failed and he

found himself out of the Navy, out of work and starting over? Would he be able to earn enough in the civilian world to keep funding his cousin? What would happen if Donovan ever asked for more? So far he never had— he'd never even acknowledged the payments Jericho made every month.

But he cashed those checks like clockwork, so Jericho knew he relied on them, even if he was too proud to admit it.

"I can see why your family thought you'd be good at tech, though," he went on. "You're damn good with numbers." She'd proved that time and time again working on the energy system with him for Base Camp.

Savannah shrugged. "I've always been good with numbers and I'm interested in what we're doing here. But I was never into what my parents were doing. Dating apps? Not my thing."

"Dating apps? I didn't know that's what your folks make."

She made a face. "That's because I don't usually tell people about it. I'm still candy-coating it, actually. Most people are familiar with their other businesses—the ones they advertise. But that's not their real financial engine." Her gaze searched his, as if she was deciding whether to trust him or not. Jericho tried to keep his expression neutral as they swayed to the music. He wanted to know what made Savannah tick, and he had a feeling her relationship with her parents could explain a lot of what was happening between them.

"They make chat bots," she went on finally. "You

know what those are?"

Jericho laughed, took in her affronted expression and stifled his reaction. He knew what chat bots were: artificial intelligence programs that stood in for real women when men entered chat rooms looking for an online encounter—or the other way around. "Are you serious? Your parents make those?" From her previous descriptions he'd painted a far more traditional view of her folks.

After a moment, she nodded, a blush stealing over her fair cheeks. Jericho found her embarrassment enchanting. Didn't everyone have a skeleton or two in their closet?

"I hate it," she burst out. "It's... wrong."

"Wrong? Why?"

"Because of the way they're used. People log on to chat rooms to connect with other people—not robots."

"I think most people are savvy enough these days to know it's a crap shoot," Jericho told her. He still wished they were having this conversation in a more private— and less noisy—place. He didn't want to risk ruining the moment by taking her somewhere else, though. They hadn't talked this much in weeks.

"Do they? Really? I don't believe that."

"It's not like people go to chat rooms for serious relationships, honey. They go looking for sex, plain and simple. And online sex isn't real no matter how you slice it."

Savannah pulled right out of his arms. "So you're one of those guys who thinks a quick wank while chatting online doesn't count as cheating?"

Jericho put up his hands. "Whoa, there." He took in the surprised expressions of the people dancing around them, took Savannah's hand and pulled her closer. "For one thing, I've never had a quick wank while chatting online," he said, making sure no one else could hear. "For another, I don't cheat—online or off. When I'm with a woman, I'm with her. When I'm done, I say so." He knew he wasn't expressing himself well, but he couldn't figure out any other way to say what needed to be said. "Here's the thing, Savannah—you get what you see with me. You've worked beside me, eaten meals with me—" he leaned closer "—made love to me. You know who I am."

She shook her head. "Do I? You're saying you have no secrets?"

He had more than he could count. "Don't you?" he retorted.

She didn't answer for a long moment, and Jericho's heart beat hard in the interval. She had secrets, all right; that was obvious.

What were they?

"I had a fiancé," she blurted. "I left him just before coming to Westfield. But I told you that already."

Jericho relaxed a little. She was right; he knew all about Charles. Just like he'd known what her parents did—except that bit with the chat bots.

After their encounter, he'd looked Savannah up on the Internet. He'd read about her music degree, looked at the few photos she'd posted of herself with family and friends. Apparently, she wasn't into social media much, but as a member of the Silicon Valley elite, local newspapers were interested in her. She appeared in a number of photos attending charity events and other gatherings. In many she was accompanied by a smug-looking man.

Charles Scott.

An angel investor from an old-money family, Charles was the natural match for the daughter of two programmers who'd brought several startups to IPOs at stratospheric evaluations. His old-money patina would take the shine off her family's new-money success—and maybe even the tarnish off their chat bot business, should that get wider exposure—and gain them entrée into the best society, while their fresh connections helped Charles's family keep picking hits to fund.

The one thing he'd never found, though, was an announcement of her engagement to Charles. He wondered why not. Had Savannah refused to announce it?

What had happened to drive them apart?

He didn't want to make the same mistake.

SAVANNAH REALIZED TOO late she'd given him an opening to talk about marriage. She couldn't believe she'd mentioned Charles again. She didn't want to think about the man, or how close she'd come to marrying him when it had been clear almost from the start he was never right for her. Like her parents, he couldn't understand her disinterest in the revolution in technology underway in her home state. Nor could he under-stand her squeamishness about the part of the business her parents had chosen to pursue.

"I'm glad you realized he wasn't the man for you," Jericho said, pursuing her. "Like I said, I'll talk to Boone. I'll make sure you've got plenty of time to practice. I admire your dedication, you know that?"

Now he was trying to sweet talk her. "That's what it takes to get the applause," she told him. Besides, the piano had always given her an escape from the world that surrounded her. She used to hate hearing her parents talk about ways to make the bots more lifelike, so she'd played loud enough to drown them out. She couldn't stand their callous conversations in which they treated sexual encounters like business transactions. It had been horrifying when she was a teenager, and even more disturbing when she was old enough to really grasp the kind of fire her parents were playing with.

"How did we raise someone so old-fashioned?" her mother had always asked when Savannah protested their latest innovations. "You should be grateful for what we do; those *sex sites*, as you call them, pay for the roof over your head."

Savannah had never been able to find it in her to be grateful. It would have been one thing if her parents had honestly tried to find ways to match people with their soul mates. Savannah could have gotten behind that and had suggested it many times.

"Love doesn't sell," her mother told her. "But sex does. You've got to go where the market is."

So Savannah's dedication to the piano became a kind of rebellion against her family and what they did for a living. Compared to the shifting ethics of the community surrounding her, her music felt pure, clean and true. She chose classical music as her concentration in college and refused to touch an electronic keyboard. To her mind, electronic music could be programmed and perfected, just like those chat bots could. But no computer could bring a human touch to music, just like no chat bot could provide a truly human interaction.

Savannah had to believe that.

Because otherwise nothing she believed in was true.

Her recitals and concerts got her through. Every time her folks wore her down and she began to feel as dumb and out of touch as they made her out to be, she let the audience's applause prove them wrong. She could stand up, take her bow and walk offstage knowing she was good enough by someone's measure.

But then she'd left school. The concerts had stopped. So had the applause.

And Savannah had gone further and further adrift.

"I want you to know I believe in what you're doing," Jericho told her, echoing her thoughts. "I see your drive and I applaud it."

Savannah's heart squeezed. If that was true, then he was the first man to do so. In the end, Charles hadn't understood anything about her.

When she'd complained to him about what her parents did for a living, he'd taken an altogether more practical view of the matter. "People are going to have sex," he'd said. "Chat bots don't pass on STDs—they don't get pregnant, either."

Was that enough to justify the other damage they could do? Savannah had wondered at the time. People were designed to forge attachments. Even men visiting prostitutes liked their regulars, didn't they?

What happened when someone formed an attachment to a bot?

"That's their problem," Charles had said.

Savannah didn't believe that was true.

Jericho pulled her close and began to sway to the music again. Did he really understand how she felt?

"When I'm working on the energy system, it consumes me," Jericho said, as if he'd heard her question. "It's hard to stop thinking about it. Is that the way music is for you?"

"Kind of." That's the way success was for her. If she was honest, she thought much more about the applause than the music. She craved approbation— which was why she'd stuck so long with Charles. Her folks had liked him instantly, and had forged a business relationship with his parents before a month was out. Everything had become so entwined, it became hard to walk away.

She hadn't told a single one of her closest friends she was going to get married, though. Her mother had pushed and pushed for Savannah to make wedding plans, but she hadn't gone ahead and announced the wedding, even though Savannah knew she'd been dying to.

Her mother liked to boss people around, but she
didn't like humiliation. She must have known Savannah
would bolt in the end.

"So I'll tell Boone you won't be working with me
anymore. That's two more hours a day to practice,"
Jericho said, interrupting her thoughts.

Savannah nodded. Soon she'd be onstage again.
And one day she'd play in a venue like Carnegie Hall.
Somewhere dazzling with an enormous audience. She
could picture the grand piano. Her fingers on the
keyboard. The bright lights. The sweep and soar of her
music. That final hush when she played her last note.

The thunderous applause.

And somehow—miraculously—her parents in the
front row, realizing how wrong they'd been about
everything. On their feet as well, clapping and cheering
her. Realizing she was worth—

"Did you hear me, Savannah?" Jericho repeated,
breaking into her thoughts. "You can have your mornings to yourself."

"Are…are you sure?" Savannah was wary of a trap.
If she let Jericho do this for her, would she end up
paying for it later?

"Of course I'm sure. Anything for you, Savannah.
You know I want—"

Warning signals flared in her mind. "I've got to go
help Riley." Savannah jerked out of his grasp before he
could mention marriage. She made it off of the dance
floor, took a wide detour around a camera crew filming
nearby, and darted into the manor before Jericho could

catch up. Pounding up the stairs to the third floor, she dashed into her room and slammed shut the door. Turning the lock, she leaned against it, breathing hard.

Safe. For the moment. She and the other women slept in Base Camp with the others these days, but they used the manor during the day. This room was still her sanctuary.

But as she thought about what Jericho had said, desire threaded through her worry. He seemed to understand her in a way no other man had and she wanted him in a way she'd never wanted another man. She could go back outside right now and be engaged to him within minutes. It was what he wanted.

What she wanted.

Her mother was right; at heart she was a traditional woman and she'd like to raise her baby with the man she loved here at Westfield, among people who shared her values. But first she had to reach her goal. She had to prove once and for all she was someone—even if she hadn't followed the path her parents laid out for her.

She had to have that one shining moment in the sun. Then she could relax her schedule. Be home more.

Be the mother she wanted to be.

Maybe if she explained it was temporary, Jericho would understand.

But she knew all too well how easy it would be for him to persuade her to wait. Base Camp was happening right now. So was the television show. He'd want her to just hold on until it was over.

But she couldn't. This chance with Redding was a

once-in-a-lifetime kind of thing. She couldn't turn her back on that.

What had her parents said when she'd graduated?

You don't have a single concert lined up. Come home and get a normal job until you can prove you can make money and support yourself.

She'd done just that. And ended up without the time to practice or to track down opportunities to play. Her career as a pianist had slipped away, just like that. So had the recognition.

And any chance of showing her family exactly who she was.

This time she wouldn't let that happen. With Jericho's ring on her finger and a wedding to look forward to—and a baby on the way—he'd say, "Wait until the show is over. Wait until after our child is born. Then start your career."

She'd lose her chance.

She had to stick to her guns. The audition first. A commitment from Redding to mentor her. Her career on rails.

Then she'd make her proposition to Jericho from a position of strength.

If he wasn't the man she hoped he'd be, she didn't know what she'd do.

CHAPTER TWO

WHEN THE SUN rose the following morning, Jericho rose with it, though he'd had little sleep. Each time he'd drifted off, he'd found himself back in his childhood home, filled with an unnamed dread. He'd surged awake searching for what he'd lost—what he needed to do to put his family back together, but found only the close, stuffy confines of his tent and the hush of the camp all around him.

Base Camp had grown since their early days at Westfield. Now the area near the bunkhouse sported more than a dozen tents—and three tiny homes built for the married couples. Boone and Riley Rudman, and Clay and Nora Pickett, had moved into two of the houses. As soon as they got back from their honeymoon, Harris and Samantha Wentworth would occupy the third.

In forty days, Jericho would live in the next small building that stood half-constructed near the others. Dug into the side of a south-facing slope, soon its large front windows would reflect the blue Montana sky, but for now it looked as blank and empty as he felt.

It was hard to shake the feeling from his dreams—that some screw-ups could never be fixed. He should never have agreed to help Savannah watch those children, but he knew if he tried to back out of it, he'd lose ground. He wasn't sure what to think about her reaction when he'd told her she didn't need to work with him anymore.

She'd seemed pleased at his offer to free her from her morning work on the energy grid, but then she'd run from him instead of dancing the night away. He'd waited for her to return. He'd even entered the manor in search of her. But Savannah had stayed upstairs in her room and he'd instinctively known that to pursue her there would mean losing her for good.

What would happen today at Crescent Hall? Would she give him the silent treatment?

Would she give him another chance?

Would a bomb drop and blow them all to Kingdom Come—?

Jesus—where had that thought come from?

Jericho raked a hand through his hair. There were no bombs in Chance Creek. He wasn't back in Yemen. The children he'd see today weren't caught in an abandoned school, unable to get home, running out of food and water—

He drew in a deep breath of air and blew it out again. Nightmares were bad enough, but these daytime visions were worse. You couldn't wake up out of them. All you could do was try to clear your mind, or work until you dropped. Sometimes he wished he could drink them away, but he'd long ago learned he had to keep a clear mind in this world. Once in a while he tied one on, but those occasions were few and far between.

Still, the thought of going to Crescent Hall today filled him with dread. How would he get through an afternoon surrounded by children without thinking of Yemen? Without thinking of Akram?

Bad things happened when he was in charge of kids. Despite every effort he made, he couldn't keep them safe.

Which is why he needed to steer a wide berth around Crescent Hall. This wasn't Yemen, but that didn't mean anything.

Danger could come from any direction.

Disaster could strike at any moment.

Even right here in Chance Creek.

Jericho turned to look up at the manor. He could corner one of the other women and ask her to take his place—

But then he'd lose his chance to get Savannah alone.

Was it worth the risk?

Jericho sighed and made his way to the bunkhouse.

"Morning," he mumbled when he reached the kitchen and found Walker there.

The big man grunted a greeting and poured himself a cup of coffee.

"Morning," Kai Green said. Another of the men of Base Camp, Kai was past thirty, but looked like he'd be more at home surfing in California than cooking breakfast in Montana. Kai was one of Jericho's crew and helped out rigging up their green energy system. He was also an amazing cook and a wizard at using ad hoc solar ovens to create gourmet, filling fare. He was as meticulous as Jericho about calculating energy use—and his cooking practices showed it. Jericho enjoyed his company, but even Kai's cheerful greeting couldn't dispel the worry that lingered in his mind.

"Those bison coming soon?" Jericho asked Walker, getting himself a cup of coffee. He figured he'd go put in a little work before Kai called them back for breakfast.

"Yep. Avery's kind of spooked." A smile curved the man's lips.

"How's her riding coming?" Jericho was grateful to clear his dark thoughts from his head. Avery was a city girl and she'd been pretty intimidated by the horses at first, too. Jericho knew Walker was teaching her, and he figured the Native American was enjoying the task. Sparks had flown between those two since the day they'd met, but Walker had some kind of prior engagement he refused to discuss with anyone—including Avery—and from what Jericho had gathered, Avery was running out of patience.

"Good." Walker took another sip of coffee. "But she isn't too happy about the idea of wrangling bison."

"You think she'll ask to be re-assigned?" Something was bothering Walker, and it wasn't the bison.

The man shrugged. "Maybe."

"You any closer to telling her about this other woman you're supposed to get hitched to?"

Walker gave him a baleful glance, but Jericho didn't back down. He was facing a forty-day deadline to marry; he figured that gave him the right to give Walker a hard time.

When Walker shrugged again, Jericho banged his cup down on the counter. "If you lose her, it'll be your own damn fault, you know." If Savannah wanted him as clearly as Avery wanted Walker, they'd be well on their way to getting hitched. He didn't know what Walker was waiting for.

"Maybe so." Walker drained his cup. "Breakfast in a half-hour?" he asked Kai.

"That's about right."

Walker left the kitchen. Jericho exchanged a look with Kai.

"What do you think his story is, really?" Kai asked him.

"I'm not sure." When they were kids, Walker had kept his reservation life separate from his life in town. He was possessive about his history and his people, and since he'd been as closemouthed back then as he was as a grown man, Jericho didn't know too much about the entanglements his friend might have taken on.

"I never heard that the Crow practice arranged marriages," Kai said lightly.

"I don't think it's a cultural thing, if that's what you mean. I think there's something else going on here. Some promise or obligation." Walker had always taken those seriously.

"Well, I hope he figures it out."

"Me, too."

"Hope you figure it out, too, dude. Time's ticking away." Kai tapped his wristwatch.

Jericho knew he was kidding, but it wasn't funny. Too much rode on these marriages.

"I'm going to get to work."

Kai nodded and bent back over the counter, where he was cracking several cartons of eggs for omelets.

Back out in the fresh August morning, Jericho tried to shake off the last vestiges of his dreams. He wasn't a child anymore. Nor was this a war zone. He could watch a few babies and toddlers with Savannah's help.

Nothing would go wrong.

SAVANNAH HADN'T SLEPT a wink last night and her anxiety kept growing the closer she and Jericho came to Crescent Hall, not because she was worried about her ability to babysit a number of young children, but because of the silence of the man sitting next to her in the truck. At first she'd worried her rushed escape the night before had hurt Jericho's feelings, but soon she realized that with the camera crew in tow, he'd have been quiet no matter what.

He tapped his thumbs on the steering wheel each time they stopped, though, as if he needed an outlet for his excess energy.

Was he nervous?

Maybe.

Did he mean to try to propose to her today?

She hoped not, but she figured she'd have to keep on her toes to put him off during their time at Crescent Hall. She didn't like the way he'd finagled things so that there wouldn't be a camera crew present with them for most of it.

Jericho turned into the drive and they continued up to a large, proud, three-story, white clapboard house at the top of a rise of ground. Savannah had only been to Crescent Hall a couple of times for neighborly get-togethers, but she understood completely why all the Halls were in love with their home. It was a prime example of Gothic architecture, from its rounded corner tower to its large wraparound porch. The front door opened, and Regan came out to greet them. She held Hugh in her arms, and Savannah's heart throbbed with the desire to take the precious little boy from her and snuggle him herself.

She turned to Jericho, took in his white knuckles, and her spirits sank further.

Was he nervous? Or angry that he'd gotten roped into babysitting? Was she a fool to think a man who'd been a Navy SEAL would volunteer to stay home and raise their baby while she toured the country playing her music?

Regardless of whether he wanted to be a stay-at-home dad or not, Savannah didn't think she could stand it if Jericho turned out to be one of those impatient men who found no child interesting until he was old enough to play sports.

Maybe she'd been thinking about this day all wrong.

Maybe babysitting the Hall kids was the perfect way to test Jericho. She'd learn right away how he truly felt about children. Then she could decide what to do next. As soon as the truck stopped, she hopped out and went to take Hugh from Regan's arms.

"I've missed you," she told him, giving him a snuggle.

Hugh gave a happy coo.

"I think he missed you, too," Regan said. She stepped out of the way as Heather Hall passed them on the porch with an infant-size car seat in her arms.

"Are you sure you want to watch all of the kids?" Heather asked. A cheerful blonde who ran the local hardware store, she had married Colt Hall after they'd been separated for years. Now they were raising their fourteen-year-old son, Richard, together. "We could take one or two along."

"It's no bother at all." Savannah sent a sidelong look Jericho's way to see his reaction. Was that fear gripping the tall, strong SEAL? That spelled trouble. While it amused her to think a few babies and toddlers could disconcert him, she'd known other men who were afraid they wouldn't hold a baby right or would accidentally hurt a toddler. If that's all this was, she could teach him what to do.

If he had an actual aversion to babies, it would be more difficult.

"Richard wants to come to the hospital, too," Heather said. "Otherwise he could have helped babysit. He's a whiz at it."

"That's just fine; of course he wants to be one of the grown-ups," Savannah told her. "Like I said, we don't mind one bit. It's going to be fun, right, Jericho?"

"Uh…sure." But the SEAL didn't look so sure. Savannah's spirits sagged some more.

"Go right on inside; I'll be there in a minute. I want to help Heather." Regan held the door open for Savannah. Savannah kissed the top of Hugh's head and consoled herself that no one could remain aloof around a baby like him. She'd cure Jericho of any shyness he had in no time.

"You are a darling," she said to the baby as she went inside and Jericho followed. "A darling, darling boy. Right, Jericho? Jericho?"

She turned to find Jericho hesitating in the doorway, the camera crew behind him. "Shut that door before one of the kids escapes," she teased him.

There wasn't a child in sight besides Hugh, but Jericho jumped into action as if a whole horde of them was racing for the opening. He yanked the crew inside and slammed the door shut.

"Jericho, relax! I was just kidding." Savannah would have laughed if she wasn't so surprised.

Why was he so nervous? Charles would have gotten the joke. Savannah shook her head at the wayward thought. The last thing she wanted to think about right now was Charles, even if he had liked to talk about kids. He wanted an heir and a spare, if you could belief the pompous indulgence of that. Just because he shared a name with a certain prince didn't mean anyone besides himself—and her parents—cared about his bloodline.

His attitude toward children—as if they were some accessory that was *de rigeur* this year—had chafed her all during their engagement. She'd wanted children some-day—but only after she'd proven herself. And only if her husband would love them as much as she would. She'd wanted to focus on each thing separately—first her career, then parenthood—because she'd known when she chose to be a mother, she'd be the kind who made her child the center of her life. She couldn't do that and be a concert pianist at the same time. Now Fate had played a trick on her. It had taken away her chance to separate her career from motherhood. Savannah glanced at Jericho again, nearly succumbing to the uncertainty that had plagued her since she'd found out she was pregnant. He was supposed to be the answer. If he would step up and help while she was traveling and practicing long hours, she could still do both things to her high standards.

Although neither in the way she'd hoped.

Savannah tried not to think about that, but it was true. She knew she'd miss her baby during her long hours of practice and time on the road.

Sometimes—sometimes she wondered if she was making the right choice.

Of course she was, she told herself. She was doing this as much for her child as she was for herself. She couldn't pass this kind of self-doubt and resentment onto another generation. Only when she was a national success could she relax and take things more slowly.

But when Hugh rested his head on her shoulder with a contented baby sigh, her heart squeezed again, and she longed to hold the child growing even now inside her.

She was grateful when Regan re-entered the house. She took Hugh from Savannah and led the way toward the living room, chattering as she went. "Everyone's been fed and should be fine until we're home again, but there are lots of snacks in the cupboard and fridge and I've written down everyone's preferences. There are bottles of breast milk in the fridge, too; those have been labeled."

They entered the large living room off the kitchen, and Savannah had to smile despite the thoughts careening around her brain. Controlled chaos was the only way to describe the scene. The furniture had been pushed to the edges of the room. Small toys were scattered everywhere, and larger ones were grouped in stations, as if the living room was a preschool. There was a play kitchen, a play workbench, a dress up area and a corner with every type of block imaginable.

"As you can see, there's plenty for the kids to do," Regan continued. "All they'll want is for you to play with them." She began to introduce the kids, who barely looked up to greet the newcomers, they were all so busy. "We have to keep Annie and Wyatt apart for now." She indicated a toddler girl and a baby boy. "Annie is biting these days, and she has it out for Wyatt. So we put one in a playpen with lots to do, and let one roam around, then switch them."

"I love the way you've got it all worked out," Savannah said. "It'll be so nice for all the kids to grow up together."

"I think so," Regan said with a smile. "Although sometimes it's a little crazy around here. Okay, all our cell phone numbers are on the fridge in the kitchen. So are the emergency services."

"We'll be fine," Savannah assured her again.

She and Jericho spent the next half-hour posing with babies, with each other, and being filmed at play with the youngsters, with various members of the Hall clan participating so that their children weren't frightened by the cameras. Mason and Regan proudly showed off their son, Aaron, along with baby Hugh, and Ella and Austin's older son, Michael. Storm and Zane played with their toddler, Gabriel, and twin babies, Wyatt and Sean. Heather and Colt posed with their twin toddlers, Nellie and Andrew, and their baby, Laurie. And Dan Hemmins and his wife, Sarah, friends of Mason's who'd settled down at Crescent Hall, too, showed off their daughter, Annie. When the crew finally headed out to get a ride back to Westfield with the Halls, Savannah sighed with relief. The kids were getting restless from all the attention. Time for a little peace and quiet.

"Are you sure you have everything you need?" Regan asked again as the Halls headed for the door.

"Positive. Go on. Ella's waiting."

"I'm so excited she's coming home," Regan confessed. "Thank you for doing this. Thank you, too, Jericho."

"Sure." Jericho nodded but kept his gaze low, watching all the kids. Savannah thought he was counting them. "Ten," he said suddenly, confirming her guess. "There are ten of them, right? We need to be able to do a head count."

"That's right." Regan was already half out the door. "See you in a couple of hours."

"Bye," Savannah called after her. "Jericho—what are you doing?" she asked when the man sprang into motion and began to move the furniture and larger toys to block the wide entrance from the kitchen into the living room.

"Securing the perimeter."

"But—"

The toddlers and infants had all stopped to stare, as surprised by this turn of events as Savannah was.

"Grab that one." Jericho pointed to a large plastic refrigerator and Savannah went to move it into the position he indicated. It wasn't a bad idea, all things considered, she supposed. It would be easier if they could corral all the kids in a single room. She wondered why there wasn't a baby gate, but with so many people living under one roof, maybe one wasn't necessary when the Halls were at home.

His barricade in place, Jericho looked around. "I only see two playpens."

"How many do you need?" Savannah's smile slid when she caught a look at the worry on his face.

"There are four babies who can't walk. Why aren't there four playpens?"

"They don't need to be in them all at once. Annie here is the only one who bites, remember?" She patted the head of the cherubic little girl in a blue dress and striped stockings.

"The other kids could step on them." Jericho lurched suddenly across the room and scooped up Laurie.

Savannah's breath whooshed out of her lungs at the sheer beauty of a baby in the Navy SEAL's arms. Jericho's long, strong fingers made the tiny child look even tinier, and the little girl gazed at him like he was the most fascinating thing she'd ever seen.

Savannah understood exactly how she felt.

She could stare at Jericho all day, especially when he was standing like that, cradling a baby girl as if he meant to keep her safe at all costs.

Would he be like that with his wife, too? Protective? Caring?

Or would he be like Charles—all charm and no substance?

Jericho took another step and scooped up Hugh, whom Regan had placed near the play kitchen, as a toddler careened by carrying an armload of blocks. "This is crazy. There are too many of them." He transferred both babies to the same arm and picked up Sean.

Juggling them all in his arms, he stared helplessly at Wyatt, who was belly crawling across the middle of the floor, evidently intent on reaching the play refrigerator.

Savannah's heart overflowed. Why had she ever

doubted this man, who obviously cared deeply about all the children placed in his care—even temporarily? Why was she withholding the news of their baby when he had every right to know?

Hadn't he proved he meant to ask her to marry him? Hadn't he shown he was willing to support her career? Maybe ten youngsters were proving too much at the moment, but he'd handle one baby with ease.

"Jericho," Savannah began in a rush, her determination to keep her secret until after her audition disappearing into thin air.

"Get him!" Jericho said.

"He's fine," she assured him, but she picked up Wyatt anyway, who promptly burst into tears at being denied his goal. Savannah hurried to the play refrigerator and soothed him by passing him plastic fruit from inside it. When she looked up again, Jericho had placed Laurie and Sean into the playpens and carried Hugh.

"Two in the pens, two in our arms," he stated, and she could tell that solving that problem had relaxed him a bit. It was sweet he was so worried about the situation. Savannah had been around kids enough to know they were tougher than they looked.

"Jericho, I've got something to—"

Annie chucked a block at Aaron just as Savannah started her explanation again. Aaron bellowed, picked up the block and chucked it back.

"Whoa, whoa!" Savannah lifted Wyatt up again and stepped in between the two of them, the long skirts of her gown effectively blocking the line of sight between them. "All right; who wants a story?"

"Me! Me!" The older children thronged around Savannah, pulling on her skirts.

"Let's see—what should we read?" Savannah strode to a bookshelf laden with picture books and chose one that looked interesting. Crossing back to the couch, she sat down and was immediately overrun by the toddlers who struggled to sit on her lap, or at least press up as close against her as humanly possible. "Jericho, could you bring the babies?"

"All of them?"

"Well, I've got Wyatt already," she said, cuddling the baby boy closer. She could barely open the book for the way the kids had crowded against her, but she managed to do it while Jericho balanced the three other babies in his arms. There wasn't room on the couch for him, so after a brief look around, he settled on the floor, his back against the couch.

Once again Savannah's heart squeezed to see the way he juggled the babies on his lap. Nellie, a sturdy toddler sitting on the couch just behind him, began to play with his hair, threading her little fingers through it and mussing it first one way, and then the other.

"Hey!" He shot a glance over his shoulder that made Nellie giggle. When he subsided again against the couch with a sigh, she got back to work.

"There once was an otter named Jake," Savannah began, and for about thirty seconds the children listened quietly to the story, and a tender feeling she hardly recognized filled her chest. This was lovely. Reading a story surrounded by children—filling their eager minds with new thoughts and ideas—stimulating their curiosity about the world—

Hugh wrinkled his tiny face into an expression of supreme concentration…

And filled his diaper loudly.

"Holy hell!" Jericho sprang to his feet, the other two babies hooked under one arm, and held Hugh as far away from his body as he could.

"Uh oh." Savannah was ready to put Wyatt down and take the offending baby from Jericho's arms, but he moved far too quickly for her.

In two strides he was across the room. He deposited Sean in one crib, Laurie in another one and whirled around to place Hugh on the changing table in the corner.

"I can—" Savannah began, trying to extricate herself from the pile of children on the couch, but she stopped in her tracks when Jericho grabbed a fresh diaper, popped several wipes from their container, lay Hugh on his back and got to work changing his diaper, as if he'd performed the action every day of his life.

Savannah watched openmouthed as he got Hugh undressed, changed and dressed again in the blink of an eye, wrapped up the dirty diaper, scooped up Hugh again and headed into the kitchen. A moment later she heard the back door open and shut.

Before she could collect herself, she heard him re-enter the kitchen and water run as he washed his hands. When he carried Hugh back into the living room, he picked up Sarah and Laurie, turned around and stopped. "What?"

"Where did you learn to do that?"

BUSTED.

Did he look guilty? Because he felt guilty—like he'd betrayed knowledge of some secret feminine rite. Jericho cleared his throat. "When I was a kid. Took care of my cousin a lot when our parents were busy." With their houses side by side, the two families spent a lot of time together. Jericho had many memories of long, drawn-out meals together and nearly nightly card games among the adults. Lots of laughter. Lots of fun.

Before the accident.

"Guess you don't forget," he said to cover the awkward pause.

"I guess you don't. Jericho, look—"

"Book! Book!" Nellie crowed.

"Yeah, how about that story? Let's hear what happened to that otter." Jericho sat down again and was glad his back faced her. He didn't want to talk about the past, or see the questions in her eyes. It occurred to him if he was going to make a life with Savannah, he probably should tell her everything that had happened. He shifted uncomfortably, trying to keep all three babies on his lap. He didn't feel like discussing Donovan with anyone.

After a moment, Savannah resumed reading, and Nellie resumed grooming him from her perch on the couch, her tiny fingers tapping over his scalp like she was writing a novel. He supposed if she was, it would be full of sunshine and laughter and joy. He remembered when his life had seemed simple like that. When he'd thought things could be good.

The first day his aunt Patty had placed baby Donovan in his arms, he'd only been seven years old, but he'd felt grown up as he'd sat on the comfortable couch in his aunt and uncle's living room and cradled the baby in his arms. It had been summertime, and in between fishing and bike riding and racing around the neighborhood with his friends, he'd spent a lot of time like that; holding Donovan while his aunt did her chores. And then holding him again while his aunt and uncle and parents played their cards at night.

Kara, his four-year-old sister, had found the whole thing excruciatingly boring and she'd spent that summer causing as much mayhem as a four-year-old could cause.

Which was a lot.

"She's just trying to get your attention. Play with her," his mother would call from the dining room.

Jericho did his best, balancing the baby and building blocks into towers for Kara to knock down.

As the months passed, the job got more challenging when Donovan started to crawl. Like Wyatt and Annie, a rivalry grew up between Kara and Donovan. He'd spent most of his time preventing Kara from "accidentally" stepping on the baby. Or tripping over him. Or dropping things on him.

"They're growing up so close it's a sibling rivalry," his mother had said. "You have to watch them. That's what babysitting is all about."

Jericho had watched them.

And watched them.

To the point his friends stopped making fun of him for babysitting all the time and just accepted it as a fact of life. As years passed, wherever Jericho went he'd be followed by his two shadows—the belligerent Kara, and the eager to please Donovan.

Most of the time, Jericho hadn't minded. Kara, for all her headstrong ways, could be a ferocious team-mate when their games called for one. And Donovan was always so happy to see Jericho his face would light up each morning when Jericho and Kara came to fetch him. By the time Jericho was eleven, Kara was seven and Donovan was four, they were inseparable.

Just like their parents.

Nellie tugged Jericho's hair. "I want a horsey ride."

"Shh, honey, the story's not over," Savannah said.

Jericho gently tilted his head away until his hair was free of Nellie's strong fingers, but as soon as he straightened again, she was back, this time clutching what little there was of it with both fists. "I want a horsey ride!"

Her demand brought him right back to those early summer days.

"I want to be the captain!"

Kara's seven-year-old voice cleaved the quiet air of a lazy August evening. They were up in the tree house his father and uncle had built earlier that year—a wide, railed platform some ten feet up in the air. This new venue had provided fodder for all kinds of games. Pirate ship was their favorite, and this argument was far from new. As the sun sunk low in the soft summer sky, Jericho had fought to keep his irritation at bay.

"It's Donovan's turn today. You were captain yesterday."

Just once he'd have liked to be captain, but like his mother always said, "You're the oldest, Jericho. It's up to you to keep the peace."

"That's right; I'm captain!" Donovan, safe on the other side of Jericho, spoke out boldly.

Kara scowled. "You're too little to be captain! I'm not taking orders from a shrimp!"

"You're the shrimp!"

"Kara—shut up or go home," Jericho had ordered. He'd had enough of peacemaking between them. Had had enough of babysitting, to tell the truth. It was one thing at seven to spend every waking moment with your family. At eleven, it was getting old. He knew damn well that Boone, Clay and Walker had ridden their bikes to the movie theater. He was missing out.

Again.

"You shut up!" Her indignant tones should have warned him one of Kara's rages was coming on. Her fits of anger were legendary in the Cook household. "She'll wear the pants in her marriage," their aunt was fond of saying.

"Make me!"

"Jericho, can I—?"

Jericho would never know what might have happened if he hadn't turned to answer Donovan's question. Would he have seen Kara coming? Could he have stopped her? Braced himself? Warded her off?

It didn't matter.

What was done, was done.

"I'll give you a horsey ride later, honey," he said to Nellie, refusing to dwell on the past anymore. "Let's listen to the story."

"You're a bad horsey." But Nellie listened through the rest of the story.

When it was over, Savannah said, "Jericho, there's something I really—"

"Horsey ride! Horsey ride!" Nellie's strident tones made it impossible to hear Savannah. Jericho handed Savannah one of the babies and put the other two in their playpens, thinking he would give Nellie a short ride and quickly get back to them.

He'd forgotten the allure of a horsey ride as far as toddlers were concerned. Forty-five minutes later he was still pacing the living room on all fours and neighing, much to the delight of the kids. Savannah was riding herd on the babies as far from the chaos of the horsey rides as she could. She didn't look too happy with the situation, and Jericho wondered if she was tiring of the job. He thought he understood. Savannah was a career woman, not a homebody. She might like to cuddle a baby now and then, but she didn't want to devote her life to caring for kids.

That was fine with him, he told himself, pushing down the voice that said that *maybe, someday—*

When the Halls finally arrived home triumphantly, sweeping Ella and her baby into the house, Jericho had never been more relieved. He'd had fun, but ten kids were a handful.

"Don't know how you do it," he confessed to Mason when the children were reunited with their parents.

"It's easier when they're family," Mason said. He smiled at Savannah when she came to stand at Jericho's side. "Thanks to both of you. We appreciate it. Our little horde isn't easy to tame."

"The kids were great, right, Jericho?" Savannah asked—as if she hadn't been frantically chasing after babies all this time.

"Yeah. Great," Jericho echoed.

"Just wait until you have some of your own. You'll see," Mason said with the complacency of a satisfied father.

Jericho laughed. "Not going to happen, man. If there's one thing I know for sure, I'm never having kids."

WAS SHE SMILING? Savannah hoped she was smiling—even though her heart was breaking in two. Jericho's words played in a loop over and over again in her mind, drowning out everything else.

Never having kids.

If the situation wasn't so awful she would have laughed. Never having kids?

How about having one in less than six short months? Thank God she'd been interrupted every time she'd tried to tell Jericho about the baby. She had no idea what she was going to do now.

Raise her child on her own?

"Want to stay and celebrate Ella's homecoming?" Regan asked her.

"Uh… we can't," Savannah managed to croak. "I've got… a thing. Back at Westfield. With the others. To… plan."

"You've got guests coming?"

Savannah stared at her blankly until she remembered the B&B. "Yes… soon. Lots to do."

She knew she was babbling. Their next guests weren't due until October. Mason was studying her. Regan's brows furrowed.

"Oh… okay. Well, come back anytime."

"That's right—any time," Mason echoed. "By the way, who's the next to get hitched over at Base Camp? Have you men drawn straws yet?"

Regan gave her husband a not-so-subtle elbow to the ribs. Savannah wanted to sink into the ground. Jericho jammed his hands in his pockets. "Uh… yeah. We've drawn straws. It's… me."

"Oh. Hell, I'm sorry; that was awkward." But Mason was chuckling. "Well… good luck with that."

Savannah turned toward the door. She didn't know what else to do. "See you soon," she called back, struggling to keep her voice even.

"See you," Regan answered feebly.

Regan had to know how uncomfortable that conversation had been. She probably felt badly for what her husband had said. Savannah was sorry for that, but she couldn't stand around and pretend her world hadn't collapsed around her. Jericho wasn't going to have kids—ever.

Except he was.

He needed to know that. She needed to tell him.

Now. On the ride home—before they were back under the scrutiny of the cameras.

But she couldn't seem to find the words, and Jericho didn't give her a chance. When they reached the two-lane highway in the truck, he said, "Look, I know what's going on."

Savannah panicked. She wasn't ready for this confrontation, no matter how hard she'd tried to convince herself she was. She wanted to go home, shut herself in her room at the manor and cry—or better yet, scream.

Now she knew she would face her future alone. And she had no idea how she'd do it. She wasn't ready to be a single mother. Not now.

Not—ever.

"You're uncomfortable because I drew the short straw yesterday morning. You know I have to marry in forty days—and you're wondering if I'm going to propose."

She nearly laughed. Of course she'd wondered those very things, but that was before she'd found out he didn't want a child. He'd better not propose now—because she couldn't say yes. Not if he didn't want their baby.

It was bad enough her parents had always been disappointed in her. They'd made no bones when she met Charles that he was the answer to their prayers—the child they'd wished she was.

This was worse. Jericho didn't want a child at all.

Savannah didn't think she could stand that.

"When you found out about Fulsom, the television show and the demands we had to meet, you were angry. I get that. But since then I feel like we've...well, made progress, I guess you could say." Jericho kept his eyes on the road. "You know what I'm offering you. What life is like at Base Camp. Curtis and Clay are building my tiny house as we speak. Once I've set up the community's energy grid I'll be in charge of maintaining it, and I'll probably build a business consulting with other communities that need a similar system. You won't have to worry about helping me. You can focus on your career one hundred percent and pursue it as far as it takes you. I'll applaud you all the way."

Jericho sent her a smile, and Savannah fought to blink back the tears from her eyes. He was saying everything she'd wanted to hear. But he wasn't saying the one thing she needed to hear.

"What about... kids?" She managed to say the word clearly. "Fulsom's demands." As if that's what she was worried about.

"There are nine other men willing to get that job done," Jericho assured her. "You and I—we don't have time for that. You, especially. You need to get out there and grab that career you want. You need to be up on stage with everyone cheering you on. Can you imagine that? Playing to a packed house?"

Savannah imagined it, just like she'd imagined it so many times before. Standing on stage. Receiving her ovation. Her parents applauding her more than anyone else.

But this time the vision took a different turn.

There was her baby in one of the aisles, crawling toward the exit, Jericho nowhere in sight. With the performance over, the crowd streamed from the seats as she watched helplessly.

The aisles were overrun, her baby lost from sight.

He'd be trampled—

Hurt—

"No!"

Jericho hit the brakes and Savannah's body snapped against the taut seat belt.

"What? Where—"

A truck rolled past them, blaring its horn. With a curse, Jericho pulled to the side of the road and parked.

"What's wrong? Did you see something in the road?"

Savannah covered her face with her hands. She wanted to jump from the vehicle and race across the fields to dispel the vision that had seemed all too real a moment ago.

She knew what her subconscious was trying to say to her: how could she care for her child and pursue such a vigorous career—one that would take her away from home, all over the country? She couldn't—not without Jericho's help.

"I'm sorry," she said. "I... thought I..."

"Savannah, I might as well say this now." He turned in his seat. "You know I have to marry in forty days. You know I want—"

Savannah closed her eyes and leaned back, defeated. A tear trickled down her cheek. He was proposing—and she couldn't say yes.

Jericho broke off. "Are you getting sick?" He reached out to lay his palm on her forehead. Savannah swallowed. His touch still affected her too much, despite what he'd said earlier. Jericho was perfect for her in every way—except this one. That's why it'd be so hard to let him go.

"Maybe. I don't know. I think I need to lie down." She kept her eyes closed—unwilling to look at the man who was breaking her heart.

A moment passed before he turned the key in the ignition. As the truck's engine fired up again, Jericho checked for traffic before pulling back onto the road. "It's all those babies," he said darkly. "They'll get you every time."

CHAPTER THREE

W HEN JERICHO DROPPED Savannah off at the manor, she climbed out of the truck without another word and trailed into the house dejectedly. Jericho wasn't sure what was wrong. She'd had plenty of energy back at Crescent Hall, but as soon as everyone had come home from the hospital, she'd clammed right up. He'd wanted to follow her into the house, but his gut told him to give her space. Maybe she was simply worn out.

He had just pulled in to park near the bunkhouse when his phone buzzed in his pocket.

"Jericho here," he said when he'd pulled it out and accepted the call.

"It's Kara. You going to Mom and Dad's anniversary dinner tomorrow?"

"Yeah." He'd already let his mother know that. He wasn't looking forward to it, though. During his time back in Chance Creek, he'd already sat through two stilted family meals. He figured after the anniversary dinner, he'd have a word with his mom and let her know she could stop trying to bring the family together again.

Too much water under the bridge. Too many memories none of them savored.

"Just making sure. You have a way of letting them down, you know. It'd be nice of you to show up."

He pulled the phone away from his face and stared at it a moment. Putting it back to his ear, he said, "You gotta be kidding."

"Like hell I am. Don't disappoint them."

Jericho burned with resentment. Of course he'd show up.

"And bring a gift this time. Flowers. Something like that."

He clutched the phone so hard he was surprised it didn't shatter. "I'll grab a bottle of wine."

The silence at the other end of the line stretched so long Jericho thought she'd hung up. "Jesus. You're the one who's got to be kidding. Jericho—you know they don't drink, right? Haven't in years."

"Since when?" They'd always drunk. Every childhood memory he had included a bottle of wine or two. At least it had before his aunt and uncle had moved away. After that his parents didn't celebrate very much.

"Since... a couple of years ago. They joined AA."

Now he was the one with nothing to say. "Then why didn't they say something?" he finally sputtered. He'd been sending those bottles of wine forever. Practically ever since he joined up. He'd thought about the quiet household he'd finally escaped and thought a little good cheer could brighten things up—just like in the old days.

His parents didn't drink?

He remembered those two strained meals since he'd been back in Chance Creek. Each time his mom had made a big fuss over whether he wanted iced tea or lemonade. It had been summer, they'd served barbecue and, in truth, he'd thought they were avoiding serving alcohol while Kara was present. His sister's moods were volatile no matter the circumstances—and alcohol never helped the situation. It had never occurred to him they'd finally stopped drinking themselves.

"Bring something else this time," Kara said.

"Sure." Movement in his peripheral vision brought Jericho's head up. Boone was approaching the truck. "Gotta go. See you tomorrow night." He ended the call before Kara could answer. He'd have to mull over what she'd said later; he didn't have time now. Didn't have time to think about Savannah's tears, either. Hell, he'd practically proposed to her and she'd started crying. What was he supposed to make of that?

Reluctantly, he climbed out of the truck and nodded to Boone. "Everything all right?"

"With Base Camp? Yeah, it's all fine." But Boone looked worried about something. Jericho waited. "It's Riley," Boone admitted finally. "She's not pregnant yet. And we've been trying—lots." He shook his head. "Don't want to dump this on you. Just don't know who else—"

"You can talk to me," Jericho assured him, but he

wished the topic was different. He'd thought about babies far too much recently, and he'd seen Mason's face when he'd declared he wasn't going to have children. Mason couldn't have made his thoughts more clear if he'd spoken them aloud. He'd looked from Jericho to Savannah and back again, as if to say Jericho might not want kids, but Savannah probably did.

Mason was wrong, of course, but everyone would feel the same way, especially given Fulsom's demands. For the rest of the year, he'd have to field these questions again and again—and so would Savannah. That would certainly put a strain on things—and they were strained enough already.

"We're going to go to a doctor today. Can't say I'm looking forward to it." Boone cocked back his hat and studied the horizon.

Jericho could imagine. "I'm sure it's not your fault."

"It's not a matter of fault." Boone's tone was tight. "It's just a matter of fixing the problem—if there is one." He made a visible effort to control his irritation. "I've been reading up. It's not necessarily a simple process, either; it can take time to figure things out. So the pressure's on the rest of you. Don't wait for your wedding night, if you know what I mean. Get to it as soon as you can." He paused. "You and Savannah have an understanding yet?"

"Not like that." Jericho swallowed. "I mean, we've talked a little—"

"She knows you want to marry her?"

"Yeah, but—"

"Good. We're due for an easy wedding for once." Boone slugged his shoulder. "Buy her a ring. Throw an engagement party. Let's get this show on the road." He pulled his phone out of his back pocket. "Gotta go see that doctor." He grimaced. "Can't wait to get this over with. Hope I'm not shooting blanks."

He climbed into the truck Jericho had just vacated.

Jericho watched him drive away.

SAVANNAH WAS STILL reeling when she let herself into the manor's front door and headed toward the front room where her baby grand piano sat. She'd wiped her tears and told herself she was ready to get back to work, despite her broken heart. With the wedding yesterday and babysitting today, she'd barely practiced. She couldn't take setbacks to her schedule like this—not if she wanted to be prepared for her audition. But when she turned into the room, she found Riley there before her, sitting at her easel and working on a large landscape painting.

At least, she was sitting in front of it. Savannah could make out golden pastures, a sweep of blue sky and distant mountains, but Riley wasn't painting.

Riley turned. Savannah noticed her eyes were red. Had she been crying, too?

"Riley? What's wrong?"

Riley shrugged, but another tear slid down her cheek. "I don't know if I'll ever have a child."

"Honey—" Savannah took the paintbrush from Riley's hand and set it down. She led Riley away from her painting and into the kitchen, sat her in a seat and began to heat a kettle of water on the stove. "Why would you say that?" She was glad to have something to do to distract herself, but she felt bad for Riley. She knew how much she wanted a child.

"I've been married two months! When am I going to get pregnant? You know I was ready to adopt before I came to Westfield."

Savannah nodded. Riley had told her all about her attempts to adopt on her own. But she'd lost her job just as the process was reaching its conclusion and her application had been denied. That was before their idea to move to Chance Creek together.

"When I got here and met Boone again, I figured Fate knew what it was doing. I thought I was supposed to have a baby with him, and that's why I hadn't been allowed to adopt. I figured things would turn out okay, but they're not!"

"Two months is nothing," Savannah assured her. "Sometimes it takes years for a couple to get pregnant!"

"We don't have years! We could lose Westfield!"

Savannah's heart ached for her friend. Fulsom's stupid goals were to blame for this outburst. Otherwise Riley loved Boone enough not to care if it took months of trying to get pregnant. But Westfield had belonged to Riley's family before Fulsom bought it. Riley had once thought she'd inherit the spread. Savannah knew she couldn't bear the thought of losing it. There was far more than a pregnancy at stake here.

"I have to get pregnant right now," Riley told her.

"Boone and I decided to go to the doctor to get checked out. We don't want to waste time. What if they find—what if—"

"They won't find anything. Look, you're letting Fulsom get in your head. There are nine other couples—or there will be. We'll get it done."

"We're three months into the year. No one's pregnant yet. What makes you think—?"

"Because I know it will happen. You and Boone go at it like rabbits, right?" Riley stiffened in surprise but Savannah pushed on. "Nora and Clay are mad for each other. And from what I heard, Harris and Samantha were sneaking off to the woods when they weren't even supposed to be together. There will be plenty of babies. Trust me."

Riley sighed. Tried to smile. "And of course you and Jericho will be next. And when you finally let that man touch you—Savannah, are you okay?"

"Yes." Savannah covered her alarm with a coughing fit. "Sorry—something caught in my throat." She busied herself pouring tea. "I'm not so sure about me and Jericho," she said. "We might want different things."

Riley, who'd just picked up the cup Savannah placed in front of her, put it down again. "Did you have a fight? I thought you two were babysitting at Crescent Hall."

"We didn't have a fight." Although her heart felt so sore they may as well have. She searched for a way to change the topic, but Riley glanced at the kitchen clock and gasped.

"Boone's going to be here any minute to pick me up. I'd better get ready."

"Good luck at your appointment."

Riley rushed from the room. Savannah sat down to sip her tea. It was cruel for Fate to give her a baby and deny Riley one. Would Riley resent her for getting pregnant so easily while she struggled?

Savannah hoped not.

But with the way things were going, she didn't count on it.

WHY ON EARTH had he convinced Boone to let Savannah skip work?

Jericho glanced at the time on his phone the following morning and cursed when it was clear she wouldn't come today. He didn't know why he'd thought she would after he'd told her she didn't have to. When he'd made the impetuous gesture the other night it had felt good to support her music career. He'd hoped she'd remember that support when he asked her to marry him.

But Savannah had kept her face turned away from him all the way home from Crescent Hall yesterday, had cried when he'd begun to propose, and as soon as they reached the manor, she'd slipped out of the truck and gone inside without saying goodbye. She hadn't appeared at breakfast this morning, either, although he'd seen her getting out of her tent and heading to the bunkhouse with Avery early that morning to help each other finish dressing in their Regency gowns. She must have slipped back up to the manor while he was visiting one of the composting toilets and she hadn't come back.

Had all those babies yesterday made her think about Fulsom's demands? Was she afraid if she married him, he'd push for children, too? She'd made it pretty clear she didn't want him to propose on the way home. Jericho supposed he didn't blame her. A truck wasn't the place for a romantic gesture. He just hoped that was the only reason she'd pulled away from him like that. She'd seemed so tired—so defeated when she'd leaned back against the seat and closed her eyes.

Was she worried she'd never get the chance to pursue her dream? Did she think they'd all pressure her to be a mom, instead?

Jericho wasn't sure how he could make it clearer he didn't want kids—and wouldn't push for her to have them. He'd stated his intention to stay childless pretty baldly when Mason had asked.

Whatever had made her so upset, he'd better go talk to her. And ask her out on a real date, too. Even though they saw each other every day—had worked with each other evey day until now—he couldn't expect her to jump straight into matrimony without a little wooing.

He trudged up the hill, sighing when a camera crew seemed to appear out of nowhere to follow him. He supposed there was nothing for it but to go ahead and talk to Savannah anyway. Even before he crested the ridge he heard the sound of her playing the piano. She wasn't thundering through a crescendo or tripping lightly over a waltz, however. Instead it sounded like she was pressing random keys without much thought to tempo or tune.

Avery showed him in when he knocked on the back door.

"I'm glad you're here. Savannah's in the parlor," was all she said as she pushed past him out the door and headed toward Base Camp. Jericho assumed she was going to meet Walker. Savannah stopped playing and watched him approach warily, frowning when the crew followed him in.

"You're not at work."

"You said you'd talk to Boone."

"I did, and it's all right. I just missed you."

She looked down at her hands. "Every hour counts."

"I guess so. What's your next step?" He was making conversation because he didn't know how to broach the topic he'd come here to talk about.

"I… have to prepare so I'm at the top of my form. Then I'll need to find venues to showcase my talent."

"So you need to practice a lot. I get it," Jericho said. It made sense, although he felt a pang as he thought about the way her career would take Savannah away from Base Camp frequently. He liked it when she focused her attention right here—on him, and his ideas for a green energy system.

He guessed he'd been fooling himself when he'd thought she might be growing interested in the technology he'd been teaching her to use during their work hours. After all, what was a bunch of physics to a woman who lived and breathed music?

"Do you mean that?" Savannah asked him. "I know you've got deadlines to meet."

"I'll meet them, don't you worry about that. I understand commitment and drive. Your career is everything for you—just like mine is for me."

"Is that why—?" Savannah broke off.

"Why what?"

"Why you don't want kids?" she asked tentatively.

Just like he thought; she was worried he'd push for children when she wanted to focus on her career. Best to get the truth right out in the open. Savannah would be relieved to know he wasn't expecting her to take on motherhood.

"That's part of it. The way I see it is you and I both have plenty to do without adding kids into the mix. Everyone else here is going to try for babies. Soon Base Camp will be as awash with them as Crescent Hall. With the career you've got planned there's no way you'd have time to be a good mom. I understand that. I support the choice you're making. When you play Carnegie Hall, I'll be in the front row and start the standing ovation. Won't that be great?" There. Now she could be in no doubt of where he stood.

He couldn't read her expression. It was like she'd frozen in place, her hands resting on the keys, her eyes staring forward but seeing nothing.

She must be overcome at how supportive he was being. After all, neither her family nor her ex-fiancé had respected her career. Jericho stepped closer, braced his hands on her shoulders, bent down and stole a kiss. "You and me—we'll make a great pair. We see everything the same way. Eyes on the prize, right?"

"Right." Savannah's voice was barely audible. She cleared her throat and repeated the word. "Right. Eyes on the prize."

She was still shocked. "So don't you worry about coming to work anymore," Jericho told her, wanting to clear up his intentions once and for all. "You practice all day. All night, too, if you want. Except tonight."

"Why not tonight?" Savannah asked dazedly.

"Because tonight you and I are going on a date. I'll pick you up at seven."

He beat a retreat before she could protest, and by the time he reached the back door his spirits had been restored. That hadn't gone badly at all.

"WE'RE GOING TO have a full house this time," Avery said later that morning when all the women except Sam had gathered around the kitchen table for a quick meeting before lunch. Savannah was finding it hard to focus on anything except the ache in her heart. After Jericho had left, she'd climbed slowly to her bedroom, shut the door and locked it—but found she couldn't cry. This was even worse than she'd imagined. Jericho didn't want kids. Not only that—he didn't think she'd make a good mother if she pursued her career. His pronouncement had sliced straight through her heart.

It was her worst fear. The thing that woke her in the

middle of the night and wouldn't let her sleep again. What kind of mother left her baby for days while she traveled? Savannah knew perfectly well people made all kinds of situations work in circumstances like hers. They hired a nanny, or brought in a grandparent to care for the child. But Savannah's mother was hardly maternal, and she'd never met Jericho's mom. And most likely wouldn't—not with his attitude about fatherhood.

She'd put all her eggs in one basket. She'd told herself a child could be just as happy and well-nurtured with a father as with a mother. Surely Jeicho could see the logic in that—unless he wasn't interested in being a father at all.

Avery had called a meeting to discuss the next round of guests who were coming to the manor—a large party of women celebrating their ten-year anniversary of graduating from med school.

"What are we going to do with a house full of doctors—in early October?" Nora asked.

"The usual things," Avery said. "But I thought maybe we should do more with Base Camp this time. I have a feeling this group of women will like learning about the science and technology behind what the men are doing there."

"Even though they're coming for a Regency vacation?" Riley asked skeptically. She'd been quiet since returning home the day before. Savannah knew the doctor had run a battery of tests on her, and now she was waiting for results.

"We'll give them plenty of Regency fun, too," Avery

assured her. "I'm already coordinating with Maud and James for a musical evening and a ball."

"At least it's in between weddings," Win pointed out. "Jericho will be married on September 28," she added with a wink at Savannah, "and whoever comes next won't marry until November."

The trill of a phone cut through the conversation and Win jumped, pulling it out of her apron pocket. "I've got to take this." She stood up and crossed to the far side of the room before taking the call. Savannah wasn't sorry for the interruption. The last thing she wanted to think about was weddings.

Riley must have understood that. "The weather is getting cooler, and we could have rain; we'd better think of more inside—" She cut off when Win raised her voice.

"No! No, I won't! You're the one who's acting like a lunatic. People don't control their grown children—this isn't the nineteenth century."

Avery raised an eyebrow. Savannah knew why; Win was wearing a nineteenth-century gown as she spoke.

"I will not come home. This is my life, Mom, whether or not you like it. You better believe I'll marry him when I—" Win frowned. "You can't be serious." She listened again, then looked up to see everyone else staring at her. "I'm in the middle of a meeting. I'll call you back later."

She cut the call and slipped the phone back into her pocket, but it was a moment before Win rejoined them at the table. "Sorry, that was my mother. I swear she's losing it. Who cares who I marry in this day and age? All of a sudden she's got something to say about everything I do. There's nothing wrong with Angus, if she would just meet him."

"She doesn't want you to marry him?" Avery asked.

"Doesn't want me to marry him. Doesn't want me to be on the show. Hates that I quit my job and broke off my engagement. Thinks it's all your fault, by the way," she said to Savannah. "According to her, your family is about as angry as mine is."

Savannah bit her lip and prayed Win would stop talking. "They're fine," she assured everyone.

Win snorted. "That's not what I heard. Mom said you were engaged, too, before you left town. That you ditched your fiancé. When were you going to let everyone know?"

"Engaged?" Avery echoed. "To who?"

"Charles Scott, one of the richest men in California," Win told her. Savannah could have kicked her— wasn't she aware of the camera crew silently filming everything? "He's an angel investor. The kind of guy who makes or breaks start-ups. Savannah here could have been Silicon Valley royalty." Win glared at Savannah. "My mother thinks you're a bad influence."

"I didn't make you stay here," Savannah said, stung. She and Win had been acquainted, but hadn't been friends before Win had come for Savannah's cousin's wedding. Once she'd decided to stay they'd become closer.

"No, but your mother is over the moon that you're

doing something that promotes your family's business. She keeps bragging to my mom about how much more air time you get than me. Of course, my mom doesn't want me to get any air time at all."

"How could you not tell us you're engaged?" Nora asked.

"That's the pot calling the kettle black, isn't it?" Savannah said tartly. "Like none of the rest of you have kept secrets."

They all had the grace to look ashamed of themselves. As well they might; it was clear that their friendships hadn't been as solid as they'd thought. Every one of them had been holding back when they arrived at Westfield.

"Besides, this isn't about me—this is about Win. What are you going to do?" Savannah went on.

"What can I do? If my parents don't like Angus, then screw them." But Win didn't sound half as sure as her words made her out to be, and as the conversation awkwardly drifted back to their guests, Savannah noticed her gaze remained distant.

Savannah didn't blame her; she was finding it hard to concentrate, too.

She dropped a hand to her belly under the table. Poor little sprite. Babies should be welcomed. She'd always felt that when she finally told Jericho about their child, his face would light up, and all her problems would be solved. It hurt her more than she could say to know that wouldn't be the case. She couldn't stand the thought of his anger. Or worse—disinterest.

She finally faced the question that had haunted her since Jericho declared he didn't want kids.

Should she leave?

Savannah bit her lip. She didn't want to; that was the heart of the matter. She didn't want to have to give up on anything. She wanted her baby. Wanted her career. Wanted Jericho.

She wanted her friends, the bed and breakfast, even her work on the energy grid.

Was she being too selfish?

"What do you think, Savannah?" Riley asked.

"Uh—" Savannah didn't even know what they'd been talking about. "I'm sorry, what was the question?"

"Should we take our guests on a hayride?"

"Uh…sure. Why not?" She glanced at Win, who was gazing out the kitchen window. Pulling herself together, Savannah added, "But let's make sure we have refreshments waiting afterward to make the outing seem more elegant."

Riley nodded. "That's a great idea."

With another glance at Win, Savannah gave her attention to the meeting. She wondered if there was more to that phone call than their friend was letting on.

Secrets, again.

How much longer could she keep hers?

CHAPTER FOUR

"**K**AI! YOU IN here?" Jericho hurried past Kai's array of solar ovens outside, and ducked into the kitchen at the bunkhouse just before noon. "Hey, I need to rustle up a picnic for later on. Can you help me with that?" He barely noticed the film crew trailing him. This far into the experience of being on a reality television show, he was beginning to take the crews for granted.

"Taking Savannah out?" Kai asked, hard at work prepping lunch.

"That's right. Got any ideas for grub?" He looked forward to the day when they'd have this whole kitchen running on solar power, along with the rest of the bunkhouse. They were getting really close.

"I'll take care of it. Glad to see you're getting a move on. I think I heard Boone say something about backup brides." He grinned, but Jericho knew Boone was capable of putting out an ad for one.

"I'm working on it. What about you? Have you found a bride yet?"

"You know, I've found that life works best when

you go with the flow instead of fighting it. I'll meet her when the time is right." Kai shrugged.

Jericho thought it must be nice to be that zen about your future. "Go with the flow, huh?"

"Things work out, you know?"

He hoped that was true. At the moment he wasn't sure if things were going to work out between him and Savannah.

"Lunch is in five minutes," Kai added.

"I'll get out of your way." Jericho headed back outside, but stopped in the doorway when he spotted Savannah arriving with the rest of the women from the manor. She was kneading her left hand with her right as she walked, as if her fingers were sore.

Maybe they were after so much practice.

Jericho moved to intercept her, happy to see the camera crew hadn't followed him outside. "Hey, come and sit a minute. Lunch isn't ready yet." Before she could protest, Jericho took her hand and brought her over to one of the logs they used as benches. He sat, and tugged her down beside him, keeping her hand in his.

"How did your practice go this morning?" He began to massage her hand and wrist, so slender and delicate compared to his.

"It was… it… it was…" Savannah's shoulders relaxed as he kneaded her hand. "Wow, that feels good," she said.

"I could tell you were sore." Jericho kept going as Savannah's expression grew distant. He'd hit on something with the massage, he realized. Something good. He'd make the most of it.

"My wrists ache when I play too long," she admitted.

"Maybe you should take more breaks." Too late he realized how that would sound to her. Savannah pulled her hand away.

"I can't," she said fiercely. "You have no idea how competitive this field is, do you? It's not like the Navy, where they'll take anyone."

Jericho recoiled. Did she have any idea of the grueling process he'd gone through to qualify as a SEAL?

Maybe she did—because Savannah now looked distinctly sheepish.

"I'm sorry," she said. "I'm just… stressed out."

He picked up her other hand, and when she didn't pull it away, he began to massage it. He chose his words carefully. "You don't have to do this alone, you know. I'm here for you. I understand why you're stressed out."

The look she gave him said he couldn't possibly understand, but Jericho wasn't going to let her push him away again.

"You're working toward an enormous goal—one that means the world to you," he went on. "Your family isn't supportive. Your situation is tricky. You've got a lot of different demands on your time." Was she growing misty eyed? Jericho rushed on. "I've got your back. I'll do anything I can to help you be a concert pianist. Whatever you need, you tell me—got it? I'll be there for you—What?" he asked when she shook her head.

"You're saying all the right words, but you don't mean them." Savannah tried to tug away from him.

"I mean them." He didn't like the way she was looking at him, like all of this was far above his head and he was too thick to understand. He'd held positions of responsibility before, and he'd thought she understood that about him.

Instead, her disdain reminded him all too clearly of his family's assessment of him.

"Not really." But she let him continue to massage her, working his way up her wrist to her forearm. That was something, Jericho decided, and he didn't stop as Savannah went on. "I can think of a dozen things I could ask you to help with that you wouldn't like."

"That's not true. Savannah." He hesitated only a moment. "I'm going to ask you to marry me soon. And when we're husband and wife, there's nothing you can ask that I'll say no to." He noticed some of the crew members exiting the bunkhouse and looking around for something else to film. Damn it; just when he'd gotten Savannah to talk to him. He hoped they'd keep their distance.

"That's an awfully broad statement. And you're getting ahead of yourself, don't you think?"

"It's not a statement. It's a promise." If he wasn't mistaken, despite her words, she was giving in. Thinking about saying yes to him. Jericho leaned down and stole a kiss while he had the chance, his whole body coming alive at her touch. God he wanted her. Wanted to know he'd get to wake up beside this beautiful woman every day for the rest of his life.

Wanted to go to bed with her every night, too.

He braced himself for her to pull back like she always did these days, but this time Savannah stayed with the kiss, as if she was testing what it felt like to be close to him.

Couldn't she remember?

He could—with vivid detail. He relived their encounter in the Russells' bathroom on a daily basis. Several times a day if he was honest. As their kiss went on, he could call up exactly how it had been to press inside her for the first time. To feel her breasts heavy in his hands. To know he was driving her to the brink of ecstasy.

"Get a room," Angus called out from the bunkhouse door in his thick Scottish accent.

Jericho jumped, pulled back an inch and met Savannah's gaze. Her lips were parted and her breath coming fast.

And he was in no fit state for company. A quick glance told him the film crew was bearing down on them.

"I'm going to go get my lunch," Savannah told him, beginning to rise.

All around them people were heading for the bunkhouse and coming out with plates stacked with food.

"Hold on," he said, a little more roughly than he intended. He clamped a hand on her wrist to keep her in place.

"But—"

"Just give me a minute, would you?" Jericho said with a glance at the crew setting up to film.

Her brow furrowed, but when Savannah looked down and took in his condition, the corners of her mouth tugged up into a smile. Despite the awkward circumstances, Jericho's spirits lifted; it had been far too long since he'd seen her do that.

"You've worked yourself into a state."

She was enjoying this, wasn't she? "I was remembering you in Maud and James's bathroom," he said honestly. "The image got the better of me."

She leaned toward him. "Shh! You want the whole world to know?"

"The world wouldn't blame me for not being able to get it out of my mind if they did. Come on, Savannah. Why won't you let me touch you like that again?" He kept his voice too low for the microphones to pick up.

A delicate blush spread over her features, but she shook her head. "I don't think that would be wise."

"I don't know about wise. It'd sure be fun."

She glanced up. "You think life is just about fun?"

"Honey, I was a SEAL for years. I know what life's about. But I say take your fun where you can find it. There's enough suffering in the world. Why not give each other some happiness when we can?" He leaned closer. "I'd like to make you happy. Why don't you marry me and let me get to it?" Jericho realized this was no place for a proposal, though. Not with the cameras rolling. "Wait—don't answer that yet. Just think about it. Okay?" He moved closer and kissed her harder this time. That would give Renata something to put in the next episode.

"Can I go get my lunch now?" Savannah asked when he pulled back a second time, her exasperation clear, although her eyes were shining.

"Not yet. Give me a minute."

IT SHOULDN'T GRATIFY her this much to know that Jericho could get hard just thinking about their time together, but the SEAL was in a peck of trouble, and she couldn't help feeling a little pride. She bent toward him, knowing the view of her cleavage could hardly help, and was rewarded when he groaned. She didn't think the cameras would pick up the swell in his pants; not when they were both sitting down. It was clear from her vantage point, though.

"Savannah…" He didn't go on, but she knew what he meant; she was driving him wild. Which was only fair, because he was doing the same to her—dangling marriage in front of her twenty-four hours after he'd declared he never wanted children. It was clear that he wanted her. She felt certain he loved her—and would never want to cause her pain. He kept talking about supporting her career. Did he think that was how to win her heart? Was all his bluster about not wanting kids real? Or—?

Savannah straightened. Was he merely saying what he thought she wanted to hear? She'd made it clear pursuing her dream was her first priority—so much so she'd jumped at the chance to stop working with him. No wonder he was acting like she'd said she didn't want kids.

She glanced down again. Jericho was totally turned on. He wanted her. Cared about her. She cared about him, too. At this point in her pregnancy, she should have suffered from morning sickness. Why wasn't she pale and prostrate on her bed?

Instead she had a healthy desire to be *in* her bed—with Jericho.

Could they slip away?

No. She squashed the impulse hard. Jericho was out of bounds. At least until they figured things out. He'd said he didn't think she could be a good mom and pursue a career, too, for heaven's sake. She couldn't fool around with him, let alone lead him on to think they had a future.

Unless…

He'd said he'd do anything for her. Couldn't that possibly include changing his attitude about fatherhood? About taking on a strong role in their baby's upbringing? Could his flippant remarks at the Halls' place—and again this morning—be just that—thoughtless, off-the-cuff statements that really didn't mean anything?

Savannah wanted to believe that—badly.

Especially since every fiber of her body was yearning toward the handsome man trying to hide his lust for her from the rest of their friends.

"What's the square root of two hundred and fifty-two?" she asked him.

"I don't know—"

"Figure it out."

Jericho hesitated. "Fifteen point…something."

"What's thirty-five times twenty-nine?"

"A thousand and fifteen," Jericho said after a few seconds.

Savannah kept grilling him until Jericho stood up.

"Okay, I got this under control. Saved by math," he said with a shake of his head.

"Works every time." She stifled a laugh, gratified she could find the humor in the situation. Despite the hurtful things he'd said, she loved this man. She thought he felt the same way. He was ready to propose to her, for heaven's sake.

Surely he'd come to love his child, too—if he got used to the idea?

She stood, too, plucking at the neckline of her dress. This late in August, the hot days were following one after another, and although mostly she felt fine, sometimes she found it hard to handle the heat.

"Kai's fixing us a picnic for dinner," Jericho said as he led the way to the bunkhouse. "I thought we'd go down to the creek. Maybe it'll be cooler there. We have a date tonight, remember?"

How could she forget? She'd give this one more try, she decided. She'd dig deeper into Jericho's reasoning for not wanting to have kids. Maybe she'd uncover some simple misunderstanding about parenthood she could put to rest. "Sounds like heaven," she said before she realized she should moderate her response. After all, she had no guarantee she could change Jericho's mind.

"I think so too."

JERICHO DIDN'T THINK he'd ever seen someone as beautiful as Savannah looked that night. She was seated on the blanket they'd spread by Pittance Creek, and as she lifted the packets of food Kai had prepared out of the basket one by one, even the presence of a camera crew couldn't spoil his enjoyment of the moment.

"Kai's packed us three kinds of salad, chicken sandwiches, all kinds of fruit and..." She pulled out a bottle. "Oh."

Jericho grinned. "Good ol' Kai. Hand me that."

Savannah passed over the bottle of wine slowly. Catching on to her hesitation, Jericho set it aside, wondering if she thought he wanted to get her tipsy and take advantage of her. The thought had crossed his mind. "We'll get to that later. Food first." He saw that Kai had non-alcoholic beverages, too. The man thought of everything.

Savannah busied herself with opening containers and finding serving spoons. Soon they each had a plate of food and began to eat. With Kai's delicious cooking and Pittance Creek rolling past, he couldn't ask for a better setting.

"It sure is warm tonight." Savannah balanced her plate in one hand and pushed back tendrils of her hair that had escaped from her bonnet.

"Why don't you take that hat off? You'd be cooler."

"I think you're right."

Fondness welled within him as she undid the ribbons holding it in place and lifted her bonnet from her head. She placed it carefully aside and caught him looking. "What?"

"You're a beautiful woman, Savannah."

"Thank you." She picked at her food with her fork. "Stop looking at me; I'm trying to eat."

Jericho chuckled. "You can't eat while I watch?" He reached over and ran a finger along her jaw.

"It's hard to look alluring while you're shoveling the most delicious potato salad ever into your mouth. I'm hungry."

Jericho liked a woman who liked to eat. "Well, dig in. I'll pretend you aren't even here."

"Perfect." Savannah scooped up a pile of potato salad and popped it into her mouth. "Yum," she said when she'd chewed and swallowed.

"Do I have to learn to cook to win your heart?" Jericho asked.

"Learn to cook, clean, do the laundry, walk the dog…" Savannah said lightly, scooping up another forkful.

"We get to have a dog?"

"Do you want one?" She raised an eyebrow.

"Sure. I love animals."

"You're not worried a pet would tie you down? Sounds like you plan to have a busy career." She licked a bit of potato salad off her finger.

A certain part of Jericho's anatomy woke up, but he made himself answer her question. "I plan to have a career, but I won't let it run my life. I'll pick and choose my projects carefully. Need to leave plenty of time to spoil my wife—which apparently means doing a lot of chores." He'd like to do a little spoiling right now. If only these damn cameras hadn't followed them like usual. He'd complained about it to Boone earlier. His friend was lucky—he'd wooed Riley before the show started.

"Are you saying you'll clean, cook, feed the dog, walk it, play with it... keep it safe?"

"Of course." Jericho bit into a sandwich. Savannah was right; the food was excellent.

"You think you can handle the responsibility?"

"Yes, I think I can handle the responsibility of caring for a dog." Jericho wondered what this was about. "And I can probably learn to grill a steak. Pretty sure I know how to dial a phone to find a cleaning service—hey!" He caught the cherry tomato Savannah had picked out of a salad and thrown at him.

"Cleaning service, my ass. You're going to live in a tiny home."

He chuckled. "Yeah, all right. Probably can keep it halfway decent if I have to. What about you—you're just going to practice day and night and ignore me and the dog? Walter might not like that."

"Wynona won't give a hoot because she'll be too busy playing with you," Savannah retorted.

"I'm pretty sure Walter will want some mommy time now and then." Jericho noticed Savannah had stopped eating. She had the most peculiar expression on her face, but she lifted her cloth napkin to wipe her lips and nodded.

"I guess she will," she said quietly.

Did she really care so strongly about whether they got a female dog or a male one? Somehow, Jericho doubted it—and he doubted she was this concerned about whether he'd remember to feed the mutt. "Savannah—are you worried about your career?" he hazarded. "Do you think you've taken on too much?"

She studied her plate as if it contained all the answers. "I have high goals," she said. "For everything I do—not just my career. It's important to me to do things right, and I'm not sure I can—without help. What if I fail?"

Jericho had never seen her look so vulnerable. "Can you fail with music? I mean—not everyone can play at Carnegie Hall, but is that really your goal? I thought it was more about having the chance to entertain people."

Savannah bristled. "It's not like I'm playing pop music."

Jericho's gut told him not to back down. Savannah was worried about something, and he still hadn't figured out what it was.

"Would it be bad if you were? Don't a lot more people listen to pop music than that classical stuff you play? That doesn't make classical music any less important—" Damn, he was really sticking his foot in it. He tried again. "Listen, play what you want to play whenever you want to play it—that's all I'm saying. Don't wait for an audience. Don't tell yourself you can't be happy unless you're headlining some big venue. It's a great goal, but—"

"But what—you don't think I'm good enough?" She set her plate on the ground.

"That's not it at all." Jericho tried to marshal his thoughts into order. "How many top-notch pianists are there? Classical ones—who get to play for audiences on a regular basis? A thousand? A hundred? Ten?"

She shrugged, her lips set in a thin line.

"When you graduated with a music degree you did something unusual. Now you're throwing your hat into an industry that employs very few people, because its audience is small. What will you do when you've won? When you're the best—the very best pianist in the world—for about a minute until the next person gets her turn? See what I mean? You can make it about that one shining moment when you're on top—or you can make it about the entire journey."

"That one moment is all I need—"

One of the cameramen swore and waved his cell phone at the others. "They're playing pickup football up near the bunkhouse—shirts and skins. Chris says it's off the hook; they want all of us there, right now."

The crew took off running up the track toward Base Camp without a backward look. Jericho and Savannah watched them go in stunned silence.

"Did…that just happen?" Savannah asked a moment later.

Jericho knew what she meant. The quiet the crew left behind was almost eerie.

"Yeah, it did. You know what this means, don't you?" He stood up, glad for the opportunity to drop the fight before it got worse.

"We should go back and watch the game?"

"Hell, no!" Jericho laughed. He knew exactly why the men at Base Camp had chosen this moment for a pickup game. Thank God for Boone—always resourceful, that man. His friend was giving him time to seal the deal with Savannah.

"What, then?"

Jericho tugged her to her feet. "Time to go skinny-dipping."

WHY THE HELL not? Savannah thought as she watched Jericho strip down to his skivvies—and then peel those off, too. Why not enjoy one last romp with this sexy man? Even if their conversation had her brain doing cartwheels? As much as she hated to admit it, the questions Jericho had raised made sense. He was right; she was tying her happiness to an achievement she could barely hope to approach. What if she never played Carnegie Hall—or similar venues? Would her whole life be a failure?

She touched her belly, then quickly dropped her hand before Jericho saw the gesture. Of course it wouldn't be. No matter what, she'd have this child.

And maybe—just maybe—a husband who loved her. She still had hope of Jericho, if she was honest. Even if she couldn't imagine backing down from her plan to impress her parents. Otherwise, she'd never be fumbling to undo the ties of her dress, then turning around to let him take a crack at it.

Jericho moved behind her and pulled at the fastenings of her dress. "Hell, this is complicated," he said when he'd gotten it off her and stood looking at her stays.

"Get busy," she told him, still trying to make sense of the desires competing within her. Fame—success—motherhood—

Jericho.

"Yes, ma'am," he said with a chuckle. He got to work and Savannah braced herself as he tugged and pulled the laces free. By the time he'd wrestled her out of them, Savannah had stopped trying to sort out the future. She was far too busy second guessing the present. Letting Jericho undress her had to be a huge mistake.

But when he reached for the hem of her chemise, pulled it over her head and turned her around, she forgot all her doubts when she saw the look on his face.

Pure desire.

His want spurred her own, but she bit back a chuckle when she saw where his gaze rested.

Not on her belly, as worried as she'd been it might give her away. Typical. She might feel every one of the four pounds she'd gained since getting pregnant, but Jericho hadn't noticed the slight rounding of her stomach.

Instead, his gaze rested squarely on her breasts.

Savannah couldn't blame him.

If she'd added some weight to her waistline, she felt like she'd gained at least that much again in her bust—a fact that had driven her to Two Willows more than once so Alice Reed could let out the bodice of her dresses.

So far she'd managed to hide that from everyone— except maybe Samantha. She'd swear Sam had over-heard her talking to Alice the last time they'd visited Two Willows, but the newest addition to Westfield hadn't mentioned it yet.

She was still on her honeymoon with Harris at the moment, so Savannah could count on a few more days of peace at least. Maybe Jericho would guess what was going on, though, given how thoroughly he was examin-ing her body.

He stepped forward, cupped her breasts with his hands and Savannah forgot everything in a wave of sensation that nearly swept her off her feet.

"Easy," she gasped. "They're... a little tender."

"Sorry." Jericho made as if to pull away, but Savan-nah grabbed his wrists and kept his hands exactly where they were.

"Don't be. It feels—amazing."

Jericho looked pleased and he began to explore her body with his hands, spending most of his time and effort on her breasts. Savannah, weak in the knees, closed her eyes and gloried in the feelings his touches and caresses spun out of her willing flesh. All she could do was brace her hands on his shoulders and let him have his way with her. It was as if Jericho knew every-thing about her—and could play her body like a fine instrument.

When he bent to take one oh-so-sensitive nipple into her mouth, Savannah thought she'd found heaven. Her body was on fire for him. The length of him bobbed against her stomach when he pulled her closer. Savannah couldn't resist sliding a hand down his hard chest, his washboard abs, to wrap around his thickness and slide her palm along him, glorying in the moan that escaped his mouth.

"Savannah," he growled against her neck as she teased him. He grew harder beneath her fingers and Savannah imagined what he'd feel like inside her.

"Mm-mm," she moaned, pressing kisses along his shoulder. "Jericho—"

He pulled her close and she could feel him scanning the vicinity, his gaze settling on the creek. "Come on."

He lifted her up and she wrapped her legs around his waist, stifling another groan as his hardness pressed against the part of her that ached for him most. She clung to him as he bent to fetch something from the jeans he'd discarded, then walked into the creek until he was thigh-deep in it and continued to wade up to their waists.

Savannah gasped as the cold water lapped over her bottom and thighs, then held on as Jericho tore open a condom wrapper with his teeth and quickly sheathed himself. "We took a chance last time," he said in explanation.

If only he knew, Savannah thought.

Both of them looked at the now-empty wrapper in

his hand.

"Don't you dare throw that in the water," she told him.

"Of course not. Hold on to me." He surged out of the water again, carrying her with him, until he could shove the wrapper back into his pants pocket. "Next time I'll open it on land."

"We could stay on land," she pointed out reasonably.

"No fun in that."

Back in the water they went, and Savannah whooped when he nearly tripped and dunked her into the creek.

"Get back up here," he told her, grappling with her thighs.

Savannah, laughing too hard to hold on, did her best to wrap them around his waist again. "You're taking too long—oh!"

He slid inside her without preamble, filling her completely. She was so slick and ready for him, Savannah nearly slid over the edge into an orgasm right then and there, but she wasn't ready for that yet. She wanted to make this last.

Wrapping her arms around his neck, she eased up and back down around him again, causing both of them to sigh.

"Damn, woman—you feel... hell, you feel like everything I've always wanted."

Savannah didn't know how to respond to that. She knew exactly what he meant. She felt it, too.

"What have you done to your breasts?" He sighed as they bobbed against his chest with their rhythmic movements. "They've always looked good. But today—"

He didn't finish his sentence. Instead, he pushed into her again, slipped a hand up to cup one and bent to brush his hot, wet tongue over her nipple.

Savannah gasped and gave herself up to the experience, her whole body swirling with sensation. Jericho was teasing her everywhere, and it felt so good she didn't want to be anywhere else. When his other hand slid down to cup her bottom, Savannah gloried in the pressure of his touch, the cool water and the heat of their connection.

Soon Jericho sped up and all she could do was cling to him while he coaxed her to the edge and brought her over into a cascade of ecstasy that pulsed through her body, bringing her bucking up against him, wanting more and more.

When he came, thrusting deep within her, Savannah knew she wasn't through with Jericho yet. He had her hooked. She couldn't imagine sharing this experience with any other man. As she rode out his ecstasy, she explored the idea fully.

She needed to be with him.

Wanted to be with him.

Was—

A shout warned them someone else was coming. Savannah stiffened, suddenly aware of her nakedness and the intimate position they were in.

Jericho swore, pulled out of her in a rush and

scanned the banks. "Come on!"

She still clung to him while he dashed for dry land, scooped up her clothes, set her down and handed them to her. "Run—into the woods. I'll come back to help you dress when I've got them away." He was fiddling with the condom, racing to get it off. When he tied a quick knot and flung it into the woods, Savannah was shocked.

"Jericho!"

"I'll get it later."

"You're littering!"

"I'll get it later! Go!"

Savannah dashed over the uneven ground, stubbed her toe in the process and danced and hopped her way into the woods, biting back a string of swear words. Couldn't they have even a few minutes alone? Was that really too much to ask?

She supposed it was, given their situation.

She'd barely made it to the cover of the trees before a woman strode down the track. Savannah caught a glimpse of her as she bolted behind a clump of hemlocks to hide. A tall, angular blonde who didn't look happy.

"Jericho? For God's sake, get some clothes on," the woman snapped.

Savannah didn't recognize her, and jealousy reared its ugly head before Jericho exclaimed, "Hold your horses, sis. If you don't want to see my bare ass, don't surprise me while I'm skinny-dipping."

"No one wants to see your bare ass."

Savannah smiled as she slipped her chemise over her head and picked up her stays. She liked Jericho's bare ass. Too much. She wrapped her stays around her waist backward and began to do up the laces in front. She wouldn't be able to get them too tight by herself, but she could do them up, shimmy them the right way around and thread her arms through the armholes, at least. Later, she could get one of her friends to help redo them.

She listened to Jericho's conversation while she worked on her complicated outfit.

"How'd you know where to find me?"

"I know you like to slack off while everyone else is working." Jericho's sister's voice was teasing, but carried an edge.

"That's not true. Besides, they're playing football."

"Game's over, I guess. One of your buddies up at the bunkhouse told me you were down here with a female friend. Where'd she go?"

Savannah froze.

"She's long gone back up to the manor," Jericho said. "Couldn't convince her to go for a swim."

"Really? That must be a first. I know how you like the ladies. One in every port—isn't that how you sailors roll?"

"Not me."

"Right. Jericho the steadfast. Excuse me if I don't buy it. You aren't exactly known for being responsible."

"Why the hell are you here, Kara?"

Savannah didn't blame him for snapping at his sister. That teasing must be growing old fast.

"Anniversary dinner? Seven o'clock? Ring a bell, Mr. Steadfast?"

"Shit! What time is it?"

"We're not late—yet. But getting mighty close. You got a gift for them?"

Jericho swore again. "You'd better go right now so one of us is on time. I'll be there in fifteen minutes. Twenty, tops."

"I'll tell them you're coming—probably," Kara said.

A minute later Jericho crashed through the trees to come to get Savannah. "We've got to go."

"Go ahead. I've almost got myself dressed—"

Jericho spun her around, yanked her dress the rest of the way down and rapidly began to do up her fastenings. "You're coming, too."

"Where?"

"My folks' place. Anniversary dinner."

"But—"

"Savannah—could you do this for me?" He spun her around to face him again, and his need was stark in his eyes.

"I—" When he looked at her like that she didn't know how to refuse him. "I guess so, but I look like hell."

"You look beautiful. We have to hurry. I don't have a gift to bring them."

"How about a nice bottle of wine?"

Jericho laughed, but it wasn't a happy sound. "No—no wine. I need something else."

CHAPTER FIVE

H E COULDN'T BELIEVE he'd completely forgotten about his parents' anniversary—especially after his sister had made such a big deal about it. By the time he found a gift, they'd be late.

"Harris would have something good if he were here," Savannah said, rushing to keep up with him. "Some bit of metalwork you could give your parents."

"You're a genius." Jericho would have kissed her if he had time. Only a week ago, he'd bought a metal wall hanging the man had hand-forged. Savannah was right; it would make the perfect gift.

After a quick detour to his tent—and Savannah's—they stopped by the bunkhouse to drop off the barely touched picnic, clean up and give a hurried explanation for their absence to Boone. They hopped into one of the Base Camp trucks to drive to town.

Jericho's parents lived in the same small, square house he'd grown up in. The front of the home looked the same as it ever had and Jericho knew from his previous visits its interior hadn't changed much, either.

The only real difference was the absence of the old cottonwood tree that once had held the treehouse out back. It had been cut down and chopped up, the stump pulled and the ground reseeded with grass, leaving no trace of where Donovan's accident occurred.

Still, somewhere in North Dakota a man's life was shaped by it, Jericho knew. He often wondered how extensive his cousin's injuries had been. He'd never brought himself to ask his parents directly, and they'd never volunteered the information, either.

"He was hurt bad. Real bad," his mother had told him the day after the accident. She'd said more to his father when they thought they were out of his hearing. Words like *surgery—paralysis—wheelchair—*

Never walk again.

Jericho had known that day his life would never be the same. Never before had silence ruled their home like it did then.

That silence never truly went away again, either. Despite the years that had passed.

It didn't matter that it had been an accident—that Jericho, Donovan and Kara were young, all three of them.

He had been in charge.

He was supposed to be watching his cousin and sister.

He'd let it happen.

"Jericho?"

Savannah's soft voice pulled him from his reverie. He got out of the truck and opened her door. "Thanks for coming with me."

"Of course. How many years have your parents been married?"

He did the math. "Thirty-five."

"That's a long time." She looked pensive. "They must really love each other."

Jericho stumbled, but caught himself. Did they love each other?

He wasn't sure.

Maybe they stayed together out of habit at this point.

They'd grown far more insular after the accident and subsequent split with Donovan's parents. The two couples had always been inseparable, but Donovan's parents held Jericho to blame, and his parents were guilty by association.

They'd never had another card party.

As the familiar guilt wound through his gut, Jericho wondered for the first time what was with those parties, anyway? Why hadn't they done other things—like going to movies, or out to dinner, or on hikes and vacations?

Didn't they have other friends?

They must have had.

Thinking back he could picture larger get-togethers—holiday gatherings, things like that. But only once in a while.

And all of them had come to a halt after the accident. His parents had stayed home. Grown quiet.

Bitter.

His fault, Jericho thought again as the front door

opened and Kara peered out. She held a wineglass in her hand. "It's about time," she said loudly as she let them in.

"Don't start," he said in a low voice, noticing that wineglass in a way he wouldn't have previously. "I thought you said Mom and Dad were on the wagon," he added.

"They are. I'm not."

He opened his mouth to let her know what he thought of that, then changed his mind. That was an argument for another time. "This is Savannah," he said instead.

"It's nice to meet you." Savannah put out a hand.

But Kara was far too busy staring at Savannah's Regency gown to shake it, and Jericho realized he'd forgotten to warn his family.

"Savannah and her friends run a Jane Austen Bed and Breakfast at Westfield," he explained.

Kara considered this. "That big, old stone house of yours would make a great B&B. But why are you dressed up now? Trying to drum up business?"

"No." Savannah blushed and Jericho kicked himself for his mistake as his folks joined them near the door, both of them trying and failing to hide their surprise at Savannah's outfit.

"Savannah runs a Jane Austen B&B," Kara told them.

"My friends and I made a vow to each other…" Savannah trailed off, looking down at her gown. "It's supposed to remind us of the goals we each set when we came to Westfield. It's a little hard to explain."

"They got rid of all the modern things that interfere with having time to pursue their goals," Jericho stepped in. "Instead of filling their days with social media and surfing the web, they're devoting their time to things like playing the piano. Savannah here is a concert pianist."

"Not yet," she rushed to qualify, but she sent him a thankful look. "I'm working toward it. I studied music in school, but took some years off. Now I'm getting back to it."

"Savannah, meet my parents, Mary and Dan Cook," Jericho said.

"And that's Andy, my better half, watching the game," Kara said, pointing in the direction of Jericho's brother-in-law, who sat on a couch in the living room.

"Hey," Andy said. He raised his hand in greeting, but didn't get up.

"That's Molly and Cam." She gestured at two elementary-school-aged children, sitting next to him, engrossed in their cell phones.

"Come in, please," his mother said. "Jericho, I wish you'd told me you were bringing a guest. Savannah, excuse me a minute while I set another place at the table."

"Let me help." Savannah followed his still protesting mother into the kitchen, leaving Jericho flanked by his father and Kara.

"Well, come sit down," Jericho's father said.

"Full house," Jericho commented as he took a seat

on one of the easy chairs. "Cam, Molly—good to see you guys."

"Hi, Uncle Jericho."

"Hi, Uncle Jericho."

Neither child looked up, busy as they were with their phones. Jericho's mother bustled back into the room to set another place at the dining room table, then hurried back into the kitchen again.

"Always well behaved," Jericho's dad commented, jutting his chin at Cam and Molly. "No need to watch those two like a hawk."

Stung by what could be a reference to the accident, Jericho bit back a sharp retort. Kara was the one who'd pushed him into Donovan. Why did everyone always act like it was his fault?

Because they'd never believed him in the first place when he'd told them it wasn't, Jericho thought grimly. He still remembered the thrashing his father had doled out for blaming his little sister for his own mistakes.

As a grown-up, he'd realized his father's pain and worry for Donovan had pushed him to the edge. His dad had lashed out, and Jericho had long since forgiven him.

Mostly.

"You're right; Molly's nothing like her mother," Jericho agreed. There. That would get his sister's goat.

Kara's eyes flashed with fury. "Watch it—"

Only Savannah's reappearance broke the spell of the tension between them. "I'm supposed to find out what everyone wants to drink," she said. "Milk? Water?

Pop?"

"I need another glass of wine," Kara said thickly.

"Babe, you've had enough," Andy said absently.

"Don't you start!"

Andy raised his hands, still keeping his eyes on the game. "Fine. Have another glass."

Kara got up and stalked toward the kitchen, muttering under her breath. Jericho's father stood up, too. "Come on, kids. Go wash your hands and get to the table. I'll pour you some milk."

When he and the kids were safely gone, Andy sighed, used the remote to turn off the television and got up. "Always good times at the Cook place," he said resignedly.

"Why do you keep coming?" Jericho asked him as they followed the others to the kitchen to fetch drinks.

"Family is family."

He'd said a mouthful, Jericho thought.

SHE'D THOUGHT MEALS with her family could be awkward, Savannah mused ten minutes later. She'd had no idea. The Cooks were a study in simmering resentments and long, uncomfortable pauses.

They discussed the weather—and agreed the summer had been dry. They discussed local politics—and agreed the town councilmen and women were idiots.

They discussed Cam and Molly—and agreed both of them were well above average. But the gaps lasted longer than the conversations did.

They didn't discuss Base Camp, or Jericho's energy

projects, his military career—or Kara's grim determination to finish the entire bottle of wine herself. Savannah had worried she'd be pressed to drink, but when Jericho abstained, no one even asked her if she wanted wine. She sipped her pop and watched the family drama unfold before her.

"Remember the time Jericho took the car and went joy-riding with Alexa Briggs?" Kara said suddenly midway through the meal.

Jericho's mother tsked. "He always was reckless," she said. "I'm surprised he made it home in one piece, all those years in the Navy."

Jericho rolled his eyes. Savannah thought his mother didn't sound completely pleased he had made it home at all.

"Then there was the time he and his friends climbed the water tower," Kara continued.

"That was our senior prank. All we did was spray paint our grad year on it," Jericho explained to Savannah.

"And—"

"And then there was the time you drank too much while your kids were watching," Jericho said pointedly.

An awkward silence descended over the table.

"More ham?" Jericho's mother asked Savannah.

"Please." She helped herself to another slice, not because she was hungry but because she wanted to cut through the thick layer of resentment so obvious between the members of this family. "You should see what Jericho's up to at Westfield," she said brightly, hoping to turn the conversation. "He's got two wind turbines up already, and—"

"Old Ned Eaton would turn in his grave to see you do that," Jericho's father pronounced. "Those turbines won't do you any good. They'll spook the cattle and—"

"Extensive testing has been done on the turbines, Dad," Jericho interrupted. "We made sure these are compatible with all the other uses we'll make of the ranch."

"Wind will let you down just when you need energy the most," his father argued. "Why do you think our ancestors jumped to make the switch to coal and oil?"

"Technology has improved a lot since—"

"Besides, what about the birds?"

"Impact on migrating birds concerns me a lot," Jericho said reasonably, "which is why I chose the kind of turbine I—"

"You never think things through," his father pronounced and turned to Cam. "How did that project of yours come out? The one about the first settlers of Chance Creek?"

Savannah couldn't believe the way he'd changed the subject, or the way Jericho sat and took the slight with barely a shake of his head. How could his father be so callous about a topic Jericho held so dear? And how dare he assert that Jericho didn't think things through?

Jericho was one of the most responsible people she knew.

"Excuse me." She placed her napkin on the table, rose to her feet and hurried off to find a bathroom before her temper got the better of her and she spoke her mind. Jericho's family was as annoying as…

Hers.

She dallied in the modest bathroom for as long as she could before she washed her hands and came out again. Back at the table, the other members of the party looked no happier than when she'd left. Cam had finished telling everyone about his project, and too late Savannah realized that Jericho's father might have asked about it to show off his grandson's brilliance to their guest.

"What do you two like to do for fun?" she asked the children as she sat down.

"There's nothing to do here," Molly complained. "Gran and Grandpa don't have any games."

"Now, that's not true," Mary said. "We have plenty of board games in the living room on the shelf."

"I don't want board games—they're boring." Molly straightened, as if hoping for a compliment on her pun. No one offered one and she sighed.

"You can always go outdoors. It was good enough for your mother and uncle," Dan said.

"There's nothing to do out there, either."

"Not anymore," Kara said grimly.

A look went around the table Savannah didn't understand.

She wished she'd stayed home.

JERICHO STARED AT his sister. She wouldn't say it. She didn't dare say it.

"Not since the accident," Kara continued.

"Accident?" Savannah asked.

What the fuck? Had his sister really just lobbed that grenade in the middle of his parents' anniversary dinner? What kind of selfish sociopath did that kind of thing?

Was it the wine talking? She'd nearly killed a bottle on her own, and the nearly empty bottle on the table brought back too many memories. How many similar bottles had he gathered up on mornings after those card games his parents played with his aunt and uncle? How many boxes of empties had he lugged to the return depot for nickels each week?

At the time it had been part of life. What one did.

Those fistfuls of nickels had been his first allowance—and his first paycheck for caring for his sister and Donovan. Again, as normal as apple pie after a big dinner. As normal as the baseball game on the TV, his father pushing the lawnmower.

As normal as daydreaming in the treehouse about how his life would turn out.

"Why did you two stop drinking?" he asked before he could stop himself. Kara's words had haunted him since they'd spoken on the phone.

"You watch your mouth," his father said.

"Drinking was never a problem in this house." His mother stood abruptly.

"Really? Not even the day that Donovan broke his back?" Kara asked and tok a healthy swig from her glass.

Savannah looked even more confused, as well she

might. He'd never mentioned his cousin—or the accident.

"He didn't break his back," Jericho's mother said.

"Jericho pushed him," Kara said to Savannah. "Our cousin. Pushed him right out of the treehouse. Fell ten feet. That's why there's nothing to do at your grandmother's house," she said to Molly.

"Kara, you're drunk." Jericho stood.

"Like hell I am. I remember—"

"You remember?" He'd had enough. "You remember the way you pushed me into him? You're the reason Donovan fell—not me!"

Kara gaped at him, fury quickly crowding out her shock at his words. "That's a lie!"

"No, it's not—"

His father stood, too. "Enough! I thought maybe joining the Navy would finally make a man of you— would stop you from shoving your faults and mistakes onto other people. Get you to use your brain for once. But look at you! Still hiding behind your little sister. Playing like a child with your toys and blocks. Still refusing to grow up. I'll have you know your sister is our greatest comfort—"

Savannah surged to her feet, grabbed Jericho's arm and practically propelled him toward the front door. "Go," she urged him.

Jericho let her have her way, although if he'd dug in his heels she wouldn't have been able to budge him. She flung the door open, pulled him right outside and slammed the door behind them.

"What is wrong with those people?" she demanded as she strode toward the truck, skirts swirling around her ankles.

"I wish to God I knew." He followed quickly after her. He had plenty more he wanted to say to his family, but maybe this way was best.

She kept quiet until they reached the truck, but when they were both buckled in and Jericho had pulled out of his parents' driveway, she said, "You need to tell me what that was all about."

Jericho supposed he did. After all, he wanted Savannah to be his wife. But he'd have done anything to keep the whole thing in the past.

"The accident happened years ago." No, better to start at the beginning. "My dad has a twin brother, Christopher. Uncle Chris and my dad were like two peas in a pod. They were inseparable. And they married two women who were best friends. They bought houses right next to each other. It's like some sappy fifties television show—except it was real."

Savannah nodded. "Sounds great."

"It was, at first. My parents had me and my sister. It took Uncle Chris and Aunt Patty a few more years to have Donovan. I was seven and Kara four when he was born. I remember the day Aunt Patty brought him home from the hospital and let me hold him for the first time. It was—amazing. This new tiny life."

Out of the corner of his eye he saw Savannah nod. "So what happened?"

"My aunt and uncle came over most nights and

brought Donovan with them. When he was a baby they kept his bassinet right in the dining room, where they played cards. He graduated to a portable crib when he got bigger. But even before he could walk, it became my job to watch him and Kara. Kara…well, she didn't like that. The more time Donovan spent with us, the more she resented him."

"Is that why she pushed you when you were in the treehouse?"

"She was pissed," Jericho agreed. "It was Donovan's turn to be the pirate captain."

"How old were you?"

Jericho kept his eyes on the road. "I was eleven. Kara was seven. Donovan was four."

"A four-year-old up in a tree house? Without his parents around?"

Jericho shrugged. "No one thought anything of it. This is the country we're talking about."

"Still." Savannah looked away. "It's a risk I wouldn't be comfortable taking with my child, I don't think."

"There was a railing. It gave way." Jericho shrugged again, but the words he'd just said bugged him. Why had that railing given away? If he was going to build a tree house, he'd make sure it was solid.

He tried to remember if his father or uncle had ever climbed up to test it once it was built. The tree house wasn't that old at the time. It must not have been anchored right.

"I don't want to be a helicopter mom, but I think I'd check the railing on a tree house now and then."

Jericho glanced her way. "Maybe I'm just making excuses. I was the oldest. I was in charge—I should have made Kara climb down if she was going to act like that."

"But she's the one who pushed you?" Savannah asked.

He nodded.

"Then, Jericho—none of this is your fault. She got angry, she didn't think and she pushed you. You fell into your cousin and the railing that should have kept you all safe, didn't. Why are you taking the blame for this?"

"Donovan's fall is only the half of it," Jericho said, turning onto the highway that would bring them back to Westfield. "My aunt and uncle were furious about what happened—that I let it happen. They fought with my parents. They moved away to North Dakota. Sold the house, just like that. Never came back again."

"Jericho—"

"Can you imagine what it was like at our house after that? My father lost his twin. My mother lost her best friend."

"That's terrible. And wrong. I'm sorry, but I think your parents and your aunt and uncle all behaved badly. Even if an eleven-year-old could keep two other children perfectly safe all the time—which I don't think is possible—it's clear the real problem was shoddy construction and your sister's temper. And two sets of parents who couldn't be bothered to watch their kids."

"That's not how they saw it."

Neither said anything for a time as they each watched the scenery pass. "You know what? I think they felt guilty. I think they still do. They know they're the ones to blame as much as you. More so," Savannah said.

Jericho pulled into the driveway that led to the manor. When he pulled up in front of the tall stone building, he parked the truck.

"I still feel responsible," he said quietly. "I always have. At the end of the day, if I hadn't knocked into Donovan, he wouldn't have fallen. The sound he made when he hit the ground—I'll never forget it. I climbed down as fast as I could to help, but he couldn't move. He was paralyzed."

"I'm so sorry." Savannah took his hand. Jericho held her small fingers in his, glad for the link to another human being—to her. His friends knew the bare bones of this story, but not all of it.

"I need to get back to work—paying work," he told her in a rush, confessing a part of the story he'd never shared with anyone else. "Ever since I was twenty-five, I've been sending Donovan money—as much of my paycheck I can spare. I paralyzed him—"

"The accident paralyzed him," Savannah corrected him. "And it really sounds like it was an accident, Jericho."

"Anyway, I've been sending him money. It kills me I waited that long, but it wasn't until then I really understood what I might have done to him. Being in the Navy—you see people get hurt. When someone you know—someone you've worked with—gets laid up for life… you understand mortality in a whole new way. It occurred to me that Donovan wasn't going to get better. I had to do something. He cashes every check like clockwork. He must need it. I can't imagine what it would be like to go through life in a wheelchair—or not be able to work at all."

"Wait—he *must* need it?" Savannnah tightened her grip on his hand. "You mean you don't know for sure? When was the last time you talked to him?"

Jericho shook his head. "I've never talked to him. Not since the day he fell out of the treehouse."

SAVANNAH COULDN'T BELIEVE what she was hearing. Her family might be messed up, but nowhere near this bad. Her parents were self-absorbed, so was Charles, and her conversations with them frustrated her to no end, but at least they talked.

Jericho's family was so dysfunctional, she didn't know where to begin to sort out the tangle of it. How could his parents blame a little boy for something so obviously not his fault? And why would they still blame him for it so many years later?

If Mary and Dan missed Patty and Chris so much, why not call them? Apologize, make amends. Hold out an olive branch? Donovan was grown up now. He must have come to terms with his life, no matter how badly he'd been injured.

That is, unless he'd died.

The thought struck her cold until she remembered

someone was cashing those checks and Jericho must have an address to send them to.

She shifted in her seat and undid the seat belt when it hindered her. "When was the last time you talked to your aunt and uncle?" she asked him.

"Never. Not since I was eleven."

Savannah thought she was getting a glimpse of the SEAL in him. He still faced forward, his expression hard—impassive. As if he'd seen so much pain he couldn't feel it anymore. But that wasn't true, was it? He'd been in pain this whole time—holding himself responsible—letting that one incident hold him back from any kind of peace.

"But you have Donovan's address. Did you find it online?"

"That's right."

"What else did you find out when you looked him up?"

"Nothing," Jericho said vehemently, finally turning toward her. "I couldn't... couldn't stand knowing how badly I hurt him. In my mind he's in a wheelchair and he's mobile, at least. He's holding down a job of some kind. Maybe he's got a family—at least friends and hobbies. What if I look him up and that's not true? What if he's a quadriplegic? What if he's hated me his whole life?"

"No wonder you can't get rid of your ghosts," Savannah said sadly. "You haven't faced them, and your family won't let you forget them." She watched the sun fade to the west. "Neither of us have had the support we need."

"I guess not." He moved his hand and threaded his fingers through hers. "You've got my support, you know that, right?"

She nodded. At least in the case of her piano playing, he'd made that clear. Maybe this was the time to tell him about the baby.

No, she decided. Not now. Not when his family had dragged him through the muck of the memories they refused to let go. No wonder Jericho was afraid of children—he'd taken on the guilt his parents had yoked him with and wore his supposed carelessness like a crown of thorns.

"I'm going to say it again," she told him. "You aren't careless. You are a man to be trusted with children. You have my support all the way, too. I'm impressed with the work you're doing at Base Camp, you know."

"Thank you." He leaned toward her across the center console, tipped her chin up and kissed her. Savannah sighed, and let herself enjoy it.

He pulled back. "Savannah, you know I want to—"

"Let's go inside," she blurted, needing to head him off. She couldn't take a proposal. Not tonight. "I'll make some tea. I could use a cup."

"Savannah—"

She opened the door and got out of the truck before he could finish his sentence.

CHAPTER SIX

SAVANNAH WASN'T READY to be proposed to yet, Jericho thought early the next morning. She'd made that entirely clear last night when she'd leapt from the truck as if her gown had been on fire, and made sure to keep moving as she prepared tea and directed him into the parlor to drink it, where the others were hanging out. When she was done, she pointedly went to the piano and began to run scales. Jericho had given up and gone back down to Base Camp. He could understand why a proposal wouldn't be welcome after the disaster that had been dinner at his parents' house.

He wondered if the incident had set him back with her even more, however. Who would want to marry someone from such a dysfunctional family? Not that hers was much better by her description. Maybe they should leave their relatives behind and start over again—with each other.

She and the other women hadn't come down from the manor until late that evening, and it had taken him a long time to fall asleep, conscious that Savannah was lying in her own tent not that far away. He wasn't sure what to make of her mixed messages. She'd taken his side against his family, but she'd pulled back hard when he'd tried to propose.

One step at a time, he told himself.

But time was passing, fast.

He thought Savannah might keep her distance from him that morning, after the awkwardness of the previous evening, but she surprised him by sitting with him at breakfast, and when she and the rest of the women headed back up to the manor to do their morning chores, she turned back to say, "I'll see you in a little while."

"What about practicing?" He couldn't have been more surprised.

"Getting this place powered up is important, too," she said.

Jericho watched her walk up the hill away from Base Camp, thoroughly confused.

Boone joined him. "You asked her to marry you yet?"

"Not yet," Jericho said. "It's only been three days."

"That leaves thirty-seven. What's the hold-up?"

"I don't know," he said honestly.

"Got a ring?"

"Nope." Jericho shoved his hands in his pockets. The last twenty-four hours had knocked him off-balance. Making love to Savannah in the creek, the disastrous dinner with his folks, Savannah's declaration that he was a responsible man, paired with the distance she insisted on keeping from him kept him too confused to figure anything out.

"Go get one. Now."

"It's pretty early, chief. I doubt Thayer's will be open."

Boone pulled out his phone, tapped it a few times and held it to his ear. "Rose? It's Boone Rudman. You in the shop yet?" He waited a beat. "Terrific. Jericho will be in to see you soon. Set him up with a decent ring, won't you?" He finished the conversation and pocketed his phone again. "She'll be ready for you when you get there."

"Why are you in such a hurry for me to buy a ring?" He couldn't propose to Savannah until she was ready to say yes.

"Why do you think? Time's a wasting. Get it done."

Jericho headed into the bunkhouse to hand his dishes to Kai, but the kitchen was empty except for Avery and a member of the film crew. Avery jumped when she caught sight of him in the doorway. "Jericho! How long have you been there?"

"Just a moment." They'd been filming, that was obvious. "Stealing a snack?" he asked her, unsure what to think of the situation. "You just had breakfast."

"No." Avery looked affronted. "Just...dropping off dishes, like you are. Come on, I need to get up to the manor," she said to Byron, who was the youngest cameraman on the set. Byron followed Avery with alacrity, and Jericho wondered what Walker would think if he'd seen them. Walking up to the manor was hardly a scintillating activity to film—unless the kid wanted to get Avery alone.

Jericho filed the problem away for later. He'd mention it to Walker and leave it at that; it wasn't his place to interfere. He dropped off his dishes, found a free truck and climbed in. But he didn't immediately turn the engine on.

He'd never bought a ring before, and it occurred to him that he should have asked Boone to come along. His friend had managed it, and Riley seemed happy enough. He didn't even know Savannah's size. He'd figured he'd propose first and take her to buy the ring with him, but Boone wasn't giving him much choice in the matter, and if he was truthful, he looked forward to leaving Base Camp for an hour, driving into town alone and clearing his head.

In fact… he was in luck; none of the camera crews had caught his conversation with Boone, which meant he was on his own for now. If he could get out of Base Camp without them seeing, he might actually be able to do this errand alone.

He had just turned the key in the ignition when Win rapped on his window. Jericho flinched before he collected himself and rolled it down. "I didn't see you coming."

"Sorry; didn't mean to startle you. Are you going to town?" Win didn't look as cheerful as she normally did.

"Need a ride? If you do, hop in quick, before anyone notices us." He didn't mind the interruption, as long as they could get out of there fast. Anything to stop overanalyzing what was happening with Savannah.

She nodded and rushed to get in on the passenger's side. "Do you have a lot of errands?" she asked as he executed a quick U-turn and gunned the engine. Renata wouldn't be happy, but he didn't care.

"Just one. Buying a ring."

She raised an eyebrow.

"For Savannah—I hope."

"Lucky girl." Win examined her hands.

"Where do you need to stop?"

"I can walk from Thayer's. It won't take long. Want to meet for coffee afterward?"

"I was kind of hoping you'd help me pick the ring out," Jericho admitted.

"Oh. I can do that."

"It's not a big deal." Something had her worried, Jericho realized. He wondered what her mystery errand entailed. "If you come to Thayer's, I'll go get us a booth at Linda's Diner while you do what you need to do."

"O... okay." Win subsided into a silence that lasted until they reached town. When he talked to Walker about Avery, he'd better talk to Angus about Win, Jericho decided, but he let her alone during the rest of the drive. She obviously needed to think something over.

Once in town, Win shook off her thoughts and brightened up. "I've never been in Thayer's," she told him as they climbed out of the truck.

"Been a long time for me, too." He didn't think he'd been there since he was a child tagging along with his mother.

Even at this early hour, the door was unlocked. Inside, a petite young woman with dark hair stood behind the counter.

"Jericho!" She came around the counter to give him a hug. "It's been years since I've seen you."

Jericho remembered Rose as a girl with dark braids and big eyes. She was a number of years younger than him, but Chance Creek was a small town and as a kid he'd known most of the other children.

"I hear you're a married woman now."

"Married the local sheriff."

"I bet you keep him in line." She'd always been a scrappy little thing.

Rose blushed a little, and she craned her neck to catch sight of Win behind him. "And here's your fiancée! You picked a pretty one, Jericho. Congratulations!" She rushed to take Win's hand, pumped it once and then impulsively gave her a hug, too. "Jericho was always such a nice boy. I'm sure you two will be very happy."

"Uh…" Damn. He should have anticipated this.

"I'm not his fiancée," Win said with a sudden grin. "I'm his consultant. He didn't trust himself to pick out the right ring."

"Oh… oh, my God! You'd think that in this business I'd learn not to jump to conclusions." Rose's blush deepened and she clapped her hands to her cheeks. "I'm sorry. Come on—come over here where I keep the engagement rings. Have a look around." She hurried to the back of the store, and Jericho and Win followed her. Rose began to pull trays of engagement rings out of the glass case for them to look at.

"What do you think Savannah would like?" he asked Win.

"She's pretty glamorous," Win said. "She needs something feminine, but striking, don't you think?"

"Striking?" That sounded expensive.

"Like this one." Win pulled out a silver ring set with a large, oval, multifaceted diamond, surrounded by small blue stones Jericho couldn't identify.

"Uh, I'm not sure about that one," he said quickly. It looked like it cost a bundle. "I'm thinking something more like…" He jabbed a finger almost at random. "That one."

It was a plain silver band set with a single, small diamond. Elegant, he thought.

Spare, even.

Win's eyebrows shot up. "That one?"

Rose frowned, looking from one to the other.

"What's wrong with it?" Jericho asked.

"Nothing. If Savannah worked at the laundromat and you flipped burgers for a living," Win said scathingly.

"It's a perfectly lovely ring," Rose intervened.

"Do you have any idea who your fiancée is? Who her family is?" Win said to Jericho.

"Yes." Of course he did, but he was also aware of his dwindling bank account and his responsibility to Donovan.

"Then you know that despite Savannah's decision to live the simple life, she's used to being wealthy. Extremely wealthy. You have to take that into consideration. She's used to the finer things in life—you can't expect her to just throw that all over in the span of a few months." As Win's voice rose, Jericho's worry grew. She was right; Savannah came from money, and he didn't want to come off as a cheapskate. But he couldn't bankrupt himself, either—not when he had payments to make.

"All I'm saying is if you want to make Savannah happy, you'll buy this one." Win thrust the fancy ring into Jericho's hand. "I'm going to go run my errand. See you at Linda's Diner. You should make up your own mind."

She walked off, and Jericho wondered why she was so angry. He wasn't buying *her* a ring—that was Angus's problem.

"What do you think?" Jericho asked Rose, but only for show. He couldn't buy the plainer ring now. Every time he saw it on Savannah's finger—if she accepted him—he'd think of the way Win had disparaged it.

"I'll take this one," he said before Rose could answer him, and held out the fancier one. Win was right; it was exactly the sort of thing Savannah would wear. The blue stones circling the diamond would match her favorite gown.

Rose took it from him, held it in her palm and for a moment her gaze relaxed, as if she was looking inward instead of focusing on her surroundings. She frowned, paused again, then shook her head.

"Jericho… I don't think you need to worry about the ring… I think there's something else. Something you don't know about."

"What do you mean?"

"I'm… not sure. I can't get a clear vision."

A clear vision? "Uh… okay." Did Rose think she was psychic? He knew plenty. He knew Win was right; Savannah would like this ring. Knew, too, there was no guarantee she'd say yes even if he bought it for her. He had a hunch of his own, as well; that it would wipe out half his savings. More than half, he realized when he turned over the little tag and saw the price.

"We have payment plans," Rose ventured.

"I'd like to see one," Jericho said quickly. That was the answer; he'd put it on credit. He'd eke what little money he had along until Base Camp was ready and he could get back to working for pay. Maybe he'd talk to Boone and the others about doing so sooner rather than later.

Rose brought out some paperwork and began to go over the terms of the monthly payments.

SAVANNAH WAS CLEANING the kitchen windows, but her thoughts were on the piano in the other room. Part of being a professional was managing the distractions that threatened to get in the way of practice time, so why had she decided to head back down to Base Camp in a few minutes to put in two hours with Jericho on the energy system?

No one expected her to. They knew she'd been forced to work with Jericho—she certainly hadn't volunteered.

But the truth was, she wanted to be near Jericho again. She liked the work—and she found it compelling to watch Jericho so focused on his passions. Like he'd told her, he was consumed by renewable energy systems and the things they did together went far beyond the grunt work she'd figured she was in for when Boone had ordered her to join Jericho's team.

For one thing, she'd found she was good at doing the equations necessary to execute the schematics. She loved it when she could run the calculations even faster than Jericho could. She'd always been good at that back at school, too.

Maybe if someone had shown her the ways math— or programming for that matter—could be used for such interesting real-world applications, she'd have taken to it when she was a kid. Instead they'd plied her with dumb computer games and simulations. Boring. But figuring out how to make the energy system as efficient as possible?

She liked that kind of puzzle.

Too bad no one cheered you on when you installed solar panels.

Savannah shook her head at the direction her thoughts had trended. She had to focus, and right now that meant practicing—as much as possible. Preparing for a concert or audition could be tedious, but that was the price you paid for those moments on stage, and she was willing to pay it.

Later.

This afternoon.

After a little break.

Savannah checked the time, quickly put away the window cleaner and rags and hurried to wash her hands and straighten her clothes before meeting up with the other women to walk down to Base Camp.

"Someone's happy to get to see her boyfriend," Avery teased.

Savannah glanced back at the camera crew that had joined them. They had definitely gotten that on film.

"I'm happy to get out in the fresh air," Savannah retorted. "How about you? Ready for another horseback riding lesson?"

"Walker's preparing me for the bison." Avery shivered. "I'm not sure there's any amount of preparation that will get me comfortable with them."

They walked down the hill chatting companionably, but when they reached Base Camp, Avery ducked away from the rest of the group. "I need something from my tent. Tell Walker I'll meet him at the stables."

"Sure thing." Savannah did so, and went on her way to where Jericho had set up a folding table and was looking through a set of schematics. Bent over the table, bracing himself with one hand, pen in the other, he scribbled something on a sheet of paper.

The SEAL was so handsome. Did he have any idea what he did to a woman?

Probably, Savannah decided. That's why he could

afford to be so forthright about his likes and dislikes; he assumed a woman would bend herself to his desires in order to be with him.

She couldn't do that even if she wanted to.

"Hey, Savannah," he said when he noticed her. "Check my work, would you? Something's not right here."

He slid the paper her way, and Savannah held out a hand for his pen. She started over with his basic equation, did the math in her head and slid the paper back with her answer written on it.

"That's more like it." Jericho checked her work. "Yep. You got it. How the hell do you do that so fast?"

"I'm not sure. I think—I think it's the music," she said honestly. "Numbers sort of arrange themselves in my mind like notes. I can feel what number should come next, like I know if a note is right or wrong in a composition."

"That's... weird." But he was smiling as he leaned closer to tuck a piece of her hair into her bonnet.

"I like it," she told him. "It's... comforting." Not frustrating like her practicing felt these days. The closer her audition came, the more her gut tightened in knots just thinking about it.

"How on earth is math comforting?"

Was he laughing at her? He was. "You must like it, too; otherwise you wouldn't have picked this job."

"It isn't the math that sucked me in. That's just a necessary evil. I like working out how to replace fossil fuels with renewable energy." Jericho indicated the turbines turning in the wind. "I do the equations because I have to—not because they sound like lullabies." He grinned down at her.

"I never said they sounded like lullabies." But his answer intrigued her. She'd assumed he felt the same way she did about numbers, but that was silly. No one had back at Boston College either when she'd tried to explain why she loved calculus. In fact, some of her classmates thought she was making it up when she explained how she felt. She did so well in those classes, her professors had wondered why she was bothering with music.

The way Savannah saw it, music was math, and math was music.

"The solar panels are being delivered tomorrow," Jericho told her. "So let's make sure we're ready for them. Kai? Greg? Come on," he called to the other members of their little team.

Savannah followed the men, in no hurry to get back to the manor any time soon.

"HARD TO BELIEVE we've come this far," Greg said to Jericho a week later when all four of them had gathered together to look at the array of solar panels on the south-facing wall of the bunkhouse roof. A knot of cameramen stood around them, capturing the important moment. Even Renata had come to watch. Jericho had done his best to evade her these past few days. He was dealing with enough without her pointed questions.

"I know what you mean." Just two months ago,

none of his green energy measures were in place. Now several turbines contributed wind power, and the solar array on the bunkhouse roof was ready to add to the power they were producing.

"Now you can cook at will, Kai," Savannah said. "No more solar ovens."

"We'll see about that; I'm kind of partial to them at this point. But winter's on its way; I'll be glad not to have to rely on them then."

"Were you worried we wouldn't get things wired up in time?" she asked.

Kai shrugged. "Things work out."

Jericho turned around when he heard the clip-clopping of hooves and the rattle of carriage wheels, and spotted Maud and James Russell driving up in their barouche. The older couple called around to the ranch often. Since the women had all sold their vehicles before coming to Westfield, James often chauffeured them around. It gave him an excuse to drive the barouche, one of his favorite activities. Jericho often thought the older couple was a little lonely. They had no children of their own and so had adopted everyone at Westfield as surrogates. He didn't mind. The Russells were eccentric, but good-hearted, and they helped out whenever they could.

"Makes sure you get this," he heard Renata snap at one of the crew members.

"Marvelous! You've got it all rigged up. How does it run?" James called.

Jericho bit back a chuckle. The man was never out

of character, as far as he could see. He knew the show's fans loved the Russells. "We're just about to fire it up. Hang on."

"*Fire it up* isn't exactly accurate," Savannah said as Jericho fiddled with the converter. "All Jericho is going to do is flip a switch."

"Sounds splendid either way." James helped Maud down from the barouche, and they waited with the rest of them for Jericho to finish the job.

"Okay, it's the moment of truth." Jericho led the way to the bunkhouse's front door. They filed inside, where Boone, Clay and Walker, who'd been clustered around a desk, joined them. The crew trooped in after them. "If the light turns on when I hit the switch, then we hooked it up right. If it doesn't, it's back to the drawing board."

Jericho had worked on enough projects to know that things like this could take a number of iterations to work out the kinks in the system, and he also knew Renata would lap it up if he failed a time or two. He held his breath and reached for the switch, waited a beat and flipped it.

The single bulb in the fixture in the middle of the room came to life.

Everyone cheered. Savannah rushed to him, wrapped her arms around his neck and kissed him. "You did it!"

"We did it. Me and you and Greg and Kai," he corrected her, more surprised than he could say. Apart from the times they'd worked together, Savannah had kept her distance from him this past week. With the ring burning a hole in his pocket, he'd sought out times to be alone with her, but she'd made sure that never happened.

"I'm going to try the oven." Kai rushed into the kitchen.

Jericho hung back with Savannah as the others followed. He knew that if the light worked, the oven would, too. "You've been a lot of help," he told Savannah.

"Thanks. I've enjoyed it."

He kissed her again, savoring the softness of her lips.

When another cheer went up in the kitchen, though, they pulled apart, both of them laughing.

"A celebration," he heard Maud crow. She bustled back into the main room, cameras trailing after her, her long gray gown rustling as she walked. "We need to have a celebration! Right here! Tonight." She waved a hand around the bunkhouse. "A dance!"

"Here?" Savannah asked, wrinkling her nose.

Jericho understood why. There was a ballroom up at the manor, and a large one at Maud and James's place. Why have a dance in the bunkhouse?

"It'll be perfect. Leave it all to me. You, young man," she collared Kai. "You'll help."

"You'll inform everyone?" James said to Jericho, beaming at the turn of events. If there was one thing the Russells loved, it was a celebration. Jericho knew it was pointless to argue with them—especially if Kai and the others were on board. Renata had packed up.

"Uh... sure." Jericho tried to muster some enthusiasm, but he wasn't nearly as pleased as James seemed to be. There was still plenty of work to do on the power grid. They had ten tiny houses to eventually bring online, not to mention the barns and outbuildings. And he'd begun to avoid Boone, sure the other man was going to start bringing up backup brides if he didn't get a move on with Savannah.

"Tell them to dress up. Maud doesn't do anything by half-measures," James said. As if she'd heard him, Maud came bustling out of the kitchen again.

"Kai understands what he needs to do," she informed her husband. "Now, we have to get busy. I've had the most splendid idea. A surprise for the young folks."

"A surprise!" James rubbed his hands together. "My dear, this is shaping up to be a wonderful day. Until we meet again," he called to Jericho and Savannah, leading his wife from the building.

"I guess we're going to have a party," Savannah said slowly when they'd gone.

"I guess so."

ALL AFTERNOON WHILE Savannah practiced, she wondered if she should be down at the bunkhouse preparing for the celebration that night. The other women were running back and forth from Base Camp to the manor, bustling around as if they were preparing for a ball rather than a small party. After a while, the crews got tired of running back and forth and clustered around the bunkhouse.

"I just heard from Mia Matheson," Avery said, bursting into the room as Savannah was attempting a difficult passage from a concerto. "Maud and James invited everyone from the Double-Bar-K to the party tonight, too."

"That's going to be a tight fit," Savannah exclaimed, giving up on the song.

"I called Maud and asked if anyone else was coming, but she said no. So it won't be too bad. We should be able to squeeze everyone in. By the way, you got an email." Avery fished the cell phone they shared from her pocket. "From some woman." She passed it to Savannah.

"Thanks. I'll come and help soon." She wasn't getting much practicing done anyway, and if she was honest, she didn't like being left out.

"Whenever you're ready," Avery said. "I admire your dedication to your work."

"How's your work coming? Your screenplay?"

"Really good." Avery's smile was secretive, though. "Better than I expected."

"I'd love to see it—when you're ready," Savannah rushed to add.

"Sure! Soon," Avery said. "Bring me the phone when you're done with it."

She left as quickly as she'd come, and Savannah settled down to read the email, grateful she wasn't being filmed. It was from Melissa Maynard, Alfred Redding's assistant, and contained detailed information about her audition.

Savannah read through it once, and then a second time, absorbing all the rules. She must not bring any recording devices to the audition. Must let them know ahead of time what she meant to play. Must not speak to Mr. Redding unless he asked her a direct question. Must not speak to the other applicants, either.

Her audition spot was thirty minutes long, and she was warned to be on time. Her place would not be held for her, nor were there any makeup auditions. If she was tardy, her place would go to one of the waitlisted applicants who would stand by hoping for that opportunity.

Savannah lowered the phone. It all sounded...

Hideous.

No—not hideous! Savannah caught herself. Of course it wasn't hideous. It was the industry. Alfred Redding was a busy man. A famous one who didn't need to take on any protégés. She should be overwhelmed with gratitude for the opportunity, not critical of his nitpicky rules. After all, she could be punctual and prepared. Any concert pianist worth her salt knew how to be professional.

She was nervous, that was all. This would be the start of her career—what she'd been aiming for all along. She'd work her way step by step to that pinnacle Jericho had talked about.

And then what?

For the first time, Savannah wondered about what

came next. In her mind she got to that fabulous concert—the one attended by dignitaries, written about in the *New York Times*. The one in which her mother and father stood in the front row and cheered on her success.

That was all she needed, she told herself. Once she'd gotten there, she'd take a breath—pull back. Spend more time being a mother, while continuing to play around the country—around the world.

But even as she pictured that, she found herself dissatisfied.

More hours at the piano. Apart from her child.

Apart from her friends as they ran the bed and breakfast.

Apart from everyone.

She rested a hand on her belly, feeling the slight swell that was her baby.

Was it the baby making her feel like this?

A sharp knock interrupted these uncomfortable thoughts and Savannah sighed, got up and answered it. She was being silly. She loved music. Loved playing, singing, everything about it. As soon as the audition was over she'd feel more herself again.

She was surprised to see Heather Hall on the other side of the door when she opened it. "Come in!" she invited the other woman, and realized how grateful she was for the interruption when Heather accepted. "Want some tea or lemonade?"

"Lemonade sounds heavenly."

Savannah led the way through the house to the

kitchen. After pouring them each a drink, she pulled open the back door and brought Heather outside to sit on the porch.

"Did you stop by to see someone in particular?" Savannah asked.

"You, actually," Heather said. "I came to ask a favor. I hope you aren't offended."

"I can't imagine you'd offend me." But Savannah felt a pang of anxiety. She didn't know Heather all that well. What could the woman be after?

"I'm looking for a piano teacher," Heather blurted. "And I know you're a professional pianist, so I doubt that's up your alley at all, but..."

A piano teacher. Savannah sat back. Heather was right; she'd never considered it. Back at school, people used to joke that piano teaching was for people who'd failed at becoming professional musicians.

"I shouldn't even have asked," Heather rushed on. "I'm sorry. But you know how it is when your kid expresses an interest in something. You want to get him the best experience. You could have knocked me over with a feather when Richard asked for lessons."

Savannah didn't want to hurt Heather's feelings, but the last thing she had time for was to teach a teenage boy the rudiments of notes and scales.

"I..." Savannah hesitated. Heather looked so mortified, she didn't want to tell her no. "Can I tell you a secret?" she said instead, wondering if she was making a big mistake.

"O-okay."

Savannah took a sip of lemonade, playing for time. "I've got an audition soon for a chance to work with one of the most outstanding pianists of our time. I'm practicing all day, every day to get ready." At least she should be. "Can you wait for my answer until that's over? Once I know how that goes, it'll be easier for me to figure out my schedule. If I have time, I'd love to teach Richard. If not, I'll help you find someone even better."

Heather let out a breath. "Thank you. I don't know why this has thrown me into a tizzy. It's just—I don't know anything about music. I never took lessons. I don't know how to pick out someone good. But if you'll help, I know it will work out. Good luck on your audition."

A few minutes later, when they'd drained their cups, Heather looked at her phone and said she had to go. "I've got to pick Richard up and get him to the dentist."

"You're a busy woman."

"You have no idea. Being a mother isn't for the faint of heart."

As Savannah stood, her dress caught on the leg of the wicker chair and pulled tight against her body.

Heather's brow creased. "I guess you'll find out soon enough, though. How far along are you?" She bit off the question and her cheeks pinked. "Sorry. None of my business. God, I'll die if you aren't actually pregnant."

Savannah quickly tugged her dress free, but she knew her cheeks were red, too. "I guess I have two secrets," she said softly. Maybe Heather would be the one person to understand. From what she knew of the woman's history, she'd kept the identity of Richard's father a secret for years.

"Congratulations," Heather said. She meant it—Savannah could tell.

"I'm in a bit of a mess," Savannah found herself confessing.

Heather tugged her back down on the wicker couch. "If you need someone to talk to, I'm here."

"It's just—the dad." Savannah lowered her voice and made sure no one else was around. "He wants to marry me, but he told me he doesn't want kids."

"Oh, no. I'm sorry." Heather squeezed her hand. "But is he sure about that? Men say the stupidest things sometimes."

Savannah nodded. "That's just it; I think he means it, but he's also wonderful with children. You saw him the other day." Too late she realized she'd just blown her cover.

"It's Jericho?" Heather laughed. "He *was* wonderful with the kids. Savannah, he'll make a terrific father."

"But he's adamant about not wanting to be one," Savannah told her. "I think it's because of something that happened a long time ago."

Heather became serious. "Then that's what you have to work on. Those old stories we tell ourselves are traps. Help him break free of it, then he'll come around. You'll see. You've told him about the baby, right?"

"No."

Heather gave her a pitying look. "You'd better not wait too long, or someone else will tell him, if he doesn't guess it himself."

Savannah nodded. "Last week I didn't have a baby bump."

"They sneak up on you kind of fast. I'd better get back, but call me any time, and I hope Jericho comes around. I think you two would make a terrific couple."

"Thank you."

CHAPTER SEVEN

"WHAT IS THAT?" Jericho asked slowly several hours later. He stood with Boone, Clay and Walker near the bunkhouse, where they'd been discussing whether to set up some metal folding chairs outside in case people wanted to come out and cool off later that evening. Coming down the long drive from the country highway was a rig the likes of which he'd never seen before.

Eight large draft-horses pulled a wagon loaded with something tall swathed in white sheets. Ropes crisscrossed it to tie it to the bed of the wagon.

"Some sort of… I don't know," Clay said, peering at it.

"That's James driving the horses," Boone pointed out. "Must be for the party, whatever it is."

"Looks heavy." Walker jutted his chin at the rig. "Horses are working hard."

He was right. Those powerful horses were straining in their harnesses to get their load down the long track. The men all went to meet James as he brought the rig to a halt near the bunkhouse door.

"Well, that's got it this far," he said jovially as he jumped down from the wagon's high seat. "Now to get it into the bunkhouse. Good thing there are a lot of strong men here." He went to the rear of the wagon and pulled out a long, thick metal ramp. He attached one end to the wagon and let the other rest on the ground. "I'll need some help."

"Of course." Jericho sprang to lend a hand along with the others. "What is this thing?" He pointed to the sheet-covered object.

"An upright piano, of course," James said. "Can't have a party without music!"

"But…" Boone began. He looked from the piano to the bunkhouse. "A piano? In there?"

"It'll come in handy lots of times," James assured him. "Now, the trick is not to let it pick up any momentum on the way down the ramp." Jericho looked to the others. Should they stop James? Refuse the gift? Boone shrugged. So did Clay. Oh, why not? Jericho thought. Opposing he Russells was like trying to hold back the tide.

The next half hour was an exercise in frustration and frayed nerves, but in the end they managed to maneuver the piano into one corner of the bunkhouse's main room. Kai came out of the kitchen to watch the proceedings for a minute before shaking his head and disappearing back into the other room.

Jericho understood how he felt. He could picture a few of the women playing a tune or two tonight, but otherwise this piano was as useless in the bunkhouse as a bikini in a Montana snowstorm. It would only get in the way.

James beamed happily throughout the process, however. "See you in a couple of hours," he called out when he left.

Several hours later, the bunkhouse was a cheerful sight, Jericho had to admit, with its door and windows thrown open to catch the light evening breeze, and one side of the large room flanked by tables laden with food and drink. The room was comfortably full of the inhabitants of Base Camp and their guests, and the camera crews, of course. Their chatter filled the air, but there was just enough room to circulate.

Jericho, keeping close to Savannah, saw her face when Maud bustled to the front of the room and clapped her hands together. "I think it's time for music, don't you?" she called out. "Savannah, won't you come and play us a tune?"

He was surprised when Savannah's shoulders slumped at the request. This was another chance for her to practice, wasn't it? He'd thought she'd appreciate the opportunity, not act as if she'd been put upon.

She sighed, though, as she threaded her way through the crowd to the front of the room where the upright piano sat. She took her place on the bench and ran her hands over the keys. Savannah was wearing her dark blue gown tonight—the one she reserved for dressy occasions, Jericho had noticed. She looked as lovely as always, but she must have been tired, because her shoulders were rounded, as if she had a stomachache, when usually her posture was so upright.

She began to play a light piece of classical music. The room remained hushed as people paused to listen, but Jericho could tell her choice of music didn't please Maud, and glancing around, he didn't think most of the others were really in the mood to stand and listen, either. Up until now it had been a boisterous, happy occasion. Savannah's music was turning it into something far more formal than a dinner dance in a beat-up bunkhouse.

"Savannah, dear, that's very nice, but I was thinking something more—danceable," Maud said suddenly, her piercing voice carrying straight through the music. She fluttered over to place a hand on Savannah's shoulder, in what looked like a friendly gesture, but Savannah stopped so abruptly he could only guess the older woman's fingers had dug into her skin.

"Something danceable?" Savannah repeated.

"You know… so we can dance!"

Savannah stared at her, but eventually she looked around, seemed to take in the nature of the gathering and nodded. She placed her hands on the keys again. This time when she began to play, more than one woman in the room exclaimed happily at the lilting music, and soon several couples had taken to the middle of the floor.

"I didn't know she knew any two-steps," Clay said to Jericho. "This is more like it."

Jericho understood what he meant; they'd grown up

with music like this. Usually coming from a jukebox or
live band, of course, but this was fine, too. Clay went to
find Nora and they joined the other couples. Boone and
Riley were already dancing, laughing as they charged
around the floor. Jericho was happy to see them forget
their troubles for a little while. A couple who could
laugh together like that was bound to make things work
out between them.

Nora and Clay began to dance, but Nora struggled
to match Clay's steps. Probably not a lot of two-
stepping going on in Baltimore, Jericho decided, but
even though they weren't as boisterous as Boone and
Riley, they still looked like they were having fun. Avery
was working on Walker in one corner, berating the big
man for not asking her to dance. All the Matheson
couples had taken to the floor, as had Harris and
Samantha, back from their honeymoon these past few
days. Soon the room was a whirl of dancers. That was
the trouble when your girl was the one responsible for
the music, Jericho decided a few minutes later. You
didn't get to join the fun.

Instead, he fetched drinks for the both of them and
went to sit beside her on the piano bench. Savannah
didn't seem to mind the intrusion. She launched from
one song right into the next, and then the next, until a
half-hour had gone by and the dancers were beginning
to flag.

"You need a break," Maud pronounced. "Riley,
come play a slow song. We'll all settle down a moment,
and this poor man can finally have his dance with

Savannah."

Jericho grinned at her. "Thanks." He didn't wait for Savannah to agree. He tugged her to her feet and led her to the floor as Riley took her place and began to play a seventies ballad he hadn't heard in ages.

"You're great at that," he said to Savannah. "I didn't know you could play happy stuff."

"Because I'm always playing classical music?" She shrugged. "That's what people want, generally."

"At your high-falutin' concerts, maybe," he teased her.

She made a face. "I guess you're right. You know what? I am having fun," she confessed. "I haven't played like that in so long—just for the joy of it, whatever I want to play."

"I'm glad you're having a good time." He snuggled her in closer, but Savannah wriggled a little until there was space between them again.

"What's wrong?" he asked.

"Just hot," she exclaimed, and she did look a little flushed. Jericho held her lightly, but as the song went on, he wished he could press her close against him. Hell, he wished they could leave and go somewhere they could be alone.

"We could slip down to the creek later. Cool off, and have a little fun at the same time."

He couldn't decipher the look she gave him.

"Don't you need to get married one of these days?"

Uh oh. He didn't like the sound of that answer. "Yeah. So? You know you're the one I want." He tried to keep his tone light; he still wasn't sure of the answer she'd give him if he proposed.

"Do you really think you know me well enough to know that?"

Her tone was light, too, but her words twisted a knot of worry inside Jericho. She was trying to tell him something, but he didn't know what.

Before he could question her further, the song ended and Riley stood up. "I want another two-step! How about everyone else?"

A cheer went up, and before Jericho could stop her, Savannah returned to the piano. He went for new drinks, realized Savannah hadn't touched the first one and set the new one beside it on top of the piano before downing his. He sat beside her on the bench again. He was going to stick close tonight. He needed some answers.

AFTER SEVERAL HOURS of dancing, Savannah sensed the crowd tiring, but she also sensed that Jericho would press her for a response to his almost proposal when the party broke up, so instead of playing another two-step, or a ballad, or stopping altogether, she launched into a song she felt sure the others knew well enough to sing along with. When she began to belt out the words like a diva on a Broadway stage, they soon joined in and gathered around the piano.

At first Savannah played and sung song after song to put off the time when she'd have to face Jericho's questions, but after a few pieces, she forgot all about that: she was having too much fun. She caught a glimpse of the cameramen exchanging grins, but she decided she didn't care.

Savannah couldn't remember the last time she'd done anything like this. She'd focused so hard on the piano, she'd almost forgotten how much she liked to sing. The tunes brought her back to high school and the yearly musical in which she'd always participated. She'd finally gotten the lead female role in her senior year, and she'd been on top of the world.

All around her, the men and women of Westfield and the Double-Bar-K belted out the tunes with varying degrees of proficiency. Maud and James had kept the punch bowl well-supplied with some sort of alcoholic mix she was beginning to think was far more potent than anyone else realized. Jericho had finally brought her a can of pop when she didn't drink any of the alcoholic beverages he kept plying her with. As the rest of the party grew more raucous, she enjoyed watching them loosen up, even while she kept her head.

Nora and Clay seemed as moonstruck as newlyweds, which she supposed they still were. Riley and Boone were competing to see who could sing the loudest. Sam and Harris were doing more kissing than singing. Avery—

Savannah blinked as she caught sight of her friend over her shoulder. Walker had dragged one of the folding chairs back inside. He was seated on it, a hint of a grin playing on his face as Avery perched on his lap, singing as if her life depended on it.

Maud trilled out tune after tune in an operatic soprano, while James backed her up with a deep bass.

Savannah couldn't help but grin as she switched to a show tune favorite and watched her friends practically fall over themselves cheering. There were going to be some hangovers tomorrow morning.

By the time the party ended and Jericho walked her back to her tent, Savannah's throat was hoarse and her ears ringing.

"That was really fun," she said to Jericho when they reached her tent. Even the camera crew following them looked exhausted but happy. She supposed they'd gotten great footage tonight. And here she and Jericho were about to give them more.

"Yeah, it was." He bent down and kissed her. She lifted up on tiptoe to meet him, and this time when he pulled her close, she let him, her whole body coming alive as his arms tightened around her. "I feel like you and I could make a life here, know what I mean?" he said softly into her ear.

She nodded. "I know. I just—need a little more time, okay?"

He pulled back with a deep sigh. "Why do you need more time?"

This man loved her. Savannah knew that with all her heart. Jericho would cherish her as his wife. He'd said it a million times; he'd do whatever it took to make her happy.

But she was keeping two secrets from him.

Maybe it was time to tell him one. She leaned in

closer, turning her head so she could whisper into his ear low enough the cameras couldn't pick up her words. "Meet me at the creek—in about an hour?"

He hesitated, then nodded. "I'll be there," he whispered back.

"I DON'T UNDERSTAND," Jericho said a little over an hour later when he'd managed to slip away to the creek undetected by Renata's minions, and found Savannah there ahead of him. The camp had been dark when he'd left his tent. He hoped everyone else was asleep.

He'd turned off the small flashlight he'd used to guide him down the dark path, and had taken a seat on a large flat rock near the water. Savannah, sitting a few feet away, had explained all about her upcoming audition and what it meant for her career.

"You already play just fine; why do you need a teacher?"

"He'll be more than a teacher. Much more." Jericho could just make her out in the dim light from the stars overhead, a dark shadow against the silvery water slipping past. "He'll groom me for my career," she went on. "You have to understand—I took years off from playing seriously. I'm rusty. Most professionals don't do that; I'm starting at a huge disadvantage."

"And you think this guy can help?" Jericho didn't like the idea, not least because his wedding day was looming. He needed all the time he could get with Savannah.

"I know he can help," she assured him.

"But—wait a minute." Jericho thought through what she'd told him. "He's in California. You're living here in Chance Creek. Just how is this guy going to mentor you?"

"I'll have to commute," she said, affirming his fears.

"Commute to another state?"

"That's right. Twice a month."

"Savannah—" He didn't even know what to say to that. Didn't she understand at all what he and his friends were working toward here?

"I'll still help with the energy system—"

"Why?" he burst out. He surged to his feet and paced away from her, stumbling on the uneven ground.

"I just told you—he'll help further my career—"

"I mean why help with the energy system when you don't give a shit about it? Your flights will cancel out half the savings we make by installing the system." A cool breeze played over his face as he turned back toward her. He wished he could see her face, but it remained in shadow. "Airline travel is one of the most wasteful things we human beings do. It's fun. It's practical. It lets us jet all over wherever we want to go, and it burns more energy than just about anything else."

"What choice do I have? If I don't commute I'll have to move there. I don't want to leave my friends." Her anguish was clear.

Jericho bit back the sharp words he wanted to say. She'd miss her friends—but what about him? What about what he was working for here? What they were all working for? Didn't she care about him—or his goals—

at all?

"I guess it's up to your conscience," he said bitterly. "Is your career more important than the health of the planet—is it more important than us?"

Savannah stood, too. Jericho moved closer, protective despite their argument.

"You told me you supported my career one hundred percent. You said you'd do anything to help me."

"That was before I knew what it entailed."

"That's bullshit," she burst out. "You knew I'd have to travel to concerts. So why the high-and-mighty act now?"

She had him there. "I thought you'd travel regionally," he confessed. "Places you could drive to, or take a train. That's not as bad."

"You thought—you thought I'd play *regionally*?" Her voice slid up an octave. "You thought I wasn't good enough to play nationally—or internationally? What happened to Carnegie Hall?"

"I didn't say—" Shit, she was twisting his words all out of shape. And he was the one who should be angry—not her. He wasn't planning to leave her high and dry all the time.

"That's exactly what you said. Or what you meant, anyway. You're just like Charles—thinking about yourself far more than you think about anyone else. I'll have you know I'm a world-class talent! Redding wouldn't give me an audition otherwise."

She turned to go with a rustle of her skirts. Jericho strode after her.

"We're talking about something far bigger than your career—"

"You're damned right we are." She whirled to face him. "We're talking about your ego, and it's enormous. And I'm through with it!" She backed away.

His ego? Jesus, she didn't understand him at all. "Damn it—you haven't seen what I've seen!" His voice was hoarse—from singing earlier, and his anger. "If you had, you wouldn't act like this!" he called after her. "Boone, Clay, Walker and I—we didn't just wake up one day and say let's stop being SEALs and build a sustainable community instead. We had a reason."

"What reason?" Savannah challenged him.

There was nothing for it but to explain it all. No matter how much he'd prefer to keep it to himself.

"I had a good career with the Navy. Sometimes I got to serve with Boone, Clay and Walker. Sometimes we were split up. But we were together when we went to Yemen."

He knew nothing he could say could express the truth of that mission. The long hours waiting. The round-the-clock vigilance for the lucky break that would allow them to reach the aid workers. "Our assignment was to rescue four men and women who worked for an NGO—non-governmental organization," he explained. "They were aid workers, trying to help those affected by Yemen's civil war. Instead, they got caught up in the fighting. They were trapped—hiding in a bombed-out school. But that wasn't the worst of it." Jericho fought the memories that threatened to overwhelm him.

"When they took refuge there they found kids there, too, unable to get home, their teachers killed."

Savannah didn't move, but he could tell she was listening.

"The aid workers shared what little food and water they had, but you can imagine how quickly that ran out. They had a satellite phone with them—solar-powered. They called for help and were eventually patched through to us. We stayed on the line all the time, taking turns talking to them, trying to keep up morale until we could get to them."

That had been the hardest. Thinking of things to talk about when all he wanted was to rush in and get them all out—especially those children.

"There was this boy." He tried to keep his voice even. Didn't think he'd succeeded when Savannah took a step toward him. "Little kid. Scrappy as hell. Knew about ten words of English, but he kept demanding to talk to me."

Jericho closed his eyes.

He'd never seen Akram. Had only talked with him on the satellite phone one of the aid workers had handed to him when the boy refused to be put off. Even trapped in the rubble of his bombed-out school, unsure if he'd ever make it home again, Akram's zest for life was unquenchable. Jericho had pictured an active boy with dark eyes and hair driven mad by the tedium of crouching for days in the rubble, waiting for a rescue that never came. Jericho knew how frustrating that was. It was the same for him pacing the halls of the forward base, waiting for an opportunity to get in there and save the aid workers they'd been talking to around the clock.

The boy had filled Jericho's ears with a string of broken English.

This is Akram. Where are you from? Are you American? American soldier? Why you not free us? Why you not come?

They'd tried to come. Tried again and again and again.

And failed.

Jericho wondered if the pain of it would ever diminish.

"What happened?" Savannah asked.

Jericho realized he'd stopped talking. He didn't think he'd ever forget this night, speaking to Savannah in the dark, only the stars and the creek as their companions. In the dim hush, telling the truth seemed the right thing to do. "He didn't make it. None of them did." He swallowed against the ache in his throat. "That war, like every war I've seen, is being fought over resources. And every time I look to see why a country suddenly starts tearing itself apart, I find climate change at the root of it. I have to do something."

Could she understand? God, he hoped so.

He thought she nodded. But she didn't step closer.

And when she turned to go, he let her walk away.

SHAME BURNED SAVANNAH'S cheeks, and her throat was raw with pain as she made her way back toward Base Camp. She was grateful for the darkness shrouding her path. Here she was worried about how having a child might interfere with her career goals. Back in Yemen, some mother had lost her son forever. If she herself was even still alive.

Savannah hugged her belly. She had so much. A home. Safety. Peace. Friends.

A man who loved her.

A talent that had brought other people joy last night.

A rustle in the undergrowth at the edge of the track made her speed her pace.

She'd been so furious at Jericho when he attacked her plan to commute to California. She'd thought he was trying to restrict her—and then she'd thought he was telling her she wasn't good enough to play nationally—or internationally.

Instead he was trying to change the world.

How could she compete with that?

Did she even want to?

Jericho was right about one thing; it made no sense for her to live on a Montana ranch when her mentor—and career—would take her far away.

She had only come to Chance Creek to practice and prepare for the next stage in her life, she reminded herself. There was nothing to stop her from returning to her original plan and leaving Westfield when she was ready to begin her career.

Loneliness washed over her at the thought of it. She reached the tents spread out to one side of the bunkhouse, realized how difficult it would be to undress alone and decided to simply wear her gown to bed. As she unzipped her tent and climbed in, she thought about all the good times she'd had here at Westfield. Leaving meant giving up her friends, their Regency B&B, the carriage rides and balls with Maud and James—

It meant being alone again—just her and the baby.

She hated being alone.

That's what had made her friendship with Riley, Avery and Nora so special back at college. They'd done everything together, and for the first time in her life she'd known what it meant to be supported at every turn. The years after graduation, when she'd gone home and bowed to her parents' pressure, she'd missed that so much. She'd had other friends. Work friends. Gym friends.

But no one who championed her talent and told her to go for it like Riley, Avery and Nora had. No one who understood her quest for success.

She fell asleep to restless dreams and when she woke again, the wan light told her it was just past dawn. She got up anyway, needing to use the bathroom like she always did these days.

"You're up early," Win said when Savannah met her at the bunkhouse.

She might as well stay up, Savannah decided. It wasn't like she'd fall asleep again if she returned to her tent. As one, they headed inside to the washroom and helped each other finish dressing. Savannah was grateful the cameras never followed them here.

"Couldn't sleep," Savannah told her truthfully as Win redid her stays.

"Me, either." Win tugged too hard at the laces, and Savannah drew in a breath.

"Hey, could you loosen those up? It's too hot for a tight lacing," she said. What was she going to do about her stays when her pregnancy progressed? For now lacing them loosely worked, but soon her belly would be too big even for that strategy.

"Do you ever think about California?" Win broke into her thoughts.

Savannah sucked in a breath, and steadied herself. Win couldn't know about her audition. "Sometimes," she said.

"Do you ever think about moving back? Living there again? It would be weird, wouldn't it?"

"Maybe." Savannah's thoughts raced. Had Win guessed something? Was she digging for information? "It is our home. Our families are there." She hardly knew what she was saying. Could she actually move back there? Face her family? Make a life there? The thought left her cold. "What about you?"

"I don't know," Win said with a sigh. "Sometimes this place doesn't even seem real, you know? It's the cameras, I guess. It's like a stage set. I keep thinking sooner or later the show will end and we'll all go home."

"The show will end," Savannah told her, "and we'll all go home—but home's right here." At least, that's what she'd once thought.

"Will that be true for everyone?" Win asked enigmatically and Savannah's heart skipped a beat. It was obvious her friend thought Savannah wouldn't be one

of them. Somehow she must know about the audition—
or the baby. Had Heather told her? Or Alice? She didn't
think either of the women were close to Win, but who
knew?

When Win finished helping her dress, she turned
around and returned the favor with shaking hands.
"What would be the hardest part for you—if you had to
go back?"

"Losing the gardens," Win said quickly. "I like
working in them."

"You can garden anywhere," Savannah pointed out.

Win laughed out loud. "I can just see my neighbors'
faces if I tore up my parents' yard and put crops in.
That's not how we roll in San Mateo."

Savannah smiled a little. They were quiet until she
finished, and when she turned to go, Win handed her
the cell phone. "Your turn to keep it today."

Savannah pocketed it. "Thanks. I'll be up at the
manor if anyone needs me."

She breathed a little easier when she'd left Win behind and was walking up the track to the manor. Had
Win been trying to warn her that somehow word of her
plans had spread, or was she just homesick? Savannah
wasn't sure.

When the phone buzzed loudly in her pocket, she
pulled it out and answered it without thinking. "Westfield," she said.

"Savannah? Is that you?"

"Mom?" Savannah swallowed hard. Damn it, why
had she picked up the phone? And how had her mother

traced her number? "Why are you calling?"

"Spoken like the little ingrate you are. I want to know how your practicing is coming."

"Practicing?" Savannah couldn't imagine why she was asking. Her mother hated her practicing—always had, and she'd certainly never called to find out how it was going.

"I hope you're practicing, young lady; otherwise you'll make a fool of yourself and me, even if your audition is really just a formality."

Savannah stopped short. She'd reached the point of the track where it crested the hill and flattened out. She turned to look back at Base Camp, which had come alive as people congregated around the fire pit waiting for Kai to serve breakfast. "I don't understand what you mean." How did her mother know about her audition?

"Savannah. Darling. Maybe you can be anonymous in that dreary little Montana town of yours, but here people know you. They know your name. *Our* name. Especially now that you're on TV."

Her mother sounded positively fluttery. Savannah remembered what Win had said; her mother loved the attention she got from having a daughter on television. Savannah didn't understand her at all.

"After you got in touch with him, your darling virtuoso called your father and I to thank us profusely for the interest our family always shows in the arts. Of course, I had no idea what Redding meant, since you didn't tell us your plans."

"Gee, I wonder why not?"

Her mother ignored her sarcasm. "I wonder, too, since you know perfectly well how helpful we could have been. But once we straightened out that little misunderstanding, I assured Redding that of course we were always interested in the arts. Interested to the tune of donating quite a substantial sum to refurbishing the Menlo Park Performing Arts Center. It's in dire need of an update, I've been saying for years."

Savannah's bullshit meter rang off the scales. Her mother had never been to the performing arts center. She could care less about the arts. But she did care about publicity. "I don't know what you think you're doing, but you don't need to donate money anywhere. No one's going to know or care if you do."

"Of course we need to donate money. You want to pass that audition, don't you? Redding made it perfectly clear what was required. I reminded him you're already a star, but that wasn't enough for him."

That couldn't be true. Savannah forced her breathing to remain steady, and struggled to relax the muscles tightening into knots at her neck. She watched the men and women below her head inside to fetch their food and come back out again to sit on the logs and chat while they ate.

"You're lying. He doesn't care about my publicity— or my money."

Her mother's sharp intake of breath belied the calm tone she used a moment later. "How much is he charging you for his time? I bet it's a pretty penny."

Her mother was right. If she passed the audition and

was accepted to study with him, Redding would charge her a hefty fee for his time. As was his right; time was precious to a pianist in as much demand as he was.

"Savannah, when are you going to learn it's money that makes the world go round? You can dress up and play make believe all you want; the truth is you're made for better things than hiding out on a ranch. The cameras found you even there, didn't they? Nail the audition. We'll do our part. Be the best. That's the Edwards way."

Savannah let her arm drop. She could still hear the buzz of her mother's words from the phone's tiny speakers, but she couldn't make them out, which was good because she couldn't stand to hear any more. Leave it to her mother to find a way to poison her one goal in life. Now her pursuit of the audition would feel meaningless.

She brought the phone up to her ear again. "Don't make the donation," she snapped.

"—coming home and... What did you say?"

"Don't make the donation. If I don't get chosen, I don't care. I don't need him. I want to do this on my own."

"Don't be silly, Savannah. I sent it days ago. It took me this long to track you down. Now, as I was saying, the Arboretum is a lovely place for a small gathering. Highly selective as to the audience, of course—"

"Mom!" Savannah was glad there was no one near enough to hear her yell.

"What?"

Savannah didn't know where to begin. "Why? Why would you donate that money?"

"Because I know what it takes to succeed, unlike you. Savannah, stop taking everything so personally. You want to move up in the world? Guess what? It takes cold, hard cash."

"If you already made the donation, why call me? Why tell me?" Savannah pressed. "You had to know no good could come from it. That I'd be angry. It would mess up my practicing—" She cut off. "That's what this is all about, isn't it? You want me to screw up. In fact, you're hoping I'll be so shocked and angry I'll walk away. Is that it?"

"Darling, don't be ridiculous—I've just been trying to tell you about the concert I set up for you to give while you're here. At the Arboretum. Like I said, it will be very exclusive—a truly lovely event. A fundraiser for cancer research. Surely you support that."

Savannah was floored. Only her mother could manage to turn something wonderful into an insult and an obligation. "I'm not being ridiculous. I'm being accurate. You're trying to throw me off because you don't want me to succeed. You've never wanted me to succeed."

"There is no success where music is concerned," her mother burst out. "Don't you see that? Not on a... piano!" She practically spat the word. "Now if you'd built an app for file sharing, or a social media outlet that focused on launching new bands.... That's a business where you could have made some real money. And this television series would have been the making of you! But regardless, it's too late for that now, so we'll salvage what we can. You'll do the concert at the Arboretum and you'll ace your audition. That will show them."

Savannah hung up. She restrained herself from throwing the phone to the ground and smashing it with the heel of her shoe, only because she shared it with all the other women. Instead, she turned it off, shoved it into the pocket of her apron and headed for the manor.

But when she reached the parlor and sat down at the piano, she found it difficult to play. Her mother had succeeded in stripping the last vestiges of joy from this venture. What had started as a goal had turned into a noose around her neck.

CHAPTER EIGHT

"**W**HERE'S SAVANNAH?" BOONE asked when he sat down next to Jericho on one of the logs. He took a big bite of the breakfast burritos Kai had served.

"I think she's avoiding me." Jericho had no appetite today. He was still reeling from Savannah's confession from the night before. After all the time they'd spent together working out the details of the wind turbines and solar arrays, he couldn't understand how she could consider a situation that required her to fly to California twice a month. It was like she hadn't given it a second thought.

Which was exactly the problem, he thought. No one did. Not really. Not when doing so meant they might have to put a plan on hold—or scrap it all together. And if someone as smart as Savannah didn't see it—or saw it and still didn't feel like changing the way she lived—how were they supposed to change anything?

"We had a fight last night," he went on when Boone didn't answer. "About airplanes."

A corner of Boone's mouth turned up. "Airplanes, huh?"

"Well, it was a little more serious than that," Jericho admitted. He recounted the conversation that had prompted the argument. "She claimed I don't think she's good enough to play nationally, but that's not what I meant at all, and I hope she understands that. I can't tell if she'd simply never thought about the implications of all that travel, or if she did and put it out of her mind."

"Savannah and the other women didn't come here on purpose to live environmentally friendly lives," Boone pointed out. "We can't exactly force them to see things our way."

"She worked beside me for weeks. You should see her figure out the calculations for the energy grid; she's way better at it than I am. But she doesn't see the big picture. And that's what I thought this was all about; showing everyone how to live a good life without using up every freaking resource this world has to offer." He wanted to toss his plate away and pace, but they were surrounded by cameras as usual. One crew member had honed in on them and was recording this conversation. Jericho didn't care. Let them record; this was the conversation that defined their time, after all. "How does the average person live in such a way that he or she honors her goals and desires—and doesn't ruin the world for future generations?"

"That's the million-dollar question," Boone agreed. "And the point of this show. But the longer it goes on, the more I realize we're not here to show people answers; we're here to get them talking about the questions. We don't have all the answers."

"The answer isn't to fly back and forth to California twice a month," Jericho said darkly.

"I don't think we get to dictate that," Boone said. "I think Savannah has to find her own solutions, and you've got to trust she's smart enough to come up with the right one."

"Right for whom? Her? Us? The world?"

Boone shrugged. "We're all just doing our best." He set his plate down. "Savannah's doing her best to figure out her future."

"I know what you're going to say next." Jericho set his plate down, too.

"Oh, yeah? What's that?"

"Time for me to consider a backup bride."

"Yep."

WHEN NORA AND Riley entered the parlor an hour later, Savannah was still sitting at the piano. She'd managed to force herself through her warmup exercises and run through the first of the pieces she'd play for Redding several times, but her fingers kept tripping over the most basic notes, and she was so distracted this practice period was doing more harm than good.

"You weren't at breakfast," Nora said.

"I wasn't hungry."

"I seem to be hungry all the time now." Nora rested her elbows on the top of the baby grand.

"Me, too," Riley said, smiling as she came to stand next to Nora.

Savannah nodded and examined her fingers. She'd have to shake this off and get back to practicing for real if she was going to play the concert—and really, how could she refuse to do a charity event when her mother had already promised she'd be there?

"Savannah."

"Yes?" She looked up, surprised Nora and Riley were still there.

"I said I'm hungry all the time now," Nora said pointedly.

"Me, too," Riley said again.

Savannah cocked her head. "There's food in the kitchen if you didn't get enough—"

"I'm pregnant," Nora burst out. "I'd been keeping it secret because I was worried about Riley."

"But I'm pregnant, too!" Riley nearly hopped up and down with excitement. "I just took the test this morning! All that worrying for nothing!"

"Oh." Savannah stood up. "Oh, my goodness! Congratulations—both of you! I'm sorry—I was lost in my own thoughts."

"That's okay." Nora grinned as Savannah hugged her, then Riley, and for the first time in ages, Savannah forgot her troubles in her happiness for her friends. "I'm so happy for both of you!"

"We're happy, too," Riley said.

"We are."

Both of them were beaming and Savannah was so

glad to hear their good news.

She bit her lip. "I've been keeping a secret too," she confessed. Was it right to spill her news when even Jericho didn't know? "I'm pregnant, too," she squeaked, unable to hold it in a moment longer.

"You are?" Riley's eyes went wide. "Savannah!"

"But you can't tell anyone. I mean it. I have to tell Jericho first."

"He doesn't know?" Nora looked shocked.

Savannah couldn't blame her.

"Only Alice does. Although, Sam might have guessed. Heather Hall did," she admitted. Three people. Five now. She had to tell Jericho soon.

"But…why wouldn't you tell him?" Nora tugged her over to the couch and they all sat down in a rustle of skirts.

"Because he doesn't want children." To her dismay, her eyes filled with tears, and her friends' shone with compassion.

"I'm sure he'll change his mind—"

"I don't know anymore. I don't think we're on the same wavelength at all." She filled them in on everything that had happened. When she got to the part where Jericho yelled at her about flying to California, to her surprise her friends looked at each other and smiled.

"You know, I'm sure Jericho was thinking about saving energy and climate change and all that—but do you think maybe he got so mad because he didn't want you to leave?" Riley asked.

"He doesn't want to lose you, Savannah," Nora

went on. "When you told him you were going to do all that traveling, he finally understood what your life is going to be like. If you become a concert pianist, you're not going to be around much. He'll have to trust you when you sleep away from home—and that's a sore spot for most men. He's going to want you around; that's how they are."

Savannah sat back. "You really think that's why he got so angry?"

"A little of both, probably," Riley said. "He cares about the world. He cares about you, too."

"I don't want to give up my goal." But her voice sounded flat even to her own ears. Her mother's interference had ruined the audition for her. She couldn't believe Redding had solicited her family. How ironic to know her parents had bought the audition that was supposed to lead to the success she needed to prove herself to them.

"I think the first step to finding a solution is to be completely honest with Jericho—about your goals and about being pregnant. Your baby changes everything, don't you think?" Riley said.

"Are you saying it means I should stop playing piano?"

"Not at all." Nora looked shocked. "I don't plan to slow down one bit."

"Me, either," Riley said emphatically. "But it changes things between you and Jericho. No matter what, you need to start making decisions together."

"I guess so."

"Go talk to him," Nora urged. "And congratulations to you, too. Think about it; we're all going to raise our babies together!"

Her friends looked so happy Savannah couldn't bear to contradict them. Because if she and Jericho couldn't work things out, she didn't think she could stay in Chance Creek.

"JERICHO?"

Jericho turned when Kara called his name, and sighed when he realized he couldn't escape the grocery store without speaking to her. For one thing, a camera crew was blocking his exit. He wondered what they'd done wrong to get stuck with such a boring assignment. Filming him walking up and down the aisles had to be the worst. He waited for Kara to catch up to him, his cart in front of him like a shield.

"I was hoping to run into you sometime," she said.

"Really?" He couldn't think why. After the dinner they'd suffered through, he didn't feel the urge to be near his family for a good long while.

"I was a little... out of line the other day. I probably drank more than necessary."

"You think?"

"Hey, cut me some slack, I'm trying to apologize." She surveyed the rows of chips on the shelves nearby and grabbed a couple of bags of salt-and-vinegar ones.

"You were pretty harsh."

"Family doesn't bring out the best in me." She dropped the bags in the cart and bent to choose another one of pretzels. "Besides, I wasn't the only one out of line."

"What's that supposed to mean?"

"What you said at the table—that wasn't fair." She dropped the pretzels into her cart, too, and faced him.

"Are you kidding? It isn't fair that I've taken the rap for you all this time! Mom and Dad treat me like I'm an asshole. Like I've lived a life of crime or something. I'm not irresponsible; I had a career in the Navy most people couldn't dream of taking on. How come I don't get any credit for that?"

"Jericho, I was seven years old," Kara burst out. "Seven! I made a mistake!"

"So you blamed it on me?"

She put her hands out to ward him off and to his surprise he saw they were shaking. "I was angry, all right? Furious. Everything was always about Donovan back then. Always! No one cared about me!"

"Kara, that's not—"

"It *is* true! Do you think I don't remember how it used to be? How our parents drunk themselves into oblivion night after night after night?"

"What are you talking about?" Jericho couldn't believe what he was hearing.

"Do you know how many times as a child I woke up, went into Mom and Dad's room and couldn't shake them out of sleep? I'd hear you snoring in your room, but not them—they'd be passed out like they were dead. I'd go downstairs and find Aunt Patty and Uncle Chris the same way on the couches. You had Donovan with you in your room. I had no one."

Memories flooded into Jericho's mind and he fought against them, but Kara was right. He'd had Donovan. And while the little boy was no protection against danger, he'd kept Jericho from feeling alone on nights when the card parties went far too long into the night, and he'd lain awake until his parents dragged themselves upstairs, their steps heavy, their voices funny. He'd hold his breath until silence reigned through the house, then reach over to touch the crib—and later the trundle bed—to reassure himself Donovan was still there.

"That's why I shoved you." Kara appeared to be struggling against tears. "Because you were paying attention to him, not me. I just wanted someone to see me—just once—and then he fell—"

"Kara." Jericho reached out for her, but she waved him away.

"I still see it when I close my eyes. I see him falling. I hear the impact—I know my life is over."

"Kara—"

"And now I'm the one drinking." She scrubbed away the tear that slid down her cheek. "I'm the one putting my kids to bed and downing a bottle of wine. I'm going to lose them. Andy's threatening to leave me."

The cameras were capturing everything. Jericho didn't know what to do.

So he did the only thing he could; tugged his sister into a rough embrace and held her as she sobbed on his shoulder. A woman with a cart turned the aisle, took one look at them and turned back.

"Come with me," he heard himself say. "To North Dakota. Let's go see Donovan. Let's make this right." As the words spilled out of his mouth, he knew it was the right thing to do. And wondered why they'd waited this long. Nothing could be as bad as the outcomes he pictured when worry kept him awake at night. Kara must be plagued by the same kind of fears.

"What do you say?" he asked her.

Kara dried her eyes. "Okay," she said finally. "Yeah, why not? What's the worst that can happen?" Her face crumpled and she sobbed against her fist. "What if I ruined his life?"

"Then we'll find a way to help him. Together."

"YOU'RE LEAVING?" SAVANNAH wasn't prepared for the way her heart fell when Jericho told her his plans later that afternoon outside the bunkhouse. She hated the thought of being apart from him even for a couple of days, but then, she'd head out for California soon. She hadn't gone down to work with him that morning, and the rest of the day had dragged. Once her initial excitement had faded about Nora and Riley's news, she'd felt worse than before. If she couldn't change Jericho's mind, how could she leave Chance Creek and not share the experience of being pregnant with her friends?

"Next Saturday. There's something I need to sort out. Donovan," he added, as if that explained everything.

Savannah supposed it did. She remembered Jericho's anguish when he'd told her about the accident that had paralyzed his cousin. "You're going to see how he's doing?"

"It's about time I did, don't you think? Kara's coming, too. Together we'll make sure he has everything he needs."

"That makes perfect sense."

"Savannah." Jericho took her hand. "I should have said this earlier. If you marry me, Donovan's going to be a part of your life, too. I'll always be financially responsible for him, which means I won't have as much to give you—"

"That doesn't matter." She could barely admit to herself how good it felt to know Jericho still wanted her, despite everything. At the same time it made it harder to stand her ground.

"It matters to me. I want to be there for you. I want to provide for you."

"That's not what I need from you." She bit her lip as soon as she said it. Now wasn't the time for that discussion; not with cameras filming them. "When will you back?" she hurried to add.

"Two days. Maybe three. Longer if there's anything we can do to make his life better right away."

"I leave for California that Friday." She could hardly look at him when she admitted that, but even knowing how he felt about air travel, she had to go through with the audition—despite what her mother had done. "I'll be there through the weekend. Mom booked me a performance without telling me." She filled him in on the phone call she'd received.

"Family, huh? They're enough to drive you crazy."

Savannah smiled. "Sure feels like it sometimes."

"Did you clear that with Renata?" one of the cameramen interrupted. "These trips you both are taking?"

Savannah met Jericho's gaze, knowing she probably looked as horrified as he did.

"Oh, hell," Jericho shoved his hands in his pockets. "Am I going to have to take a passel of you along with me?"

Savannah's heart sunk. Was she going to have to do the same?

"Yep." Ed nodded firmly. "You both better come talk to Renata right now. She's not going to be happy."

"She never is," Jericho said.

CHAPTER NINE

"**Y**OU SHOULD HAVE told us," Boone said late that night as Jericho sat with him on a log near the fire pit. Overhead, stars glittered in the wide open sky.

Jericho wondered what his troubles would look like from out there. As important as those of a beetle or an ant—or a microbe—he supposed.

"Didn't seem like something I could share." He'd finally told Boone the whole truth about Donovan's injury and the fact he'd been sending his cousin money all this time.

"I remember that summer." Boone braced his hands behind him and stared up at the sky like Jericho was doing. "You changed. I knew that. Why didn't I ask why?"

"You were a kid. We both were."

"It was like... you gave up. Like you stopped trying to get things right. Started going through the motions instead. You didn't really perk up again until you came up with the idea to train to become a Navy SEAL."

"Guess that about sums it up. I couldn't get anything right if I tried. My parents decided I was bad news—so I acted like it."

"Not really, though." Boone turned his way. "You never really fucked up. You kept up your grades all those years. You didn't get into drugs. You picked a solid career. Guess you couldn't mess up if you tried."

Jericho turned this new assessment of himself over in his mind, finding it hard to make it fit with the way his family had always viewed him. "So how come I feel like I've messed up everything?"

"Because you haven't dealt with the past yet. Sounds like you're about to, though. You know all of us will help any way we can, right?"

"Yeah." He did, now that Boone had said it out loud. Why had he kept everything a secret for so long? He supposed it was his family's way. They all acted like they had something to hide.

"What?" Boone asked when Jericho remained silent.

"I can't help thinking that if my parents never told us what happened to Donovan, it must be pretty bad."

"Huh." Boone chewed on that. "You already know he was paralyzed. How much worse could it be?"

"I don't know."

"Want me to go with you?"

The offer surprised Jericho. "You'd do that?"

"Of course I'd do that. You agreed to join me in building Base Camp, agreed to be on Fulsom's stupid TV show. Agreed to marry and try to have a kid—how could I refuse?"

Jericho swallowed. He wasn't planning to have any

kids, and it killed him to keep that secret from Boone. What if they didn't meet Fulsom's demands? What if they lost Base Camp because of him?

"Boone—"

"Should I pack my bag?"

"No." Jericho shook his head. "I've got it covered. But thanks."

"I've put out an ad for your backup bride," Boone said. "I'm just telling you," he added when Jericho flinched. "When you're back from North Dakota, make things right with Savannah. You two belong together."

Jericho hoped he was right.

THE FOLLOWING FRIDAY, when Savannah opened the tall wooden door to the San Mateo Performing Arts Center, where Redding was holding auditions, her nerves were dancing so hard she wondered if she'd keep down the plain piece of toast she'd managed to eat for breakfast. Just like Nora, she felt hungry all the time these days, but not this morning. She was trailed, as usual, by a camera crew, which made her doubly conspicuous, although she'd changed to a conventional outfit once she'd left Chance Creek. No Regency gown for the audition. Renata had worked long and hard with Redding's people to get him to waive the restrictions on recording the audition, but as Renata confessed to Savannah when she was done, the musician seemed rather pleased at the thought of his cameo on *Base Camp*.

Her knee-length skirt and modern blouse felt

strange after months in Regency clothes. She could breathe free without her stays, but she felt exposed in the clingy garments. She'd left her dresses with Alice, who'd promised to let out their seams again and return them to Westfield before Savannah came home. She'd also managed to sneak off to the doctor's the day before she left for California. So far so good as far as the baby was concerned.

Savannah was grateful the audition would be over before noon. She had the rest of the day free to practice for her performance the following evening. She'd made it clear she had no time for a family visit—at least not until after the concert. She was afraid if she entered the same room as her mother, her blood pressure would skyrocket and that couldn't be good for the baby.

She signed in with a young woman at a desk, and was ushered into a room where Savannah was surprised to see rows of chairs occupied by men and women who appeared to be prepared to play, too. Though the cameras followed her, she was happy to note they were attempting to keep out of the way. Ed had interviewed her several times during the flight and at the hotel last night, but this morning he must have taken pity on her, because while he was filming everything, he kept out of her personal space.

"What's going on?" she whispered to the woman sitting next to her, who was dressed in a navy pant suit with a string of pearls around her neck.

The woman frowned and made sure no one was paying attention before answering in equally low tones.

"Auditions. To work with Redding. Isn't that why you're here?"

"Yes, but—" Savannah tried to hide her confusion. "I didn't expect so many—"

The woman rolled her eyes. "There's a fee to take your chance, isn't there? Look around and do the math."

Savannah covered her shock at this cynical answer by pulling out her phone and looking at the time. "But why is everyone here at once?" she whispered. "I'm supposed to audition at ten-thirty."

"Good luck with that. Didn't you do any research? Everyone knows these things take all day. He'll have you sitting here until five o'clock, most likely. And they don't serve lunch. Hope you brought a snack to tide you over. You'll need it."

Savannah hadn't, and she hoped she wouldn't need one; it didn't seem like a good idea to leave the audition waiting room to go fetch food, even if she might be here for hours. She took her seat and fidgeted, so anxious she could hardly breathe.

But as she sat and waited, and hours passed, her nerves changed to irritation, and then downright anger. She was pregnant and the baby had a way of making its needs known. It was three-thirty when she was finally called to the inner sanctum where Redding and a half-dozen other men and women sat near a grand piano. Savannah expected her nerves to flare up even higher, but the truth was she was hungry, thirsty, tired and more than a little cranky at the whole process.

When one of the women asked her to announce herself, Savannah kept it brief, sticking to her name and the titles of her audition pieces. She sat down without waiting for instruction and began to play, bringing some of that anger to bear on the music. It was a vigorous piece, which helped quite a bit, and after a few minutes she found her equilibrium.

This is it, she told herself. *Do your best.*

But the audition was nothing like she'd thought it be. To her own ears, her playing felt flat, and Savannah's desperation grew. This was her chance—she wouldn't get another one.

But when her stomach growled loudly, Savannah bit back a laugh. How could she help it? The whole situation was ridiculous. Hadn't her mother already paid for her to become Redding's protégé? Or was there a bidding system she didn't know about? Maybe helping fund the performing arts center renovations wasn't enough. Maybe someone in the waiting room had built a mansion for Redding himself.

She wondered why he bothered with auditions at all. Why not auction off his time to the highest bidder?

What was left of her nervousness disappeared, and after a while, her anger did, too. Whether or not Redding could further her career, she didn't care.

She didn't want him to.

Look at her now—the way she was playing like an automaton, far too tired and hungry to give her music any life. She was sick of these pieces anyway.

When she'd chosen her music she'd played it safe—

again.

The way she kept playing it safe her whole damn life.

Even now when she'd run away from home to re-create herself at Chance Creek, it had hardly turned out to be a grand adventure. All she did was practice—morning, noon and night. Where was the spontaneity?

Where was the joy?

Savannah permitted herself a glance at Redding, who gazed at the ceiling with his lips pursed, his whole face pinched up like he was in pain. He didn't seem to be enjoying himself any more than she was.

She glanced back down at her fingers racing up and down the keys. Once she'd been able to lose herself in music. To inhabit the songs she'd played. To escape the life she hated.

But maybe—maybe—

That was the problem.

She didn't hate her life anymore. In fact—

She loved it.

Loved getting up early to find herself part of a camp filled with friends. Loved eating breakfast at the fire pit, heading up to the manor and doing her chores. Loved coming back down to spend a couple of hours with Jericho before an afternoon spent on her own pursuits.

Loved it when guests came to the B&B.

Loved hosting weddings.

So why did she feel so awful now?

Because this was all wrong, Savannah realized, even as her fingers continued to run over the keys.

She couldn't respect a mentor who required a bribe to take her on, and she couldn't learn a thing from a man she didn't respect.

That's why she'd learned so much from Jericho about the energy grid. He didn't teach for money—

He taught for love.

Savannah brought both her hands down on the keyboard in a discordant bang, stood up and pushed back the bench.

"I'm done."

She marched out of the room on shaky legs, reminding herself she didn't need any of them. Back in the waiting room, she gathered her things and made for the door as quickly as possible.

The camera crew followed her. She'd almost forgotten about them. "Savannah—what are you doing? Where are you going?" Ed called after her.

Savannah ignored the question, strode through the halls, burst out the front door and spotted a taqueria across the street.

Time to eat.

"READY FOR THIS?" Jericho asked Kara when they exited the motel they'd booked for the night in Fargo and got back into the truck they'd driven from Chance Creek. With a pared-down two-man crew crammed in the backseat, the situation was far from perfect from his point of view. He would have preferred to do this alone with Kara. He had no idea what they'd find, and he'd warned Renata, and the crew members, Byron and

Craig, they would have to ask Donovan's permission before they filmed him.

"Sure, man. I'm not going to make money off someone who's been hurt," Craig had said, showing more understanding than Jericho thought possible. He'd figured Renata and the crew would go after a story with the kind of sensational elements this one might have.

Jericho had a new respect for the man.

"I'm ready to throw up," Kara said. "You realize we could do an Internet search and save ourselves a trip."

"We talked about that. We need to do this face-to-face. We can't chicken out now."

"If it's really bad, we'd be prepared," Kara argued. "Shouldn't we know what we're going to face?"

"We're going to face our cousin. Someone we both used to love. We don't have to *prepare ourselves*."

That was a cop out. The truth was, he'd gotten su-perstitious about it. He felt like doing an Internet search was a shortcut—one that wasn't seemly for either of them at this late stage in the game. "We need to look him in the eye and own up to what we did together. Whatever happens, we'll get through it." He was even more aware than usual of the cameras capturing this whole conversation. Byron and Craig had been weird all morning. Ready to go even before they were. Almost jaunty. Jericho wondered if they meant to go back on their word.

They'd pay if they did.

"Okay. Let's do this."

A half-hour later, however, they were still driving

around in circles, trying to find the address to which Jericho always sent his payments. The GPS took them to a street on the outskirts of Fargo, but they'd driven down it twice and hadn't seen a home marked with the correct number.

"See anything?" he finally asked the crew.

"Nah, man," Craig said. "And don't talk to us. We aren't even here."

Jericho rolled his eyes. The cameramen were most definitely here.

"Maybe we have the wrong street," Kara said.

Jericho understood what she meant. The whole area wasn't what he expected. The homes were set far back from the road with neat, long driveways, impeccable landscaping and mature trees.

He turned the truck around and went to where the GPS said the house should be. "It's got to be this driveway," he said, looking askance at the blank break in a tall stone fence that lined the edge of the road for a good three hundred feet. There was no street number. No marking of any kind. But nor was there a closed gate, either, which Jericho took for a sign it was all right to turn into the driveway and see where it led.

"You think he lives back here?"

Jericho noticed his sister gripping the armrest. Was she nervous? He was, he admitted to himself. Chances were his cousin wouldn't be happy to see them. Jericho dreaded an ugly scene and wondered now why it had been so important to drag Kara along with him. He could have spared her this.

The driveway wound a lot farther through the land-scape than Jericho would have guessed, and the property widened out around them, as if someone had bought a normal lot that abutted the street and then several more behind it, putting them together to make a large parcel.

Jericho pulled up in a cobbled courtyard in front of an attractive Spanish-style home and parked the truck.

"Think this is the right place?" Kara asked.

"Let's go see." They all climbed out and Jericho led the way up the steps with more than a little trepidation. He pushed the doorbell. Quick steps sounded from the other side and a pretty woman close to their age opened it. Her eyes widened when she took them in.

"Oh, my God."

Jericho braced himself for her anger at the film crew who were capturing all of this, but to Jericho's surprise, she smiled. "Come in. Oh, my goodness. I can't believe you're all here. Please, come in and sit down. I'll get my husband."

More bewildered than before, Jericho followed her inside slowly. There must be some mistake, because the woman obviously thought she knew him. "Forgive us for showing up like this, but I'm—"

"I know who you are. Jericho Cook. And Kara. You look so much like yourselves I would have known you anywhere. Please, have a seat in the living room. I'll be right back."

"What is going on?" Kara hissed the moment they'd taken seats on an immaculate leather sofa and the woman had rushed off again. "Who is that?"

"I don't know."

"How'd she know us? Did you call ahead?"

"No." Jericho was as surprised as she was, and he turned to confront Byron and Craig. "Did Renata?"

Craig shook his head.

When the woman reappeared, Jericho surged to his feet to question her, but before he could, a man rounded the corner into the room.

A man he recognized from the strong family resemblance.

Kara gasped.

"What took you so long?" Donovan asked.

"YOU INVITED CHARLES?" Savannah hissed at her mother twenty-four hours after her audition, when she stood in the wings of yet another well-appointed room, this one a large round concert hall with a beautiful grand piano on a raised dais that faced a semi-circular audience. The Arboretum was known as the best private venue around for occasions hosted by non-profits and wealthy society matrons. Savannah knew she had every right to bail on this concert like she'd walked out on her audition, but while she disapproved of her mother's tactics, she knew if she did, she'd let down a cause that needed everyone's help. She'd play the concert and return to Chance Creek, where she vowed she'd do a thorough re-think of her plans.

"Of course I did," her mother said. "What did you expect?"

"The impossible; that you'd have some respect for my feelings." She'd felt giddy after walking out of the audition, although grateful no one else knew what she'd done yet. But once her initial relief wore off, Savannah had realized she hadn't made her life any easier. She still had to figure out what to do about Jericho and the baby—and had to figure out what to make of her career now that she wouldn't be working with Redding.

"What did Charles ever do to you? You're the one who stood him up with hardly any warning. You haven't spoken to him since you walked out, as far as I've heard. He's the one who's showing remarkably good manners given the circumstances."

"You mean, he's the one who's still rich."

"For God's sake, Savannah, get over yourself. So we hoped you'd make a good match. What parent doesn't? You walked away and we didn't lock you in your room in chains. Stop pretending to be the misunderstood princess."

Savannah turned to go, but her mother caught her arm. "There are a lot of people here whose contacts are worth cultivating, no matter what you do with your life. If you wish to pursue music, then pursue music. We've thrown our support behind you. We're standing by you despite the way you handled ending your engagement. Stop throwing temper tantrums and act your age." She smoothed her hair and Savannah realized her mother was preening for the camera crew—and probably trying to sound wise for them, too.

"You have no idea what's important to me, do

you?" She would have preferred to have this confrontation in private, but her mother didn't seem to mind airing their dirty laundry for all to view.

"Do you?" her mother countered. Her voice sharpened. "Or are you stuck in a loop of retribution because we weren't the picture-perfect parents you hoped for?"

Savannah hesitated, hearing what sounded like pain in her mother's voice, but her mother got control of her emotions again as quickly as she'd lost it. "Maybe you should consider that we know more about you than you know about yourself."

And there it was again—that self-centered attitude that made it impossible for them to discuss anything. Savannah's anger gripped her more tightly, even as her mother's words tangled together in her mind. Loop of retribution—wasn't that exactly what her parents had set in motion by undermining the process of auditioning with Redding? They weren't setting her free; they were trying to tighten the leash around her neck.

Unwillingly, her thoughts returned to the picture Jericho had painted of Yemen—of those children in the school. In a world where you could lose a loved one in an instant, shouldn't you think through all your actions? Shouldn't you at least take a breath before you stepped in and tried to destroy what mattered most to that person?

She turned her back on her mother, and with a pang wondered if Jericho had felt this bad the day she'd told him about commuting to California twice a month. Had it seemed like she was taking aim at Base Camp and trying to thwart their progress through her thoughtless-ness?

She hugged her arms across her chest. He had to know that wasn't it at all; she was working to further her career—not hurt his.

Looking back, she saw her mother had turned away. Lines of fatigue etched her face. Was she thinking the same thing even now? That Savannah should under-stand she was only trying to forward her businesses' interests, not undermine Savannah's desire to be a pianist?

If so, Savannah was perpetuating a loop after all.

So now what should she do? How could she prove anything to anyone with the way it had all gotten tangled in knots?

Giving up, Savannah paced away to find a drink of water before the concert started. She wished she was back at Base Camp now, doing something simple—like calculations for Jericho, laughing at him when she reached the answer more quickly than he did, shrieking when he tried to snatch a kiss. Mucking around in Pittance Creek measuring water flow and counting fish. Tracking the path of the sun over various positions of their settlement. Sharing meals at the fire pit, doing chores with her friends, making plans for the next batch of guests at the B&B.

Anything but playing this concert.

Not because she didn't love music—or getting that applause.

But because she didn't know anymore what she was

trying to prove.

She looked at her hands. She'd thought she'd known exactly what they were for, but so many varied projects and tasks fulfilled her these days.

She'd thought she wanted her parents to under-stand—

But that was impossible, wasn't it? It was never go-ing to happen.

"Ms. Edwards? You're on in a moment." A woman whose name tag proclaimed her to be Carla motioned her to hurry. Savannah followed her back toward the circular concert hall. First things first, she supposed. She'd said she'd play and she'd follow through with the obligation.

"Nervous?" Carla asked as they waited in the wings. Savannah's mother had taken a seat between her father and Charles in the front row. The camera crew had positioned itself close to the stage but off to one side. The corners of Savannah's mouth tugged up at the way this moment echoed her dream of playing in Carnegie Hall. There was her family—front and center as she waited to take the stage. There were the cameras.

There was the grand piano waiting for her to play.

Just as it had been the day before, the fluttery, jittery feeling that always sent her into fits of nerves right before a concert was absent. She had nothing to lose. She'd put her heart and soul into preparing for the audition with Redding, and then had realized he was nothing but a fake. She'd realized nothing she could do now would change the way her family thought of her, either.

As for the rest of the audience, she didn't know them. She'd do her best to entertain them, but it wasn't like playing for her friends back home.

Savannah lifted a hand to her mouth as understanding crashed over her. How could she have missed it before? Why hadn't she realized it wasn't fame she was after—or even approval?

It was connection.

Playing Carnegie Hall would be a great honor. Gaining her parents' approval might have healed so many past hurts. But playing for her friends at Base Camp— watching them dance to her music—listening to them sing along with her—

That was everything.

She'd built a life for herself back in Chance Creek that she loved. With friends she cared for truly and deeply—who saw who she was and accepted her for it. With a man who loved her despite his flaws and fears— and despite hers, too.

Even if she crashed and burned today—if she was booed off the stage—she had something to go home to.

This was abundance, she decided. Having multiple options, multiple talents. Knowing that no matter what befell her she could make a way in the world for herself and her child. Knowing already that her music brought pure joy to those she loved.

"It's time," Carla said, touching her arm. Polite applause from the gathered crowd signaled she had been announced. As Savannah crossed the stage, she took in the formal arrangement of the seats and the position of the piano and the audience. As she sat down on the bench and adjusted it to fit her needs, she remembered the crowded venue of the bunkhouse. The whirling dancers. The shouted, off-key show tunes. Her heart warmed at the memory, but as throats cleared and feet shuffled in the silent concert hall, Savannah met her mother's eyes and saw the worry there, quickly masked by the lift of her chin.

What was worrying her? That Savannah would embarrass her? That the event wouldn't be the hit of the social calendar? That she wouldn't make exactly the right connections to seal the latest round of funding one of her ventures required?

As Savannah lifted her hands to place them on the keys, compassion flooded her heart. She felt…sorry for all the people in this room. Every one of them carried his or her burden of pain and fear. Most of them were probably here because they had to be, not because they wanted to be.

Many hoped to be seen—and be counted as important enough for others to cultivate.

What was this life?

And what role did music even play in it?

Did it matter?

Savannah decided it didn't. She decided the only gift she could give her audience today was transcendence. She could offer them a few minutes in which to forget their fears, forget themselves—and simply be.

But in order to do that with such a sophisticated

crowd, she was going to have to knock their socks off.

Savannah brought her hands down in a crash of notes that made every member of the audience jump, and she continued to play with the vivacity and fury of a woman possessed by Valkyries. No soft, tender interlude for these movers and shakers of modern society. Let them remember what really counted: passion. Vigor. The daring it took to truly be oneself.

Not once did Savannah glance at her audience. She played as if her life depended on it. Played as if she could pour her heart into the silent, precise, hemmed-in vessel that contained these people's lives and break it wide open with the splash of her chords.

The small hall rang with sound, and as her fingers ran over the notes releasing an avalanche of sound, Savannah stopped being a woman who played piano and simply became music itself. The rest of the piece passed smoothly. Only when it ended again in another crescendo of chords did Savannah come back to herself. To her body. To the hall, where silence reigned absolute.

Until a man leapt to his feet and began to clap. In a moment the whole audience joined in, and this time she wasn't the one creating the thunderous sound; she was the recipient of it.

"Bravo!" a woman in the back called out. A man on the far side of the room echoed the word. Savannah bowed her head in the face of the wave of approbation that flowed toward her. Maybe she still needed a little of it to heal all the wounded places in her soul—because it felt good.

When she looked up again, her mother, father and Charles were all on their feet, too. All of them sharing the same dazed expression, so shocked she almost had to laugh. They began to clap, too, slowly at first, but speeding up.

A smile broke over Charles's face—a truly open smile she hadn't seen since the beginning of their relationship, before their marriage somehow became *fait accompli*.

He nodded to her and Savannah's heart eased. He'd forgiven her. That was clear—and he'd done it because he finally understood what he'd missed for so long: her true passion.

She thought back to the days when they'd first met. The way they'd hung out together at the get-togethers they'd both found so boring and stilted. She remembered the time they'd snuck into the basement at one of their parents' friend's parties and discovered an old boom box and a stash of mix tapes from the eighties. The party upstairs had been so crowded and loud no one had heard them crank up the old tunes downstairs. They'd belted out the lyrics and gyrated around like they'd seen in the movies from their parents' childhood.

Savannah smiled back at him, turned back to the piano despite the continuing roll of applause and began to play a new song.

A pop song.

Charles's favorite eighties ballad.

The audience quieted with a few confused titters

and exclamations, but they dutifully dropped into their seats to listen.

Savannah wasn't having that. Her singing might not match the quality of her playing, but this seemed to be a day for taking chances. She hummed the opening line of the song to get her bearings, then quavered through the first couple of words, found her voice and sang it louder. At first she thought no one would understand— but suddenly Charles's baritone rang out and backed her up.

Heartened, Savannah sang louder and, pretty soon, a third voice joined in, and then a fourth and fifth. When a few bars later the entire room began to sing along, Savannah couldn't help the grin that spread over her face. First she'd surprised them. Then she'd engaged them.

No one would forget this concert.

Which was good, Savannah decided, because who knew when she would play at another public event after the way she'd walked out on Redding. She wasn't going to let her mother buy her concerts anymore.

That didn't matter, though. Because in the last twenty-four hours, she'd realized it wasn't her parents she needed to impress. It wasn't Charles—or Jericho, either.

The only opinion that really mattered was her own.

And she liked doing this: playing. Singing. Entertaining.

She didn't need a mentor to do this. She already knew how.

Just like the evening not so long ago in the bunkhouse, one song led to another and another and another until the afternoon ended in more applause. All around the hall, Savannah saw audience members laughing and talking to one another and she understood that not only had they connected with her, by singing together they'd connected with each other.

As Savannah stood up, received her ovation and walked off the stage, Carla was waiting to escort her.

"That was amazing," she gushed. "I've been here two years and I've never seen anything like that. Nothing you played was on the program for the evening."

"I improvised," Savannah told her.

"It was awesome."

"Savannah! Savvy!"

Savannah turned around when her mother called out the nickname she hadn't heard since she was a girl.

"It's Redding!"

Her mother held up her cell phone, and finally caught up to where Savannah and Carla stood. "He couldn't get through to you, so he called me. He wants to take you on. Can you believe it?"

No, she couldn't. What did he want? More money? "Tell him no," Savannah heard herself say. "I'm not interested anymore."

"Savannah!" Her mother stared at her open-mouthed. "What on earth? Where are you going?" she called as Savannah whirled away and kept walking.

"Home."

CHAPTER TEN

"**D**ONOVAN?" KARA ASKED before Jericho could say a thing. "Is that really you?"

"It's really me. And look at the both of you—only took you guys twenty years to come find me."

Jericho braced himself. Here it came—the recriminations. But Donovan only crossed the room, kissed Kara on the cheek, shook Jericho's hand and sat down on the edge of the couch. He nodded to the cameramen who had filed into the room behind them. "Go ahead and film," he said to them, as if this happened every day. He turned back to Jericho and Kara. "Well, what was the hold up? You obviously knew where to find me."

"You're walking!" Kara blurted.

"Actually, I'm sitting right now, but yes, I can walk." He looked from one to the other of them. "Is that what this is? A guilt visit?"

"No!" Kara said.

"Yes," Jericho said more slowly. Because that's exactly what it was. "We thought you'd been injured severely when you fell out of the treehouse."

"I was—or so Mom and Dad tell me. Had a bunch of operations over a couple of years. I don't remember all of that." Donovan sat back, as if settling in to tell the story. "I remember rehab more—took a long time to get fast enough to keep up with the other kids. Jackie here, especially." He smiled and took his wife's hand.

"We met when we were both seven," she told them. "I beat Donovan in the fifty-yard dash. He was the only boy I knew who wasn't faster than me, and I didn't let him forget it. Compassion wasn't my strong point back then."

Donovan squeezed her hand. "Back then I didn't want compassion; I wanted to run circles around you. Which was good; I got a lot more focused on my rehab after that. Blew everyone away with the way my coordination improved. Didn't make a full recovery, but good enough."

"Why…why didn't anybody tell us?" Kara asked.

"Why didn't you ask?" Donovan returned. For the first time his face fell. "Why did your whole family turn your back on me when I got hurt?" He looked at Jericho. "I waited for you to come see me, you know. In the hospital and at home."

Jericho wasn't sure how to answer him. He was still trying to figure out the sequence of events in his own mind. Didn't his parents know Donovan had made a full recovery? Why had they kept away when it was clear things weren't so dire after all? He glanced back at the camera crew, saw Craig's grin and understood; Renata had done exactly what he and Kara hadn't. She'd researched Donovan, and knew exactly what to expect.

"Your family left town. Your parents made it clear they didn't want us in their lives. They never got in touch—not once," he sputtered.

"It was like I lost everyone all at once," Donovan went on as if he hadn't heard Jericho. "You were like my big brother, you know. And even if we didn't get along all the time," he said to Kara, "I thought of you as my sister."

Jericho rubbed his chin with the back of his hand. "I don't understand. If Mom and Dad knew you were fine, why didn't they say so? Why all the secrecy? Did they feel responsible—?"

Donovan snorted. "Drunks don't feel responsible."

Jericho's throat constricted. "Drunks?"

"Come on. I've known my parents were lushes since I was ten. Yours are, too, from the looks of it. I found a photo album my mom hid in her closet back then. All those photos of Mom and Dad and your parents playing cards. And drinking. Man, they did a lot of drinking."

Jericho nodded slowly. "I guess they did."

"You guess?" Kara huffed. "There's no guessing about it. Remember going to the bottle depot?"

He did. Remembered all the change he'd received when he dragged his weekly haul there. It had been hard work carrying those bags of bottles on his bike.

"It slowed down after your parents left," he told Donovan. "A lot," he added as he thought about it. Gone were those hauls to the bottle return depot. He'd gotten a paper route instead when the money went dry.

"And then it stopped altogether a few years back. They're in AA now," Kara said.

Donovan sat still for a long time, lost in thought. "You guys were lucky then. Mom and Dad never did sober up."

Kara exchanged a look with Jericho. "They didn't?"

"No. Kept right at it. They still get drunk a couple times a week." He tapped his finger on his knee. "God, I've been a fool, haven't I? I've been angry at the wrong people."

"What do you mean?" Jericho asked.

"I always thought your parents were hard hearted—that's why they stayed away. That's what my folks always said—that they thought they were too good for us. Now I know why."

"I don't think I follow." Jericho didn't like the pain in his cousin's voice.

"They were protecting you. But they didn't think to protect me, did they?"

"Donovan—" His wife put her hand on his arm.

"Protect you…?" Jericho trailed off, as it all came clear. He remembered again the nights when his parents had drunk themselves silly, the heavy tread on the stairs as they'd gone to bed and passed out cold. What Kara said about trying to wake them up, and returning to her room alone.

Back then he'd been there to keep his cousin company. After the accident, Donovan had been on his own.

"How bad…?" Jericho trailed off again, far too aware of the cameras.

Donovan followed his glance and shrugged. "They can film this; I don't care. How bad was it to grow up with a couple of drunks? It sucked, what do you think?" He surged up from the couch and paced the room, while the rest of them watched. Kara was pale. Donovan's wife bit her lip, tracking his movements around the room with her eyes. "Hell, it could have been a lot worse, I suppose. Dad held on to his job. They took me to rehab. I got through school. I didn't like to be at home a lot, so I joined every club and after-school activity I could. Got into finance, which turned out to be an interesting line of work. I've done well for myself so far." He flopped back down on the couch and took his wife's hand.

"I see that." Jericho relaxed a little.

"And when things got tough, Jackie was always there. Once we stopped competing all the time we figured out we had a lot in common."

"We never stopped competing." She nudged him with her shoulder. "It kept going right through high school. We both got full scholarships to the college of our choice—which just happened to be the same one. We were married sophomore year at business school and haven't looked back."

Jericho shook his head.

"What?" Donovan asked.

"Here I pictured you miserable. Struggling. Hell, you're way ahead of me. You've got a wife, a house, a career…"

"That's right. Where's Savannah? You popped the question yet?" Donovan asked with a grin.

Jericho froze; how the hell did his cousin know about Savannah?

Then he remembered the TV show. "Oh, hell—don't tell me…"

"We watch *Base Camp* faithfully every week," Jackie said with a grin. "I feel like I know you already, but it's wonderful to meet you in person. We've waited for you to show up for a long time."

"But—" This was all too much for him to wrap his head around. "If you wanted to get in touch with me, why didn't you call? And if you're doing so well, why keep the money—"

Too late he remembered Kara knew nothing about the monthly payments he'd sent to their cousin. She turned to him. "What money?"

Donovan raised an eyebrow. "Kara doesn't know?"

"No one knows," Jericho said. "Well, hardly anyone," he added, realizing soon the world would know because he'd mentioned it to Boone while they were being filmed. Still, he understood that while Donovan hadn't been paralyzed, he'd still had a difficult childhood—partly because of that fall. So he didn't begrudge his cousin keeping the money if it had helped him in any way.

Donovan put his hands on his knees. Leaned forward. "Look, Jericho—when I got your first check, I was…well, I was angry."

"He was pissed," Jackie agreed, but she was smiling.

"I'd waited all those years to hear from you. I figured sooner or later your family would break down and come after us. Then when you finally reached out—it wasn't to ask how I was, or to come see me. You just sent a check."

"I explained it to him," Jackie said.

"She did." Donovan reached over to tussle her hair. "She said there had to be a misunderstanding. You had to think the damage was worse than it was."

"I told you to ask your parents what really happened—why the two sides of the family didn't talk anymore," she told Donovan tartly.

Donovan nodded. "Thing is, I don't ask my folks a lot of questions. Don't talk to them much these days."

"I don't talk to my folks much either," Jericho admitted. "Or, we talk—but we don't say a whole hell of a lot, if you get my drift. When I was young—"

"Our parents blame Jericho for what happened," Kara said baldly. "They think he pushed you."

Donovan's fingers spasmed. "That's why you sent the cash? It was guilt money?" He hesitated. "Did you push me? I can't really remember that part."

Jericho didn't know what to say. Donovan's question felt like a sucker punch to his gut. "If you think I could push you, why did you ever want to see me again?"

"Like I said, you were my big brother—the only brother I had. I... loved you."

Jericho's hands balled into fists. He struggled to stay

in his seat. He wanted to move. Do something. Anything.

But before he could figure out how to react, Kara suddenly burst out, "I did it. I pushed Jericho. I was mad and I pushed him—hard. He fell into you, the guard rail broke and over the edge you went. I never, ever meant to hurt you—either of you. I'm so sorry—it was an accident."

"Of course it was," Donovan said quickly, looking from one to the other. "Guys, I always knew it had to be an accident. I knew it in my gut. But are you saying your parents don't know that? They think you did it deliberately?" he asked Jericho.

Jericho nodded slowly. "They think I was irresponsible. A boy."

"Jesus." Donovan shook his head. "What a mess. What a fucking mess." He looked like he'd get up and pace again.

"Baby," Jackie said.

"So I was right; this was guilt money. But not for not reaching out to me sooner; because you thought— what did you think? You knew you didn't push me!"

"I knew that. But I was in charge. I should have stopped Kara—"

"Oh, leave it!" Kara exploded. "We were all kids. Just kids! You pissed me off—I wanted your attention, I pushed you, you fell into Donovan, Donovan fell out of the tree house."

"And all of us wasted twenty years feeling bad about it. All of us," Donovan said again. "And not just us—

our parents, too. They're still together? Your folks?"

"Yeah," Jericho said. "They're together, but—"

"But it's never been the same," Kara finished.

"My parents act like...like..." Donovan struggled for words.

"Like they could be hauled in for a crime at any time," Jackie exclaimed. "Like they're hiding something. I've never seen anything like it."

"Ours, too," Jericho said, leaning forward.

"That's because they are," Kara blurted. She clapped her hands over her mouth and shook her head.

"What do you mean?" When Kara didn't answer, Jericho asked her again. "Kara? What are you talking about?"

"Oh, fuck." At first Jericho thought she'd refuse to say any more. She dropped her head into her hands and stayed silent for a long moment. "I never told anyone." Her voice was muffled by her hands until she straightened. "Mom told me never to tell—and I think she thought I was so young I would forget what I saw, because she never mentioned it again after that night—"

"Mentioned what?" Jericho couldn't stand not knowing.

"When Donovan fell—" Her voice cracked. "We knew it was bad. You ran so fast to get help. Then they sent you back to the house with me, remember?"

Jericho nodded. He remembered all too well. "That's when they got you to the hospital," he told Donovan. "You were unconscious."

"No," Kara said. "You're wrong." A tear slipped

silently down her cheek. "They didn't take him to the hospital. Not until the following morning. I saw—I saw from my room."

Jericho pictured her room at the rear of the house. One window faced the backyard. The other their aunt and uncle's place.

"I couldn't sleep," Kara went on. "I could never sleep in those days and that night I was terrified. I was in bed and I heard something; all the windows were open—it was summer, remember? I looked out and saw Aunt Patty and Uncle Chris in their house moving around Donovan's room. The light was on. They were bending over Donovan's bed; I could tell he was still there. I thought he was better and I wanted to go see him. Mom caught me in the hall. She told me it was just a dream, and not to tell anyone."

"Why—why would they wait?" Jericho asked. He didn't understand that at all. Donovan had been unconscious. Obviously hurt. Possibly badly—

"They were drunk," Donovan said slowly. "They were drunk when it happened, weren't they?"

Kara nodded.

Jericho's head reeled. "But—even so—" He couldn't fathom it.

"Donovan could have died. I know," Kara said. "I've thought about that so many times. They took that chance in order to save themselves."

"No wonder they can't look each other in the eye—any of them," Jackie said.

Jericho's gaze stayed on Donovan. His cousin's features were slack. His eyes glassy.

"I hate them," Kara burst out. "I hate them for do-ing it—and for making me a party to it. I hate them for never talking about it—never making amends!"

He watched his cousin struggle with the new knowledge. Finally, Donovan shook his head. "You know what? I'm tired of being angry. I just feel…sorry for them."

"They could have killed you," Kara cried out. "I could have killed you. Why don't you hate me? I hate me!"

Donovan lurched across the space between them and caught Jericho's sobbing sister in his arms. "Hating you wouldn't do me any good. It wouldn't make me feel like I've found a family. It wouldn't give me hope for the future."

Kara couldn't stop crying. "I don't know how it all got this bad," she sobbed. "I kept hoping the problem would go away, and instead it got bigger and bigger. It's taken over everything. I can't stop drinking. I'm a terrible mother—"

Donovan held her until Kara had sobbed herself out on his shoulder. When she finally pulled back, he turned to include Jericho in his gaze. "Here's the thing. The three of us—no," he broke off, gesturing for Jackie to join them. "The four of us can stop this right now. We can change the course of the future—the future of this entire family. We can forgive each other, and our parents, and each other's parents. We can erase the slate and start over. Then maybe our children will have a chance."

"Our children—?" Jericho interrupted. "Do you two have kids?"

Jackie placed a hand on her belly. "I'm three months along," she said with a smile.

"That's right; I'm going to be a daddy," Donovan announced with such pride Jericho's heart flip-flopped in a funny way. He wanted to feel that kind of pride—to know his family would continue on—

But that wasn't his path. Maybe Donovan was okay, but Akram wasn't. He would never heal from the bombs Jericho hadn't been able to save him from. "I'd like that," he managed to say. "To put the past behind us and move forward—as a family."

It was a start.

"I'd like that, too," Kara said. "If you're sure it's possible." She could barely look at Donovan.

"It's already done," Donovan assured her. "My body healed a long time ago. I've made a good life for myself. The only thing I could wish for was my parents to stop hating themselves long enough to heal, too." He nodded again, as if to himself. "Now that I know what really happened, I think there's hope for that."

"I hope you're right," Jericho said. "I know Mom and Dad still miss your folks."

"Then let's do whatever it takes to get them together again, all right?" Donovan asked.

"Deal," Jericho said.

"Tell him what you did with the money," Jackie urged her husband.

"It doesn't matter," Jericho rushed to assure them.

"Sure it does. I donated it in your name, anyway," Donovan said. "To a foundation that helps wounded veterans. I have a lot of respect for your service," he added. "That's the one thing I've always regretted about my injuries; they kept me from being able to join up. So I did what I could."

"How did you even know…?"

"There's this little thing called the Internet. Ever heard of it?" Donovan challenged him.

"Yeah. Guess I should have used it, too." He and Donovan could have mended fences years ago. He'd really been an ass.

"We've matched every penny you ever sent," Jackie said proudly. "We were happy to do it."

"It's a good cause," Donovan said.

"You're a good man. I'm proud to be your cousin," Jericho told him.

"Don't you go turning on the waterworks, too," Donovan chided him. "Come on. Who wants barbecue for dinner?"

"SAVANNAH. CAN I have a word?"

Here it was—the moment Savannah had dreaded for months. She'd hoped she could slip away after the concert, but that obviously wasn't going to happen. She'd made it down the hall after leaving her mother behind, but Charles had caught up with her. She turned to face him and did her best to compose herself.

"You played—wonderfully," he said. "I'm sorry I

ever doubted your ability."

"Funny how you made up your mind without ever really listening to me play," she couldn't help say. Charles's lack of interest in her passion had hurt her a lot back when they were together.

"You're right; I was—so caught up in making money, I lost sight of everything. I lost sight of you." He took her hand. "When you left, I had to do a lot of soul-searching. At first I was angry. Embarrassed. People kept asking why you'd gone. I finally had to ask myself that. I realized it was because I'd behaved so badly. I'm sorry for that. Can you forgive me, Savannah?"

She didn't have to forgive him, Savannah realized. He couldn't hurt her anymore. She knew now she'd never loved him in the way a wife should love a husband.

Jericho was the one for her.

"Of course I forgive you," she said. And meant it. She wanted to free Charles from the past, too, so he could move on and enjoy his life.

"I knew it!" Her mother was on them before Savannah even saw her coming again. "I knew if you two had a moment together you'd patch things up. You're made for each other! Oh, I'm so happy!"

"Mom—"

"Let's make the announcement right now. Everyone's waiting for you. This is so exciting!"

"Mom!"

"I'm game if you are." Charles hugged Savannah roughly. "I knew you couldn't stay away from me for long; what we've got is special. As soon as I heard you play our song, I knew you were coming back to me. This is perfect. Don't you think?" he said to Savannah's mother. "We can announce the new partnership between our families, too." He urged Savannah farther down the hall. She tried to wriggle away, conscious of her pregnancy—conscious she'd inadvertently given him the wrong impression.

"Charles—"

They rounded a corner into the lobby, and came face-to-face with a crowd far larger than Savannah could have expected.

"Who are all these people?" she gasped.

"The ones who didn't get into the concert. You're famous, darling! You're a TV star, remember?" her mother said, a smile plastered on her face. "Now get up there and start talking. Everyone's dying to know what you plan to do next. Tell them about Charles. Tell them about us, for heaven's sake. We could use a little publicity."

"But—"

Before she could protest, her mother pushed her forward, and the crowd erupted into cheers. To Savannah's consternation, there were press people in the crowd along with spectators. Her mother was right; there was no way this many people could have squeezed into the little concert hall earlier. The thought that they'd waited for her here—simply to hear her make an announcement—struck her dumb as Charles tugged her to a lectern where several microphones had been set up.

The small crew Renata had sent along with her came around the corner, too. Afer a quick look at the crowded hall, Ed elbowed his way in front of the lectern and began to film.

"Wait!" Savannah realized what was happening. Knew she had to stop it, but even as she tried to pull away, Charles gripped her wrist and leaned toward the microphones. "Everyone, we have a wonderful announcement."

"We love you, Savannah," someone yelled from the back of the crowd. Cheers and whistles erupted from several areas.

"Isn't she wonderful?" Charles said, his amplified voice ringing around the hall. "I love her, too."

More cheers erupted.

"And I have wonderful news," he went on. "Savannah and I—"

Savannah wanted to run, but it was far too late for that. Running wouldn't solve this—it hadn't solved anything so far. If she wanted to take control of her life, she needed to try something different.

She surged forward and nearly knocked Charles away from the lectern. "Hello, everybody!" It was weird to hear her voice so loud. Weirder still to wait while the crowd cheered her on.

"Savannah. What are you—?"

Savannah blocked Charles and leaned forward again. "I came here today to do a concert to raise funds for the San Mateo Radiology Center. It makes me so proud to know so many people care about this important cause."

The sudden silence in the lobby confirmed her be-lief that very few people had come to support the cause she'd mentioned. They'd come for the chance to be near someone they'd seen on TV. Savannah's resolve stiff-ened. "As most of you know, back home I'm involved in another important cause—an experiment in sustaina-ble living dedicated to show ways we can all have a good life without consuming resources unnecessarily."

Charles shifted beside her. She knew he didn't like the reference to Chance Creek as home. He muscled in on her space, leaned in and said into the microphone, "And I know wherever she goes, Savannah will always be determined to help others out. That's one of the things I love about her so much."

An expectant hush filled the lobby, before several voices called out at once.

"You two getting married?"

"That true, Savannah?"

"What about Base Camp? Have you told your friends?"

"Are you leaving the show?"

"What about Jericho?"

When Charles leaned in again to answer, Savannah lost her patience and elbowed him hard. No one got to call the shots for her anymore. Not Charles. Not her parents. Not even Jericho, as much as she loved him.

She gripped both sides of the stand to make sure she could keep possession of the microphone. "Charles and I are not engaged. We will not be married." She rushed on despite his muttered exclamation. "Nor am I engaged to Jericho Cook. I am single. I am returning to Chance Creek tomorrow. I want to thank you all again for coming out today."

She pushed her way through the crowd as quickly as she could, leaving Charles sputtering behind her at the microphone. As if she'd dropped a load of bricks from her shoulders, she felt lighter and surer of herself than she'd felt in years. A smile tugged at her mouth as she pushed through the throng of people still trying to ask her questions. For the first time, she faced her future unencumbered by the past.

She had no obligations to her parents or Charles. Nothing to prove to anyone but herself.

She wanted to be with her friends, play her music, have her baby and then set up concerts within easy reach. She wanted to look into all the other ways she could use music to brighten the lives of the people who mattered, the people close to her. If she ended up some day at Carnegie Hall, so much the better, but she'd play for her own enjoyment, not to prove something to her parents.

For now, she'd enjoy her pregnancy. Her friends.

Her home.

And she'd tell Jericho the truth, expecting nothing.

Hoping for everything.

Savannah cut down a corridor that led through the building, sure that somewhere there had to be a back entrance through which she could slip away. Renata's crew could try to catch up—but she wouldn't wait for them.

But as she rounded the corner a man grabbed her elbow.

"Savannah Edwards? Would you come with me a minute?"

AFTER CHATTING WITH Donovan and Jackie long into the night, getting to bed at half past two and waking up again before seven to head back home, Jericho was exhausted, but instead of driving straight back to Westfield, he and Kara had decided to go directly to their parents' house. When Jericho pulled into their driveway, he steeled himself to conduct yet another confrontation while being filmed, but when he turned to face the camera crew, he realized Craig had fallen asleep on the long ride.

"Go," Byron mouthed.

Jericho didn't wait for him to change his mind, or for Craig to wake up. He and Kara slipped out of the truck as quietly as they could and hurried up the walk.

Jericho's parents didn't bother to hide their surprise when they answered the door.

"Come in," their mother said, but her tone wasn't exactly inviting. She knew something was up, Jericho thought. Something she wouldn't like.

When they were all seated in the living room, his father cleared his throat. "What can we do for the two of you?"

"We just went to visit Donovan," Kara said bluntly.

"We thought it was about time," Jericho added.

His mother pursed her lips and his father swallowed. Neither of them said a word.

"Did you realize both of us thought Donovan was paralyzed?" Jericho asked.

"Paralyzed?" his mother scoffed, animated again. "Why would you think that?"

"Why wouldn't we?" Kara said. "We saw him fall. Saw him lying there lifeless. And you said he was too hurt to come see us anymore."

"I never said he was paralyzed."

"He was hurt badly," their father put in. "Needed a great many operations. It was easier for your aunt and uncle to move near a city so Donovan could get the care he needed."

"We've got cities in Montana," Jericho pointed out. "We think there's another reason they moved." He didn't feel like playing any more games, and he wasn't interested in finding out how far his parents were prepared to go to cover their tracks.

"There's no other—" his mother began.

"You were drunk. All of you. And you didn't even call an ambulance when Donovan fell," Jericho said before his sister could. He knew whoever brought it up first would bear the brunt of the consequences and he didn't want it to be her.

"Jericho Randall Cook, you watch your mouth. Of course we did." His mother stood up, two ugly splotches of red coloring her cheeks.

"Not at first. Not for hours."

"I saw you. I know," Kara said before either parent could deny it.

Their mother's face fell.

"Mary, sit down," his father said tersely. "Yes, we'd
had a few. That wasn't a crime. Not in our own home."

Jericho's mother sat down with a thump.

"We weren't drunk," his father went on. "Just—
tipsy. It's not like we went out to a bar and drove home
under the influence. All we did was play cards with my
brother and his wife. Have a few laughs. We all worked
hard, didn't we?"

Jericho nodded. "You did. But that doesn't change
what happened."

"It seemed safe to let you watch the others," his father said. "You have to realize that. You were eleven.
Tall for your age. Kept your sister and your cousin in
line. What was the harm of letting you play outdoors
while we played a hand or two? If you had any problems
you'd come get us." He shrugged. "Seemed sensible.
Until the accident."

"Donovan fell. He was hurt. You should have called
for an ambulance."

Jericho's father heaved a sigh. His mother was studying her hands in her lap. "That's what we wanted to
do. But Chris said no. He wanted to sober up first.
Donovan was breathing. He was resting—"

"He was unconscious," Jericho asserted.

"You're right," his father said helplessly. "He was
unconscious, but my brother wouldn't listen. Just a little
while, that's what he said. He needed to sober up before
the ambulance came. He was afraid. He didn't want to
lose Donovan. Didn't want Social Services to come and

take his child away. Your mother and I didn't know what to do. What if they took you away, too?" he demanded. "We'd all heard stories about foster care. What kind of father would allow his child to be put in danger that way? As soon as it happened we changed our ways. You know that. Cut back on the drinking. Watched you more carefully. Hell, your mom has us going to those AA meetings now. You can't say we didn't own up to our part in the problem and change. Because we did."

"What about Aunt Patty and Uncle Chris?" Jericho challenged him.

His father leaned back, defeated. "It was harder for them. They didn't stop. We fought about it, believe you me."

"So you let them move away?" Kara asked softly.

Their mother looked up. "Let them? Fought them, more like it. Begged them to stay. Begged them to see reason."

"You let them take Donovan, after they didn't take him to the hospital."

"They got him there. Maybe an hour or two late, but—"

"It was longer than that. What if there had been internal bleeding? What if he'd died to protect the four of you?" Kara demanded.

"We told you, we were afraid of you being taken away—all of you!" his mother protested.

Jericho shook his head in disbelief. "So you risked his life?"

"Who's fault was that?" his father thundered suddenly.

"Dan—" Jericho's mother put a restraining hand on his arm, but his father lurched to his feet.

"No—if we're having it out, let's really have it out. Whose fault was it he fell? What kind of eleven-year-old pushes his cousin—"

"I pushed him," Kara cried out, rising to her feet, too. "I pushed him, Dad. Not Jericho. I mean, I pushed Jericho—I knocked him over. He bumped Donovan and Donovan fell. It wasn't Jericho's fault!"

"But—" Suddenly their father looked every one of his fifty-five years.

"I lied, all right? I lied when it happened and I've been lying ever since. I thought you would stop loving me if I told you the truth, the way you stopped loving Jericho!"

Their father gaped at her. "I—I didn't—I—"

"Didn't you?" Kara demanded.

Their father's chest heaved. A moment later, he turned and strode from the room. They heard the back door slam.

"See what you've done?" their mother hissed at them and went after him.

When they were alone, Jericho faced his sister.

"That went well," Kara said.

"TELL MY MOTHER I'm not interested," Savannah said, twisting her arm out of the man's grasp.

He chuckled, a response that stopped her in her

tracks. An older African-American man with gray strands in his hair, he was impeccably dressed in pressed pants, a button-down shirt and a blazer. Had he been in the audience? She wasn't sure.

"I'll be sure to do that if I ever meet her," the man said. "I'm Simon Brashear. I'm with the Sunwest Group. We're a development company with a strong interest in sustainable building and remodeling. We've been watching *Base Camp*, and were hoping to start a dialog."

"Oh." Savannah could feel a blush staining her cheeks. "You want an introduction to Jericho and the rest of the guys."

"Eventually. We thought we'd start with you," Simon said. "You work with Jericho on the energy grid, right? We're hoping you can answer a few questions."

"I can try," she said with an anxious glance over her shoulder. "But really Jericho's the one you want to talk to."

"Jericho's not here," Simon reminded her. He began to walk toward the exit and Savannah kept pace with him, happy to leave the building before she was caught by either her mother or the press. "Rather than flying him out, I wonder if you have time to come take a look at a property we're considering? See what your opinion is. Later we can video chat with Jericho, too. How long will you be in San Mateo?"

"I leave tomorrow," Savannah said.

Simon's face fell. "Oh. Well, I'm sure you'll want to spend what time you have with your family."

"Not really," she said candidly. "How about we take a look first thing in the morning?" Her flight didn't leave until the afternoon.

Simon brightened. "Absolutely. Here's my card. I've written the site's address on the back. Meet you there at ten?"

"Sounds perfect." Savannah said her goodbyes and hurried to find her rental car before her mother could catch up. Jericho would be pleased. He wouldn't have to use any extra fuel to fly out since she was here already, and she knew he wanted the work. As she hustled through the parking lot, Savannah wondered how Jericho would handle jobs like this. He'd be tempted to put his knowledge to use wherever it was needed, but how was that any different than her flying back and forth to meet with Redding if he ended up having projects around the country?

She tried to think how Jericho would answer and had to grin. Research. That's where he'd start; he was always big on research. First he'd try to do away with travel altogether, perhaps by partnering with a local company to do the *boots on the ground* type work. If traveling became necessary, he'd use the most sensible approach. He might even turn away a job if he didn't think he could pursue it in a way that wasn't deleterious for the environment. "I'm not the only one who can rig up a solar array," she could almost hear him say. That was Jericho all over: not stuffy or stuck-up even if he had the right to be.

That was the man she loved. One who thought

about the big picture, even if it wasn't convenient for their own small lives. A man who had principles and held on to them.

The father of her child.

That thought stuck with her the next day as she paced the length and breadth of Brashear's property, trailed by the camera crew who'd caught up with her at her hotel, unfortunately. She'd managed to call up all kinds of information about Base Camp, the siting of the houses and the various elements of the green power system she'd helped Jericho build. Jericho's values had already become hers. Was the same true the other way around?

Was there any hope for them at all?

CHAPTER ELEVEN

W HEN JERICHO FINALLY made it home to Westfield, he pulled into the driveway that led to the
manor rather than parking down near Base Camp. He
couldn't wait another minute to see Savannah, and he
hoped she was home from California. After witnessing
the heartache and pain that both sides of his family had
endured for so many years, he'd decided he didn't want
to waste any more time arguing with her. He wanted to
make her his wife. Savannah was a kind, generous,
loving woman with a goal that was beautiful and
important to her. Only one aspect of it clashed with his
ideals. Surely there was a way around that.

Trailed by Byron and Craig, who weren't speaking
to each other after Craig had woken and realized he'd
missed Jericho and Kara's confrontation with their
parents, he opened the manor's front door when he
found it unlocked, and stepped right into the entryway,
expecting to find the women at their various pursuits.
But inside the house was strangely quiet. He walked
quickly through the first floor, but no one was in the

front parlor or the kitchen, or the large ballroom they rarely used. He climbed up the staircase to the second story, but he knew these rooms were reserved for guests, and there weren't any at the manor at the moment. He climbed to the third floor more tentatively, the camera crew still following.

"Savannah?" he called.

No one answered, but just as he was about to turn around, a choked sound brought him rushing up the final steps.

"Savannah?" he called again when he reached the landing. Three of the four doors to the bedrooms on this level were open and a quick look into each of them showed them to be empty. He knocked on the fourth door, and when he got no answer, he slowly turned the handle.

"Riley?" Jericho rushed into the room when he saw Riley's prone form draped across the bed. The old memory of Donovan's lifeless body flashed into his mind, but he quickly shook it off and when he got close, he saw that Riley was breathing. Sobbing, actually, lying on her side, her arms clutched over her middle, her knees curled up nearly to her chin. She was crying in great, aching gasps that made Jericho brace for the worst.

He sat down on the bed beside her and placed a hand on her shoulder. "What's wrong? Do you want me to get Boone? Do you need to see a doctor?"

She only cried harder, and Jericho, not knowing what else to do, took her hand and held it. Her fingernails dug into his skin, but he figured he could bear a little bit of the pain she obviously felt.

"Riley, what happened?"

"I lost... I lost the baby," she cried.

Jericho scooped her into his arms, wanting to take away all the anguish he heard in her voice. He hadn't known Riley was pregnant. Several weeks ago, she and Boone had gone to the doctor. The last he'd heard, they were waiting for the results of the tests. A glance toward the crew told him they were as surprised as he was.

"Does Boone know?" His friend should be the one here. He knew Boone would do anything for Riley.

"Yes," Riley sobbed. "But he doesn't know—he doesn't—I haven't told him—"

Jericho rocked her, not knowing what else to do. "I'm sorry. So sorry." He didn't have any words to console her. All he could do was be here for her, but he wished to God there was action he could take. It seemed to him the worst pain in the world was never physical; it was the pain people felt in their hearts. And those were the wounds hardest to heal, too.

No wonder they all kept secrets and held themselves apart from one another.

"I'm sorry," he said again. "I know what it's like to lose someone you care about—a child who never hurt anyone—"

Riley, whose sobs had been subsiding, looked up sharply, pushed away from him, scrambled out of his lap and right off the bed. "You know what it's like?" she cried, her voice rising to a shriek. "You know? You haven't lost anyone! Your baby's still alive!"

She dashed from the room, leaving Jericho speech-less—the damn cameras still trained on him.

His baby?

His—?

His mind flashed to making love to Savannah in the Russells' bathroom—taking a chance because she'd said she was on the Pill. Flashed to the way she'd pushed him away ever since.

Could she be—?

He thought about her trips to Alice Reed's place.

About the way she'd tried to tell him something the day they'd babysat at Crescent Hall.

Was she—?

Pregnant?

Was Savannah pregnant?

"Avery? Riley? Anyone home?"

Jericho jerked when he heard Savannah's voice on the landing. He hadn't heard steps on the stairs, but she was just outside the door. Savannah—the woman who'd lied to him.

The woman who was carrying his child.

Nausea climbed into his throat, choking him with a claustrophobic feeling that rang in his ears like bombs falling on a far-off warzone.

His child.

"Riley? That you?" Savannah opened the door and came face-to-face with him. Her eyes widened. "Jericho? What are you doing—?"

"You're pregnant?" The words came out far harsher

than he'd intended, but then he had no idea what he'd meant to say. The film crew was still capturing all of this. He couldn't stand it—couldn't do this—

He knew it was true before she even answered. She was carrying his child. A child he could never protect. A child who could get hurt—or paralyzed—or killed—any number of ways, no matter what he did to protect it.

Savannah's mouth dropped open. "How—?" She stopped herself. Took a breath and nodded. "Yes, I'm pregnant."

Jericho shook his head. It couldn't be true; none of this could be true. He saw Donovan's body on the grass again, watched the bombs fall in Yemen. "No," he said. "No—"

"Jericho, I didn't mean for it to happen. It just—"

"You said you were on the Pill."

"I was!"

"You said you were safe!"

"I was on the Pill. I didn't miss a single day—I checked afterward. I don't know how it happened. It just—happened." She had reached her hands toward him. She was begging him to understand.

But Jericho didn't understand. He didn't know how any of this could have happened when he'd worked so hard to make sure it didn't. He'd never taken that chance before with another woman. Had always used condoms even if they were on the Pill. He'd fucked up once.

Once.

"I can't—" he said. "You know that. I can't—"

Savannah, unshed tears glinting in her eyes, nodded. "I know," she said softly.

She stepped back, hugging her arms over her chest like Riley had just minutes earlier. Protecting her heart, Jericho realized. Holding in the pain.

Damn it. He'd never wanted to cause her pain.

But a child—

He couldn't do it. Couldn't.

"I can't be here." He pushed past her in two long strides, pushed through the door and pounded down the two flights of stairs and out the front door. He couldn't breathe—not even outside. He needed to get away—far away. From the sound of Donovan's body hitting the ground, the silence at the end of the phone line back in Yemen—the sound of Savannah's tears.

Jericho began to run.

"I'M SORRY," RILEY said, slinking out of Avery's bedroom to meet Savannah in the hall, tears slipping down her face. "I'm so, so sorry. I didn't mean to spill the beans."

"He doesn't want the baby," Savannah said, facing her friend. "I guess I knew that, but I'd hoped—"

Riley embraced her, her body shuddering with sobs. "I lost my baby today. Jericho found me crying and tried to help, but I yelled at him. I'm so sorry," she said again.

"Riley—" Savannah didn't know what to say. She noticed the cameramen still filming. "Get out," she told the crew. Craig began to protest but Byron pulled him out into the hall. She shut the bedroom door, locked it and led Riley to sit on the bed. "I'm sorry, too," she said, and drew her friend back into a hug. "Oh, God—I'm so sorry."

For a moment they cried together, until Riley drew a deep shuddering breath and pulled back.

"I guess it just wasn't meant to be," she said.

"I'd do anything for us to be able to do this together," Savannah told her. Her heart was breaking for Riley's loss, despite her own pain.

"We *are* going to do this together," Riley said fiercely. "Whether or not I get pregnant, I'm going to be there for you, because you're my best friend in the world. What I said to Jericho—how angry I was at him for having a living baby when I didn't—isn't really how I feel. You know that, right?"

"Of course I do. But I understand if you're upset. What are you going to do now?"

"Go back to the doctor. Tell her what happened. See what she says." Riley grew teary again. "Do you think the universe is trying to tell me something? That I shouldn't be a mother?"

"Of course not." Savannah took her in her arms again. "Our bodies aren't weapons that take aim at us. They're just bodies. Sometimes they work right, sometimes they don't."

She felt Riley relax a little. "I hate my body right now."

"How far along were you?"

"Not very far at all," Riley admitted. "I took the test as early as I possibly could. If I wasn't thinking so much about being pregnant, I might not even have known. But I did know. I felt pregnant."

Savannah nodded. Riley was a sensitive person. And she'd wanted a child for a long time.

"What about you? What are you going to do?" Riley asked her.

"I'm going to have this baby and raise it right here surrounded by all my friends. I'm going to see what I can do with my music here in Chance Creek and around Montana. I've got lots of ideas." She tried to sound braver than she felt.

"What about Jericho?"

"I honestly don't know. I don't think there's a whole lot more I can do now," she confessed. "I think Jericho has to make up his mind about how much he'll want to participate in our lives."

"He has to marry," Riley pointed out.

"You know what?" Savannah said, suddenly exhausted. "That's his problem."

JERICHO WAS PACING the banks of Pittance Creek when footsteps behind him had him whirling around. He was prepared to face Boone, or maybe Clay or even Walker, who had a bad habit of popping up when a man needed to be alone with his thoughts.

Instead, his father approached him. Jericho stopped and waited for him to catch up. "What're you doing here?" he asked when his dad got close.

"Looking for you. One of your friends told me I might find you here."

"What do you want?" Jericho was in no mood to fake a hospitable mood. All these years his father had believed the worst of him. All these years he'd thought of himself that way, despite knowing damn well Donovan's accident had been just that.

"I wanted to let you know—well, I guess if you think I'm a failure as a father, you're right. Seems like I've done everything wrong."

"Dad—"

"No, let me get this out. I've tried to shut down everything that caused me pain. I've pretended it wasn't there. Hid from it. Hoped that if I didn't mention it, it would actually go away. When my brother refused to change his ways, I didn't know what to do. I thought if I kept my distance, he'd smarten up. Or that Patty would straighten him out." He sighed. "It didn't work. Days went by. Then months. Years. We'd started down a path I didn't think we could go back from. I shut down. You're right; I didn't save Donovan. I didn't save you, either. I let everyone down."

"You know what I think?" Jericho said, disarmed by his father's admission. "I think we don't have half as much say in our lives as we think we do. I think most of the time we're only one thread in a story. We can only play our part. And no matter how hard we try to control the ending, the story's going to go the way it goes."

"I think you're right." His father jammed his hands in his pockets. "I hope you're not pacing because of me. I'm not worth it."

"We're all worth it, Dad, but it's not about you this

time. It's about me. I made a mistake. A big one."

"That sounds heavy." His father waited. Jericho hadn't meant to tell his father about the baby, but somehow the words spilled out and he found himself telling his dad about his encounter with Savannah—and the results. "I never meant to be a father. Never," he finished up. "I can't do it. But I don't know what to do now."

For a long moment, his father didn't speak. When he did, his shoulders sagged. "You don't want to repeat my mistakes. I understand that."

"It's not that, Dad. Bad things happen when I'm in charge of kids," Jericho burst out, putting into words for the first time something that had haunted him for years. "I mean—look what happened to Donovan. And I know, I know, it really was an accident, but what you've always said was true, too. Why didn't I see it coming? Why didn't I stop it? I was in charge." He swallowed. "And that's just the tip of the iceberg. There's Yemen, too. I let more kids die there."

His father stilled. "You never said anything about that."

"You already thought I was a fuck-up." His voice hit a rough spot and Jericho had to clear his throat. "Didn't want to prove you right."

He felt his father's hand on his shoulder. "Tell me what happened."

"We were trying to save a bunch of aid workers," he began. Once he'd started, the story spilled out more easily than he'd thought possible. Their repeated attempts to launch a rescue. The days that had slipped by in which they made no progress. The long conversations they'd taken turns having with the aid workers to keep up morale. Akram demanding to talk to him.

"Boone was talking on the phone when the bomb dropped. But just a few hours before, I'd spoken to Akram. I'd promised him—" Jericho's voice cut out again. "I was supposed to save him. And I couldn't. No matter what I did, I couldn't—"

The grief he'd held in all this time welled up and he fought it until his father turned him around and clapped him into the only embrace he could remember receiving from the man since he was a child.

"It wasn't your fault. None of it was your fault." His father's words became a mantra as Jericho finally let out the sorrow he'd kept in his heart for so long. There was no one in the world he thought he could expose such weakness to. But when he realized his father's shoulders were heaving, too, he knew it was worth it. His father needed to heal as badly as he did.

"I let that boy lie there—unconscious," his father said, his voice broken with remorse. "I let Donovan wait—I didn't know if he'd live or die—because I didn't know how to say no to my brother. I didn't want all the good times to be gone. I fucked up. I fucked up so bad."

It was Jericho's turn to support his father as the man's grief ran its course. He'd never seen his father cry before. Knew they'd never speak of it again when it was over.

"Maybe it's time we all moved on," he said some minutes later. He didn't know how he'd ever come to the creek again without remembering this day. But maybe the rushing water could carry away their pain and bring some form of healing he couldn't even imagine for their future.

"Maybe," his father agreed. "That means you, too," he said. "If Savannah is carrying your child, it's not a matter of whether or not you want to be a father. You already are. Don't walk away from that. Don't miss the good while trying to hide from the bad. You'll regret it."

Jericho's gut twisted. His dad was right, of course. "What if I fuck up again?"

His father clapped him on the shoulder again. "Luckily for you, Savannah's one smart woman. She'll step in if you go off course, don't you think?"

Jericho chuckled despite himself. "Yeah. Maybe you're right." Maybe he was thinking about this all wrong. He wouldn't be alone in raising his child. Savannah would be at his side. So would his friends— the men he trusted the most. And Savannah's friends, who he was coming to know almost as well.

Just as his father said, it was too late to decide whether or not he was a father. If the die was cast, he wanted to do his best by his child.

And Savannah.

He loved her. Missed her.

Wanted to be with her.

"Thanks, Dad."

"For what?"

"For helping me figure out what's right."

SAVANNAH WAS SITTING at the piano in the parlor when the front door opened. She had a piece of lined paper on the top of the piano and was playing with chords and sequences of notes, popping up to write them down, then sitting back down to play some more. Boone had come a half-hour ago to collect Riley. Left alone, a song had come to Savannah while she'd washed her tears from her face earlier, and she'd come down to try it out. She'd been thinking of what it would be like to build a life without Jericho. How no matter how bad things got, her love for his baby would see her through. She saw her child as a ray of light in a dark, stormy sky. The image transferred into music in her mind and she'd wanted to test the tune before she forgot.

Now that it was all out in the open she'd decided she could bear the pain she'd thought might rip her apart. She loved Jericho, but she'd survive if he couldn't be with her. For now, all she could do was honor her feelings, and play with this simple tune.

It didn't matter if the song had any merit. The only person she'd play it for was her baby—which meant she could pour her heart into it. And that felt good.

"That's pretty. Sorry—didn't mean to startle you," Jericho said.

Savannah pressed a hand to her heart. "I didn't hear you come in."

"I need to apologize for how I acted before."

"You were surprised. I don't blame you." She

turned around on the bench.

"Why didn't you tell me sooner?" he asked, crossing the room to stand near her. "You must have known."

She nodded. "I've known for two months."

He smiled and she wondered why. She didn't have to wait long for an explanation. "Donovan's wife is three months pregnant."

"Donovan's…wife?" She brightened. "So he's all right?"

"Yeah, he is." When he moved closer, Savannah slid over on the bench. Jericho sat down beside her and gave her a quick recap of his visit to North Dakota.

"That's wonderful," Savannah said. "I'm so glad for all of you."

"I talked to my dad, too," he said. "We sorted things out."

"Really?" Savannah couldn't believe it. She waited for the bad news. There had to be bad news.

"Savannah, I've been an ass." Jericho took her hands. "I let my head get out of the game. I—"

"You had some awful things happen to you," she said softly. "You reacted to those things. I understand."

"I don't want to let you down like that again. I don't want to let down our child—ever. I won't shut down like my folks did. Or try to harden my heart so I won't feel it if something happens to you or the baby. Because that's not really living. You have to risk pain to be there for the good stuff."

Savannah's heart throbbed with love for this man. Jericho was willing to face his deepest fears for her. "I promise I'll think about the bigger picture when I make decisions. You'll have to help me—"

"We'll help each other. But you have to know I don't want to make you unhappy. If you want to travel, that's up to you. If you need to commute to California—"

"I don't." Savannah told him all about her trip. Her audition, the concert, the way her mother kept trying to pull the puppet strings, the way Charles had tried to slip back into his old role—and make her slip back into hers. The way she'd realized she needed to connect with her audience, not be revered by them. The way she'd played for the hearts of the crowd at the concert.

Then walked away from it all.

"I found you a new client," she said. She told him about Simon Brashear. "He's interested in working with us—remotely."

"That's my girl." Jericho drew her close for a kiss.

Savannah melted against him. She'd missed this so much.

But when a strange feeling fluttered low in her belly, she pulled back.

"What's wrong?" Jericho followed her, trying to embrace her again.

"The baby—" It fluttered again. Tears pricked Savannah's eyes. That was her baby. Inside her—

But before she could explain, Jericho leapt to his feet and scooped her up so fast Savannah gasped and clung to him as he ran with her across the room. "We'll get you to the hospital. It'll be okay—"

"Jericho!" Savannah shrieked as he whipped her sideways and rushed her through the front door, nearly cracking her head on the frame. "Jericho, stop! I'm fine! The baby's fine!"

"But you said—" Jericho stopped short, and Savannah nearly slid out of his arms.

"Put me down," she commanded him gently, but she kept her hands on his shoulders as he set her on her feet. "The baby. I can feel it. Here." She took one of his hands and pressed it against her belly where she'd felt the little butterfly kiss of sensation deep inside. "It's moving in me. You won't be able to feel it yet, but pretty soon you will." She reached up on tiptoe and kissed Jericho again. "We're having a baby," she whispered against his neck.

He pulled her close and she felt the current running through him. Jericho was shaking. Her big, strong SEAL was shaking.

For the first time she truly realized how much he loved her—and the child they'd made together.

He loved them so much he was terrified. Terrified of losing them.

She slid her arms around his neck and held him close. Her warrior. Her man. He'd do anything he could protect them. And she'd do everything she could do to keep him right here, in the moment, not consumed by worry for their futures.

They'd make a home together among their friends. Make a life together.

"I love you," she told him, and realized it was the

first time she'd said the words out loud.

Jericho pulled back and searched her face with his gaze. "I love you, too," he said finally, his words warming her heart.

CHAPTER TWELVE

"**I** CAN'T WAIT until Donovan gets to meet you," Jericho said several days later when Savannah came down from the manor to work on the power grid. Kai and Greg had begun to measure out an area they could use for a solar installation. Since the tiny houses were built into the hillside, their roofs weren't well-situated for solar panels.

Meanwhile, Jericho relished the thought of having a moment alone with Savannah.

Something had changed in her these last few days. When he'd asked about it, Savannah had told him she relished these mornings with him. Now that she'd expanded her definition of success when it came to music, she'd been able to relax and realized she had plenty of hours to divide among her interests. She'd still practice a lot, but she wanted to try composing. She'd committed to a three-month trial of teaching Richard Hall to play the piano, too.

"It's going to mean a lot to you, having your family back in touch with each other, isn't it?" she asked him.

"Some of it, at least. I don't know if my aunt and uncle will change anytime soon, but Donovan and Jackie will be part of our lives. I think Kara's going to get help, now, too. And my parents already seem happier now that they're not hiding a secret."

"I know I am. I hate having secrets. All that slipping away to doctor's appointments and dress alterations. I'm glad that's over now."

"I'm glad it is, too. I want to be here for all of it," Jericho said.

"Do your aunt and uncle know they're going to be grandparents?" Savannah asked.

"No, not yet."

"Maybe wanting a relationship with their grandchild will be the impetus they need to change."

"Do you really think people can change?" He wasn't only thinking of his aunt and uncle. He had a feeling she realized that.

"I really think they can. If they want to."

"I want to," he told her.

"Me, too."

"Donovan and Jackie want to come visit soon. I was wondering… if maybe it could coincide with a wedding." He braced himself for her answer.

"Wedding?" Savannah tilted her head to look at him.

"Our wedding," he said. "Savannah, I have wanted to be with you since the very first moment I saw you. I will never forget the day we pulled up outside the manor and you came dashing out the door, your skirts swirling around you. You looked so beautiful. Like something out of a storybook. So sweet and innocent in that getup and so... not innocent, at the same time."

She smiled up at him in a way that made him stop talking and start kissing her until he remembered he hadn't actually popped the question yet.

"I love you. I want to be with you. I want to raise this baby with you—and maybe have more children, too." He took a deep breath. "I want to work with you—if you want to keep working with me. And whatever you want to do with your music—anything you want—I will support you, no matter what."

Love for him shone in her eyes, and something in Jericho eased. He pulled the small box from his pocket—he'd been carrying it now for weeks. He opened it up to show her the fancy ring Win had helped pick out, and asked, "Savannah, will you do me the great honor of becoming my wife?"

Heart in his mouth, he waited for her answer.

SAVANNAH COULDN'T TAKE her eyes off the ring in Jericho's hands. It was beautiful. Really beautiful. Far more lavish than she'd imagined Jericho would choose. He wasn't a man who valued expensive things for their own sake. "It's lovely," she breathed. "Jericho, it's too expensive."

"Answer the question," he growled. "You're killing me."

"Yes! Yes, of course I'll marry you!" The ring forgotten, she threw her arms around his neck and kissed him soundly on the mouth. "I thought you'd never ask!"

He slid the ring on her finger, and frowned when it nearly fell right off again. "I guess we'll have to get it resized."

"Later. Right now all I care about is you." She put the ring carefully back in its box, tucked it in Jericho's pocket and tugged him close. "Make love to me."

"Now?" He looked around. "Here?"

"Not here. Up at the manor."

"No one's filming us." Jericho thought it over. "Let's go for it."

Savannah laughed when he tugged her toward the track that led up the hill. Jericho was right; no camera crew was haunting them at the moment. Kai and Greg would cover for them if their absence was discovered. "Hurry. It's been too damn long since we've done this."

"That's one thing we agree on." He picked up the pace and they ran the rest of the way up the hill. When they finally reached the top floor of the manor and let themselves into her bedroom, Savannah was happy they had the house to themselves. She didn't want to hold back.

She pulled him inside the room, shut the door and turned the lock, then laughed when Jericho palmed both of her breasts at once through the fabric of her gown.

"I've missed these," he told her.

She led him toward the bed. When she felt the mattress against the back of her knees, she sat down and let him urge her to lie on her back.

"They've missed you, too," she said truthfully. Jericho's hands on her breasts always felt so good. As he climbed onto the bed, too, straddled her and lowered his weight on top of her, he hesitated.

"I don't want to hurt you."

"You aren't," she assured him and pulled him closer. Kissing him was like coming home, and for a long time they reacquainted themselves with each other. As his kisses grew more ardent, Jericho sighed and pulled back.

"You need easier clothes. Or you need to wear them less often."

"I'll see what I can do." But she chuckled as he turned her over and got to work on the fastenings of her gown. She knew Jericho was resourceful enough to eventually get her out of it. Meanwhile she'd enjoy the feeling of his fingers working at the ties of her gown and then her stays after he peeled her top garment off.

Jericho took his time, pressing kisses along each inch of skin his hands exposed and soon Savannah was almost wriggling in her desire to turn over and pull him close. When she was finally unclothed, she did so, pushing his unbuttoned cotton shirt off his shoulders and arms and helping him peel the T-shirt he wore underneath up and over his head.

As they lay back against the pillows, the tenderness in Jericho's eyes nearly undid her. There was so much love there. So much wonder, too.

"What?" she asked when she grew self-conscious under his gaze.

"You are beautiful. I don't know how I thought I

could stay away from you under any circumstances." He ran his hand down her body, over one breast and across her stomach. He traced a finger over her abdomen and pressed his palm down again. "Our baby."

"That's right." She lay her own hand on top of his. "Ours."

"You really didn't miss a Pill? I'm not accusing you," he added, holding her gaze with his own. "Just curious."

"I really didn't," she told him.

"Then this must be meant to be." He cupped her belly with both hands and bent down to kiss her abdomen. "Grow big and strong," he whispered to the baby.

"But not too big. Not until after you're born," she added with a grin. She tugged Jericho back up. "Make love to me."

"All right, all right." Jericho pulled her over on top of him, and when she straddled his hips and settled on top of him he groaned, a smile tugging at his lips. "You've made me wait for this far too long. I'm not promising finesse."

"You don't need finesse. You just need to hurry up," she told him. As she bent to kiss him, her breasts grazed his chest and the sensation sent shivers of desire through her.

She wanted this man. "Are you really going to be my husband?"

"Absolutely." Jericho gathered her closer. Savannah rocked against the long, hard length of him, unable to stop her body from demonstrating what it wanted. Jericho lifted her up and poised her over him. "I don't think I can wait any longer."

"I don't think I can, either." She moved into place and sank down, taking him inside and gasping with the sensation. As they began to move together she knew he was right: this wouldn't be fancy and it wouldn't be long. They would do what it took to take the edge off their desire so they could spend the rest of the night exploring each other.

Loving each other.

Savannah arched back as they moved in tandem, biting her lip to hold on at least a few more moments. As she rocked above him, she felt the care Jericho was taking. He didn't want to hurt her. He wanted to protect her—and the baby, too. Forever.

He was right, she thought as the sensations built up to the point where thought became difficult. They would have to stop trying to control everything. They would have to give in to what life gave them, accept it and keep moving on as best they could.

"Jericho—" She crashed over into ecstasy as pulse after pulse of her release blazed through her, sensations rushing through her until she lost herself among them. Jericho followed her swiftly, his groans mingling with her cries until they both subsided, breathing heavily.

Afterward, he cradled her tenderly and stroked her hair.

"Are we still going to do this when I've got a belly out to here?" She demonstrated with her hand.

"We're going to do it all the time," he assured her. "Every chance we get."

"I'll be so big you won't even be able to reach me."

Jericho chuckled. "I'll reach you one way or the other." He tightened his embrace. "I'm not letting you go again. When I think of how I nearly lost you out of my own stubbornness." He shook his head. "What an idiot."

"What a man trying to do what he thought was best," she corrected him and stole a kiss.

"Only a couple of weeks until our wedding. Boone's going to be happy to hear about this. He was starting to look for a backup bride."

"Oh, God; not another one of those. Someone needs to stop that man."

Jericho kissed her. "I'll let you handle that."

"FULSOM'S HAPPY," BOONE announced when he entered the bunkhouse early the next morning. Jericho had parted from Savannah a half-hour ago with yet another kiss, glad no one had come to give them hell for spending the day—and night—up at the manor rather than tending to their work. He'd already begun to spread the news of their engagement, and without fail everyone he told was both relieved and unsurprised he and Savannah had been able to work things out.

"You two were meant for each other; anyone could see that," Kai had said. Boone had gone to phone Fulsom with the news. Now people were gathering at the empty fire pit, waiting for breakfast to be served.

"I wonder who will be next?" Jericho said. "Maybe you, Angus. Win must be getting sick of waiting."

Angus shrugged.

"Hope it's not me. I haven't met a woman since I've arrived here," Anders said.

"You've got to work harder. I think I've met every woman within a hundred-mile radius," Curtis said.

Jericho didn't doubt it; ever since Harris had stolen the bride Boone had found for Curtis, the man had been tireless in his pursuit of women. He was at the Dancing Boot in town several nights a week, and Jericho had heard he even traveled to Silver Falls on occasion to try his luck there, as well.

"Meet anyone suitable?" Anders asked him.

Curtis gave a sharp shake of his head. "Not yet," he said darkly.

"What about you?" Anders asked Kai, when he stepped out of the kitchen to announce the meal was ready. "Have you met a woman you'd like to marry?"

"I'm going to trust the Universe to provide me a wife at the right time," Kai said serenely. "I find when I fight the current, all I do is make waves."

Angus turned to Boone. "Since you're the one who finds the backup brides, I guess that makes you the Universe. Found Kai a wife yet?"

"Not yet, but I'll get on it now that he's put me in charge."

Kai put up with their good-natured teasing and everyone headed inside for breakfast. Jericho spotted Savannah approaching from the direction of the manor.

"Good thing you sent Riley up to help me dress," she said.

"Figured Riley would know what to grab from your tent for you." He took her hand in his and kissed it. "No second thoughts?"

"No second thoughts," she assured him.

"Good, because everyone knows already—including Fulsom. Boone called him right away."

"Ah, the couple of the hour," Renata announced as she approached them, followed by a bevy of cameramen. "Let's get a brief statement to post on the website. We'll have a rough cut of the next episode by the end of the day."

Jericho groaned. He knew what that meant. There'd be a screening tonight.

"Can't this wait until after breakfast?" he complained, but he and Savannah submitted to her instructions good-naturedly. Nothing could spoil this morning, he decided. Not as long as he was by Savannah's side.

Once they finally got their meal, they settled on one of the logs near the fire pit, and one by one the other members of Base Camp stopped to congratulate them—both on the wedding and Savannah's pregnancy. Jericho basked in their happiness, finding it harder and harder to remember why he'd fought against this so hard.

"There's Win," Savannah exclaimed. "I was beginning to wonder where she'd gotten to this morning. She's the only one who hasn't come to wish us well."

"She going somewhere?" Jericho asked. Win had a suitcase with her, and it looked heavy. Sam had already gone to talk to her and the two women were deep in conversation.

"Not that she mentioned to me." Brow furrowed, Savannah set her plate aside and stood up. Jericho followed her. They reached Win and Sam just in time to hear Win say to Angus, "Could you drive me to the airport?"

"Is something wrong?" Savannah asked.

Win nodded, her face pale. "It's Mom; she's in the hospital. I've been called home."

Savannah reached for her. "I'm so sorry. Do you want me to come with you?"

"I can drive you to the airport," Sam said. Jericho knew the two women had gotten close during Sam's time at Base Camp.

"I'll drive her," Angus said firmly and the rest of them nodded, understanding his wish to have a moment with her before she left.

"You need to plan your wedding. Don't worry; I'll be fine."

"Tell her to get well from me. I'll send a card as soon as I can." Savannah hugged her again.

"Thank you."

Soon Angus had driven her away, leaving the camp in a far more somber mood than it had been just minutes earlier.

"I guess it's time to get to work," Jericho said.

Savannah nodded. "Guess so."

"Nope," Nora said. "You're coming with me to Two Willows, Savannah. You don't have much time before the wedding; you need to commission your gown."

"And later we'll go get that ring of yours fixed," Jericho promised.

"YOU'RE GOING TO be a beautiful bride," Alice Reed said two hours later when they'd gone over wedding gowns and she'd taken all the necessary measurements. All of Savannah's friends had come with her to Two Willows, and now they were climbing into James's barouche to head home again. Savannah felt she was floating on air as she walked; Alice's initial designs for her wedding gown were wonderful.

"Thank you so much—for everything," Savannah told her. "You'd better make the dress big enough for an alteration or two. I'm putting on weight—and not just up top anymore."

"You'll look like a princess," Alice assured her. She'd sketched a Regency style gown with a fitted bodice and straight skirts that would hide the small baby bump Savannah had begun to sport and emphasize what had become an imposing bosom, as Alice had put it. She'd shown Savannah several elegant fabric choices and they'd decided on one that suited her perfectly. What was even better, Alice had sketched her hair done up with a trailing veil and a small but beautiful tiara.

"Where are you going to find a tiara?" Savannah had asked her.

"I have my sources," Alice said. "Just you wait and see."

"A tiara!" Avery exclaimed when she saw the drawing. "I want one of those, too, when I marry. If I marry," she added glumly.

"You'll marry." Savannah had given her a squeeze. "Meanwhile, I think my bridesmaids deserve tiaras, too. Don't you?"

"Absolutely," Alice had said.

Savannah said her goodbyes and climbed into the barouche, took a seat next to Riley and leaned back as James clucked to the horses and they began to move. She sighed with contentment, but remembered that Riley wasn't having nearly as easy a time of it as she was. She took her friend's hand and squeezed it. "You all right?"

"Yes." Riley squeezed her hand back. "Boone says we'll keep on trying. He says it's going to be okay."

"I'm sure it will be." But the ride home wasn't quite as happy as she'd hoped it would be. Savannah was worried for Riley. Despite the brave face she'd put on the situation, she knew her friend was hurting, and she longed to comfort her. She was worried about Win, too. She'd never seen the woman so distracted and upset as she'd been this morning.

"Uh oh, something's wrong," Nora said when they pulled up back at Base Camp some time later. Savannah shook off her reverie and craned her neck to see. Men stood gathered at the fire pit instead of working. Savannah and the others climbed down from the barouche as quickly as possible to see what had happened. A few moments later they joined the semi-circle of men standing around Angus.

"I don't think she's coming back," Savannah heard Angus say.

"Did she tell you that?" Boone demanded. He reached for the envelope in Angus's hand, but Angus passed it to Savannah instead.

"This is for you. I told Win I'd deliver it."

"For me?" Suddenly cold in the warm September day, Savannah took the envelope in fingers that had lost their strength. She opened it and pulled out a note. Savannah recognized this type of formal stationary—her mother had bought some once they had begun to rise in Silicon Valley's society—even though as a programmer she disdained *snail mail*, as she called it.

She opened the letter and read:

Dear Savannah,

Don't think of me too harshly as you read this. You'll understand far better than anyone else why I'm doing this, since you know my background. You may have turned your back on your family, but I find that I can't. Mom isn't just ill—she's got cancer—and she's not going to recover. And her wish is that I take my place back at home where I belong. She's backed up this threat with a big stick, just in case appealing to my daughterly guilt isn't enough—

Win's handwriting grew wobbly here and Savannah had to squint to make it out.

She's threatened to write me out of her will. In fact, she's already done so. I'm required to leave the show permanently and spend the rest of the year in California before she'll think of reversing her decision. She wants me to miss the deadline to marry Angus, so that he'll have to marry someone else. She says it's because he's against everything my family stands for, but I know that's not it: she thinks I'll be unhappy with him.

I can picture your reaction—your confusion. You thought I'd already given all that up. That my love for Angus would overcome everything else.

You're right; I love Angus. More than anyone I've ever loved before.

But not enough; it turns out it's one thing to leave your money behind—and it's another thing altogether to have it taken away irrevocably.

At the end of the day, it turns out I'm just as shallow and selfish as everyone ever thought I was. I can't do it. I can't be poor. I'm not clever like Angus, or talented like you. Wealth is all I've had. It's all I know.

I hope you won't hate me too much. I hope you'll realize what this is costing me. Please tell Angus—tell him I love him. I really love him. But he's better off without me.

And please, please—marry Jericho with your heart high. Don't worry about me. I've made my bed and I'll sleep in it. Be happy, Savannah. For my sake.

Love,
Win

Savannah looked up and met Angus's stricken gaze.

"They've taken her from me," he said, his accent even thicker than usual. "They didn't have to do that—I didn't want her money. I've plenty of my own. Maybe not a fortune, but—"

"I know." Savannah reached for his hand. "Don't give up on her, Angus. She doesn't mean this. She can't."

He nodded, but his eyes told a different story. "Thing is, lass, I think she does."

CHAPTER THIRTEEN

"RILEY—WOULD YOU AND the other women excuse us for a minute?" Boone said.

"Of course."

Jericho squeezed Savannah's hand before she walked away with her friends. He knew why Boone wanted the men to meet alone, but he hated the way Savannah's happiness had drained away as she'd read Win's letter. He wanted nothing to spoil their wedding.

But it wasn't just about the wedding. They could lose Westfield over this if Angus gave up and left the show. All ten of them had to marry before the year was up—that was Fulsom's rule. There wasn't a substitution clause that would allow them to find a man to take Angus's place. All or nothing.

Their future hinged on what came next.

A camera crew filed into the bunkhouse with them. Jericho wanted to push them out the door, but the show stopped for nothing and no one. That was the problem.

Angus knew that as well as anyone.

"Angus, I'm sorry Win's gone," Boone began when

everyone was situated. He jammed his hands in his pockets. "Maybe Savannah's right. Maybe she'll come back."

Angus shook his head. "I don't think so. She was pretty clear."

"I don't understand why she's changed her mind. She seemed perfectly happy here," Clay put in.

"She was play acting. Like playing house," Angus said. "Dressing up. Playing at doing all the chores her... *servants*... used to do for her."

Jericho wasn't the only one who winced at the bitterness in the man's words.

Angus rubbed a hand over his face. "Ah, don't you get it. She's not rich—she's wealthy. There's a difference. She's in a whole different league than I ever could be—"

"Don't say that," Jericho said.

"Why not?" Angus rounded on him. "Why not put it plain? She's too good for me. Her mother knows it. She knows it. I know it."

"It's not like that anymore," Harris tried.

"Isn't it? Really? Are you saying there's no class system here? Because I see it." He gazed at them each in turn. "Isn't that what Base Camp is partly about? The rest of us trying to salvage a world the rich have plundered?"

"It's not that simple," Boone said quietly.

"I think it is to a lot of people. You're always talking about resources," Angus said angrily. "Well, who owns those resources? The poor? Of course not—but we're asking them to bear the brunt of the solution, aren't we?"

"That's not true," Clay said. "We're trying to show people how they can live with less—"

"What people?" Angus demanded. "People like Win? Like her family? You think they're going to give up their mansions and move into a box dug into a hillside? The oil men, the mining companies, the billionaires—they're not going to join us!"

Jericho told himself it was the man's grief making him so angry, even though he couldn't deny the truth of what Angus was saying.

"Fulsom's funding us, for God's sake!" Boone pointed out.

"And where did his money come from? Originally? Did you ever look into that?"

"Tech," Boone answered him. "Like everyone else this century—"

"Bullshit." Angus paced the floor. "Fulsom was born rich. His family has had money forever. Dig deep enough, and you're going to find something you don't like, Boone."

Boone lifted his hands. "Sounds to me like what you're saying is you're done. Which means we're all done."

Angus met his gaze. Held it. "What I'm saying is I don't know what the fuck I'm doing anymore."

Jericho stepped back to let Angus walk out.

WHEN THE MEN filed into the bunkhouse, none of the

women needed urging to turn and head up to the manor. Savannah understood perfectly well why the men wanted some time alone. Everyone had expected Angus to marry Win when the time came. The two had been inseparable almost since the day Win came to Westfield for Savannah's cousin's wedding. Win had changed so much since then—dropping her haughty, money-is-everything attitude almost overnight when she realized there was another way to live.

But she hadn't really dropped it, had she? Savannah's strides slowed as she considered this. In the end, money had won out. Was it so important to Win to feel better than everyone else? She was a businesswoman herself—couldn't she have made her own fortune…?

No, Savannah supposed. Not here in Chance Creek, most likely.

Not like the fortune she stood to inherit someday from her mother, anyway.

But what a devil's bargain, she thought, taking in the camera crew trudging after them, filming even now. Could Win stand to lose Angus forever for money in the bank?

Savannah felt claustrophobic just thinking about a life like that. She was happy she'd faced her own demons and found peace and happiness with what she was building here. Win would have to start all over again, and after seeing her with Angus, Savannah couldn't believe Win would be happy with anyone else.

How could money trump love?

"What if Angus leaves?" Avery said.

"Then we lose Westfield," Riley said, her voice wavering.

Savannah's heart squeezed for her. Riley's roots here went deep. She loved Westfield and she'd faced so much pain lately.

"He has to stay," Nora said fiercely. "We can't lose all of this."

"We can't force a man to marry someone he doesn't love," Savannah said.

"Then we have to find someone for him to love," Avery said.

Savannah wasn't sure that was possible. Could Angus's broken heart heal fast enough?

"He'd better not draw the short straw when it comes time," Samantha said quietly.

The group finished their walk in silence.

Please, Savannah found herself praying. *Please let us not lose Westfield. Please let Angus find a way to stay.*

She didn't think she could take losing all of this just when she'd finally found her home.

JERICHO WAS PACING the banks of Pittance Creek again when Angus stumbled down the path late that night and they both came to a halt when they spotted each other. All day and evening conversations had been muted and people carried out their tasks in a watchful silence. Long after everyone settled in their houses and tents, Jericho had lain awake, until he couldn't stand it anymore. He was glad the camera crews had called it a night by the time he'd slowly climbed out again. He'd been as quiet as he could coming down to the creek. He needed time to think.

"I can leave you alone," Jericho said when it looked like the other man would turn and retrace his steps.

"You don't have to." Angus heaved a sigh. "Got myself in a right mess, haven't I?"

"It's not your fault."

"No. It's no one's fault."

It seemed to Jericho Win shouldered a lot of the blame, but he didn't say that out loud. Angus still loved her.

"It's hard for her," Angus said. "I should have seen that. Done more to bridge the gap between her old life and this."

"It's a big change for all of us."

"Really?"

No, Jericho had to admit. It wasn't for him—or for the other men, who'd all served in conditions that made Base Camp look palatial.

"It's hard on all the women," he amended. "They didn't come here for austerity. But I feel like Base Camp isn't all that austere." They'd done so much to make life interesting. The work, the meetings, the meals around the fire pit all energized him.

But Win was different, he supposed.

"Do you think Win would have been happy here long term?" Jericho asked.

"See, that's the hard part," Angus told him, pacing away. He stopped a few yards off, then turned to face Jericho. "If I knew for certain she'd be unhappy, I could let her go. It would be the right thing to do. It would hurt, but then it would be over. But I don't know for certain... Not yet."

Uneasiness prickled down Jericho's spine. "Win came with me to pick Savannah's ring," he said, even though he wasn't sure he should.

Angus waited for him to go on.

"I picked out a plain one. I don't have a lot of cash," he explained. He saw Angus nod in the starlight. "Win got angry. She told me it was a mistake. She said a woman who was used to wealth wouldn't be happy without it. She picked out a far fancier ring—one I had to get a payment plan for. I don't mind that," he rushed to add. "Savannah deserves a beautiful ring. And Donovan doesn't need my cash after all. But Win was adamant about it." He hoped Angus understood what he was trying to say.

Angus nodded again. A moment later, he sighed. "I have to let her go, don't I?"

"I don't know. She was wrong about Savannah—"

Angus wasn't listening. "I have to let her go."

"HE TOLD BOONE he'll stay. He said when the time comes, Boone can find him a bride," Riley said the following morning when the women had come to the manor to do their chores. Even though they didn't live there anymore, it took a lot of work to keep up such a big house. Dust settled on flat surfaces no matter how many times they wiped it off. Floors needed sweeping, windows cleaning. They did a little every day and kept on top of it.

Today no one went to grab a broom or mop, however. They gathered in the kitchen to talk over their future.

"That's brave of him," Avery said. "Most men would have left."

"He still believes in Base Camp," Riley told her.

"Win could come back," Savannah pointed out.

"Would he want her if she did? She left him," Nora said.

Savannah couldn't answer that. Was Angus that proud? Some men were.

"I don't think I'm going to breathe easy until the year is up," Riley said. "There's too much that could go wrong."

"I know what you mean," Avery said.

"Well, it's time to focus on happy things," Nora said resolutely. "We haven't lost Westfield yet. There's still time for Angus to find a wife whether Win comes back or not. Meanwhile, we've got to prepare for Savannah's wedding."

"And our guests coming next month," Avery said, rallying.

"You're right; we've got lots to do," Riley said. "And I've got a list for each of you…"

Savannah groaned along with everyone else. Riley and her lists. But she took hers gladly. Nora was right. They had to keep going no matter what.

Her baby fluttered inside her and she touched her belly. "I don't ever want to leave," she said.

"No one's leaving," Samantha assured her. "This is too important."

"She's right," Avery said. "You all mean so much to me."

"That's how I feel," Riley said.

"Me, too," Nora chimed in.

"Then we won't give up," Savannah said. "Not on Win, or Angus, or our future. Somehow we're going to work this out."

Because she wasn't willing to give up this community no matter what.

A knock on the back door startled her.

"Meeting at the bunkhouse," Byron said when he poked his head into the kitchen. "We're screening the next episode."

"Oh, lord," Nora groaned, but all the women stood up. There was no getting out of these meetings, they'd learned.

Fifteen minutes later, they all sat on folding chairs in the bunkhouse while Boone and Renata fiddled with a laptop and large monitor. When the episode started, Savannah sat back and crossed her arms, knowing she wouldn't like it.

It started with a recap of the men drawing straws before Harris and Samantha's wedding, an awkward scene that left Savannah wriggling in her seat as she watched Jericho realize he'd drawn the short straw. There was footage of their discussion with Regan about babysitting, and then the wedding itself, which drew ooh's and aah's as Samantha walked down the aisle in her beautiful gown. The show moved on to the photo shoot at the Hall's place. The party at the bunkhouse. There was footage of Jericho meeting Donovan. Of her waiting for her audition with Redding.

But as the episode went on, Savannah realized something was missing.

It took nearly the whole show for her to realize what it was. When the episode ended, and the bunkhouse stayed quiet, Renata walked to the front of the room.

"Do you see the problem?" she asked.

Savannah straightened. So it wasn't just her?

Renata's gaze took them all in one by one. "Savannah? You look like you have something to say."

"You left out most of the important parts."

"That's right." Renata nodded. She was far more subdued than Savannah had ever seen her before. "In fact, I don't know what those parts are. But I can tell they're missing. And why is that?"

"You should be telling us, don't you think?" Clay asked.

"Because none of them happened on screen," Savannah said.

"That's because the important parts are personal," Jericho said.

"We don't all want to air our dirty laundry on film," Angust put in.

"Why should we expose ourselves like that?" Avery agreed.

"Because we're trying to show people what's important," Savannah said. For the first time she almost felt a kinship with the director. "You didn't get my conversation with Jericho about commuting to California to work with Redding. We talked about whether or not it was right to travel so much when we're supposed to be living a sustainable life here."

"That would have been interesting," Renata said.

Jericho frowned. "I don't want to be filmed while we argue."

"But it was an argument people need to hear," Savannah told him.

"Maybe."

"You didn't find out I was pregnant until I lost the baby," Riley said softly.

"There's no need for something like that to be on the show," Boone said. "You were upset."

"Of course I was. But miscarriages are more common than people think," Riley said. "And yet women feel so alone when it happens to them."

"You didn't film me confronting my parents about the past, either," Jericho said slowly. "Or me reconciling with my dad."

"Some people might have benefitted from seeing that," Renata agreed. "Look, I know it seems like we go for sensational—"

"You do go for sensational," Boone overrode her. "Don't even pretend you don't."

"Okay, I won't. But we also go for real, heartfelt and true. And if you all would be a little more brave—"

"We might end up helping people," Savannah said.

"Maybe," Nora said.

"Yeah, maybe," Avery echoed.

"Think about it," Renata said. "Tomorrow's another day. Get out there and be real."

JERICHO WAITED A couple of days before he brought up resizing the ring with Savannah again. He didn't want Angus's unhappiness to spill over onto their future, and he was already worried that the ring wasn't right. It made him uncomfortable that Win had been involved in the process of picking it out, when he thought she might have already been thinking about leaving Westfield. She'd been so angry when he'd chosen the plainer ring. He figured that anger had been about her own situation—not his and Savannah's.

"Let's go to town," he said to Savannah after lunch one afternoon. "I'll get Kai and Greg set up for the next hour or two and we can head to Thayer's."

"Okay."

In the truck fifteen minutes later, Jericho cast a backward glance at the crew that had joined them, sighed, and decided to follow Renata's orders. He'd be real.

He handed Savannah the velvet box that held the ring before starting the engine and pulling out toward town.

"Better check it out again—decide if it's really the one you want," he told her.

"The one I want?" She turned to him in surprise. "Of course it's the one I want; you gave it to me."

"Maybe you wanted to pick out your own."

"Jericho, the only reason I haven't worn it is because it would fall off. It's too big." She clutched the little box as if she was afraid he'd take it from her.

"Maybe that's a sign—that it's not the right one."

"It's not a sign... otherwise people would only get to buy rings that already fit them. What's this really about?"

Jericho's hands tightened on the wheel. What was this about? Without having to send payments to Donovan, he could afford the ring she held in her hands.

"Is this going to be enough for you?" he finally asked. "Westfield? Base Camp?"

"Yes," she said without hesitation. "Absolutely. I'm happy here, Jericho. Happier than I've ever been anywhere else. I'm not Win," she added.

"Win helped me choose the ring. Actually, she told me the ring I picked was wrong. She was right," he went on quickly, realizing it was true. "The ring I picked was all wrong. And you know what?"

"What?"

"I like the one she chose," he admitted. "She knows her stuff."

"Win does know her stuff," Savannah said, laughing. "She wears beautiful jewelry. I'm always envious. But if the ring is too expensive—"

"It's not," Jericho told her. "I just want it to be right. I want us to be right."

"We're perfect," Savannah told him. She leaned over and kissed him. "And so's the ring. If you're sure."

"I'm sure."

He was. About everything.

WHEN SAVANNAH ENTERED Thayer's, with Jericho and the cameramen right behind her, she spotted Rose Johnson behind the counter helping another customer, and remembered the rumors that swirled around the woman. She supposedly could get a glimpse of a couple's future if she held the bride's engagement ring.

Was that what had happened? Savannah went cold. Had Rose held the ring when Jericho bought it and seen... something bad?

Suddenly, she didn't want to approach the counter. She cast around for something to slow their progress. The path to her engagement to Jericho had been so rocky, she didn't think she could stand any more obstacles.

"Look," she said, pointing to a pair of diamond-studded cuff links. "Maybe you should get something like those while we're here."

"I don't think so." Jericho shot her a funny look.

"No, I guess not." Savannah hung her head. What was she saying? She'd just convinced Jericho she wasn't like Win. He'd doubt her intentions if she kept acting like this.

"Maybe... Maybe we shouldn't get the ring re-sized. Maybe it fits," she tried again.

"Savannah." Jericho stopped and peered down at her. "You just said it would fall off."

"I could..." What could she do? Wrap it with yarn?

He was right; the ring needed to be fixed.

"What's going on?" he added.

"What did Rose say about our future?" Savannah demanded.

She thought Jericho would laugh the question off, but he blinked, and suddenly Savannah knew she was right. Rose had held the ring; she'd seen something.

Something bad.

"She told me… there was more going on than I knew. And you know what?" He laughed. "She was right."

They both stared at the petite woman still helping another woman at the counter. Rose looked up, smiled and waved at them. "I'll be with you in a minute," she called.

"She'll have to hold it again in order to fix it," Savannah told him.

Jericho nodded slowly.

"We could go somewhere else," Savannah suggested.

"Yeah." But Jericho didn't move.

"Well?"

"Are we really going to let someone else tell us how things turn out?"

She saw his point. Shouldn't their relationship be stronger than that?

"I say we stay," he said. "Let's do this. I love you. That's not going to change."

"I love you, too," Savannah said. "You're right. No one else can determine our future." She lifted her chin.

She was committed to making their marriage work.

He took her arm and they walked together to where Rose had just handed a bag to the other customer. "Have a good day, now. Thanks for shopping at Thayer's." She turned to Jericho and Savannah. "Hey, you two. I'm so glad to see you. How do you like your ring, Savannah?"

"I love it. But it's a little big." With shaking hands, she pulled the ring from its box, took a deep breath and handed it to Rose. "Can you fix it?"

Rose took it and closed her eyes.

A broad grin spread over her face. "I can make it smaller, but I don't see anything that needs fixing here."

CHAPTER FOURTEEN

I 'M NERVOUS," SAVANNAH said the evening before their wedding. Jericho stood with her in her room at the manor preparing for the rehearsal dinner that was to take place downstairs in a matter of minutes. Maud had sent Mrs. Wood, her cook, over to prepare the meal, and a banquet table had been set up in the ball-room. Her parents had arrived in Chance Creek just after noon, and Jericho had already met them at a stiff, but passably friendly, afternoon tea at the Cruz ranch guest house where they were staying. He felt he could face them tonight without worry. His parents, sister and brother-in-law would attend the rehearsal and dinner, as would his aunt, uncle, Donovan and Jackie. He was far more worried about how that might go.

After much debate, they'd decided not to serve al-cohol at dinner. His parents were sober, and Kara was only newly so. Savannah couldn't drink because of the baby, and he didn't want to put the temptation in front of his aunt and uncle; according to Donovan, they'd begun to discuss the possibility of seeking help once they found out they were going to be grandparents. Jericho worried the affair might be stilted without the social lubrication that alcohol provided, but when he'd expressed his fears to Maud and James, the couple assured him they'd thrown many such parties successfully.

"The key is the food," Maud swore, "and with Mrs. Wood preparing it, you won't have to worry. A well-prepared appetizer can be the equivalent of several glasses of champagne. You'll see."

Jericho wasn't sure he believed her, but it was too late now. "We'll be fine," he told Savannah. "All families have their issues. Why should ours be any different?"

"If it gets too bad we'll run away and elope."

"Then Avery won't be able to wear her tiara," Jericho told her.

"Lord, we don't want that." Savannah laughed and Jericho's heart throbbed. He loved it when his fiancée was happy. "You're right," she went on. "No matter what happens we have to make this work because I'll never hear the end of it otherwise."

Jericho had wondered what it would feel like to see his aunt and uncle after so much time had passed, but when the moment came, it was as if he'd seen them only yesterday. His aunt cried out happily when she caught a glimpse of him, pulled him into an embrace and hugged him hard. "Jericho, look at you. Just—look at you!" There were tears in her eyes as she hugged him again. His uncle shook his hand briskly when she finally released him.

"Glad to see you. You've grown into a fine man. Very proud of you."

"We always watch your show," Patty said.

Jericho introduced them to Savannah. "This is my fiancée. Savannah, meet my aunt Patty and my uncle Chris."

He had another moment of trepidation when it came time to introduce the families to each other, but to his surprise, Donovan stepped in and made it all easy by cracking jokes, and giving them each a moniker that soon had them all in stitches. He kept control of the social reins through the evening, bossing around all the guests so skillfully, Jericho was able to sit back and enjoy the rehearsal, and the meal, something he hadn't anticipated doing.

When Savannah's mother tilted her head back and roared with laughter at one of Donovan's off-color jokes, he knew everything would be okay. He took Savannah's hand under the table. "I love you."

"I can't wait for tomorrow," Savannah said.

"Me, neither."

After dinner, under Avery's urging, a number of the men worked together to roll the baby grand piano from the parlor to the ballroom. Others worked to move the rest of the furniture in the room aside, and soon Savannah was able to take a seat on the bench and begin to play a boisterous waltz. Jericho, not willing to let Donovan take center stage all evening, asked Savannah's mother to dance. Donovan asked Jericho's mother, and soon a half-dozen couples swirled around the room.

When Savannah's father tapped on his shoulder and claimed his wife again, Jericho went and grabbed Avery and whirled her briskly around the floor.

"Thank you. I hate sitting out dances," Avery told him, laughing as he turned her more abruptly than was strictly necessary and her dress flew around her ankles.

"My pleasure." He'd like to have been dancing with Savannah, but since she was busy providing the music, he figured he'd squire around as many of the other women as possible. A sharp tap on his shoulder startled him and he stumbled when he found Walker glowering behind him. "Don't get your feathers in a ruffle," Jericho told him. "You snooze, you lose." He pretended he was going to keep dancing and laughed out loud when Walker gave him a hard shove that knocked him into Clay and Nora. "Sorry," he told them and made his way to Savannah's side, happy that the big man had taken the bait and now wouldn't leave Avery's side for the rest of the evening.

"You handled that well," Savannah said over the lively music of the waltz.

"I aim to please."

"You are rather pleasing." She looked him up and down.

He kissed her, and the notes of the song went a little funny for a minute or two. No one seemed to mind.

As his parents spun by, dancing together now, his father nodded at him, obviously enjoying himself. Savannah's parents came by only moments later.

"I get it now," her mother called out.

Savannah botched another set of notes and looked up at Jericho. "What did she mean? Look at her—she's smiling!"

Jericho watched Savannah's parents dance, and wondered how many lives had been changed in the course of their coming together. "I think she's happy," he told Savannah.

"I know I am."

"I ALWAYS KNEW I was meant to wear a crown," Avery said the following afternoon as they gathered in Savannah's room to prepare for the wedding.

Savannah was so happy she felt fit to burst, but thankfully Alice had measured well and her gown fit perfectly and camouflaged her pregnancy. Not that it mattered, she thought. Everyone knew her condition. But still, she was glad to retain her figure for the photographs she knew she'd cherish for the rest of her life.

"You look very regal," Savannah told her. "We all do." No matter what tradition dictated, she'd told Riley and Nora they had to stand with her as her bridesmaids, too. They'd gone into this adventure together and she needed them by her side now that she was marrying the man she loved. As the four of them stood together, their graceful tiaras glinting in the sunlight filtering into the room, she thought all of them looked regal, but it wasn't the tiaras that did it; it was the wisdom they'd gained in the months since they'd come to Westfield. They'd endured hardship and pain and change in addition to the normal ups and downs of life. They'd all grown stronger—more resilient.

She knew she was ready to face whatever life might throw her way. It made her proud to know that downstairs lay a hand-written copy of the first real song she'd ever composed. A lullaby for her baby. One she'd be able to play and sing when her child was born. A special song belonging only to them.

She had more music in her—she knew she did. And her schedule was already filling with events and occasions at which she'd been invited to play. Some in town, some several hours away. She could see she'd keep very busy without even straying too far from home.

The more she sang, the more she realized she wanted that to be a part of her life, too, and she'd joined a local choir. This wasn't college; there weren't any tests or grades, so she didn't have to worry if she wasn't perfect. This was simply life—and she'd found she could do whatever she liked in it.

"Tonight you'll sleep in your very own tiny house," Riley reminded her.

"I can't wait to see it," Savannah said. She'd watched with interest as it had been built, of course, knowing it would soon belong to Jericho, but it had become a tradition for the wives not to see inside their houses until their wedding night, and Savannah was on pins and needles. All the tiny houses were beautifully made, and she'd share this one with Jericho. "I love it here," she exclaimed suddenly.

"I do, too," Riley said.

"Me, too," Nora agreed.

"Me, three—or make that four," Avery said.

Savannah grabbed Riley's hand and reached for Nora, who took hold of Avery, who reached for Riley and completed the circle. "Look at us. Look how far we've come. We're doing everything we set out to do and so much more. You three saved me from myself. I was creating a life that didn't suit me at all. I'd never have known Jericho without you. I'd never have embraced a life of music without you. Together we make miracles. And we'll keep making them, I swear to all of you. We won't stop making miracles until we're all happy."

"Hear, hear to that," Avery said loudly.

"Group hug!" Nora cried and they all fell into each other's arms.

The door opened and Savannah's mother poked her head in. "It's time."

"UH-OH," ANDERS SAID loudly when Walker entered the second-floor guest bedroom of the manor, where the men had gathered to ready themselves for the wedding.

Dressed in the old-fashioned uniforms they always donned for these occasions, they looked like a regiment prepared to march off to fight in the Revolutionary War. They'd worn them enough that most required few adjustments, but Alice was taking her time over Jericho's uniform, making sure it was just right.

"We all know what time it is," Boone said, following

Walker into the room.

Walker held up a fistful of twigs, all equally long—or so they appeared. Someone would draw the short straw in a minute. Or rather, short twig. Jericho was grateful he no longer had to worry about that.

"Four married, six to go," Boone intoned. "Angus, Anders, Kai, Curtis, Greg, let's go."

"What about Walker?" Curtis muttered.

"He's already here," Boone said.

The big man held out his fist toward Anders, who stood closest to him. With a sigh, Anders picked a twig, and chuckled when he held up a long one. "That's another forty days of freedom."

Greg picked next, and drew a long one, too. Angus stepped forward almost angrily, and grabbed one randomly from Walker's fist. Jericho was relieved for him when it turned out to be long, as well.

Kai was next and he choose his without a fuss—

But when he held up a short twig, his expression changed. His gaze caught Anders's, Jericho's, and Boone's in succession, and he paled.

"But—"

"Congratulations!" Boone clapped a hand on his shoulder. "One wife on the way, just like you ordered. I've already got a batch of responses from that ad for Jericho's backup bride."

"But—"

"You don't have a fiancée hidden away, do you?" Boone challenged him.

Kai shook his head.

"Then like I said, I'll be happy to provide one for you." He gave Kai's shoulder a friendly shake. "All right—it's time. Let's get out there and get this done." He stopped by Jericho on his way toward the door. "Do us proud."

"I will." Jericho wasn't nervous at all. Not like Kai, who looked about to have a breakdown. Or Walker, who still stood contemplating the last two twigs in his fist.

He was about to marry the woman he loved.

And he couldn't be happier.

MAUD AND JAMES had provided a string quartet for the wedding, and as the musicians struck up the chords of the traditional march, Savannah took a deep breath, knowing this truly was the happiest day of her life. Just a few short weeks ago, she'd despaired of ever winding up with Jericho. She'd thought she'd have to navigate her path through life and parenthood alone, but she'd found she was surrounded by friends who'd become her family—and would never let her be lonely for long.

She understood how much bravery it had required for Jericho to face the fear he couldn't protect their baby. She knew the depth of his love both for her and their child. She hoped she could show him how to keep that worry at bay long enough to live in the present and enjoy his family, but from what she'd seen, Jericho was already halfway there.

And now she didn't feel the need to prove her talent to her family, she'd found her days were all the richer

304 | CORA SETON

for the variety of tasks she took on. Whether it was playing the piano, singing, teaching, preparing for the next guests to stay at the bed and breakfast, or working with Jericho on the energy grid, she found herself energized and loving the busy complexity of her life.

Life would get even busier—and more complicated—when their baby arrived. But there would be countless hands to help ease the work—and countless hearts to share her triumph.

As the music struck up, first Avery, then Nora, then Riley stepped forward to walk down the aisle. Finally it was her turn.

"I'm proud of you," her father told her. "Proud of the way you held your ground and made the life you wanted to live. I'm sorry we caused you so much heartache, honey. Your mom and I got off track. We got tied up in an image of success that isn't serving us well. I think you'll see some changes from us, too. Big ones. We want to get back to our roots. Back to innovation. We stayed up talking all last night—so we might be tired today, but we're happy. Really happy—for the first time in a while." He kissed the top of her head.

Savannah's heart was full as she took the first steps of her journey down the aisle to where Jericho stood waiting for her, so handsome in his old-fashioned uniform. Boone, Clay and Walker stood with him and her heart swelled with the knowledge of how much it meant for him to have them by his side. They'd been there at his darkest moments, and now they were with him at his brightest. Love and gratitude filled her until she thought she'd burst.

As she took her position by Jericho's side, and her father kissed her and went to take his seat, she blinked back tears of happiness.

"Dearly Beloved," the minister began, and Savannah knew she'd truly come home to where she belonged. Her baby fluttered inside her and she placed a hand on her abdomen, full of anticipation for the life she was about to lead.

She loved Jericho.

She couldn't wait to be his wife.

WHEN JERICHO TOOK Savannah's hand and repeated the vows Reverend Halpern spoke, he thought his heart would burst with love for the woman beside him.

The last few months had been so tumultuous they'd had few quiet times together to solidify their relationship, and he looked forward to waking up with her every morning and going to bed with her every night. He knew it was the small things that would make all of this real. Sharing a home with her. Making decisions with her.

Holding her in his arms at night.

Jericho's whole body was aware of the beautiful woman next to him and the knowledge that she was pledging her heart to his—forever—humbled him in a way he'd never expected.

He swore he'd always protect her—and their child—to the best of his abilities, and he wouldn't let past failures cloud his mind or judgement.

He swore he'd keep his heart open, too, even when he was worried for what the future might bring. He didn't want to separate his heart from the ones he loved. He knew firsthand how painful that could be.

He swore he'd work twice as hard to make Base Camp a success and to find his place in spreading its message to the world. He knew it was still important— maybe more so than ever. Now that he'd have a child to inherit the world he made, it was paramount to protect that world, too.

But most of all he swore he'd be there for Savannah, now and forever. He swore to love her. Always.

"I now pronounce you man and wife. You may kiss the bride."

Jericho thought he'd never heard sweeter words in his life. He turned to face Savannah and found her looking up at him, her eyes wide with wonder and hope and... love.

That was enough, Jericho decided as he leaned down to kiss her and the crowd behind them cheered.

That was everything.

To find out more about Harris, Samantha, Boone, Riley, Clay, Jericho, Walker and the other inhabitants of Westfield, look for *A SEAL's Purpose*, Volume 5 in the *SEALs of Chance Creek* series.

Be the first to know about Cora Seton's new releases! Sign up for her newsletter here!

www.coraseton.com/sign-up-for-my-newsletter

Other books in the SEALs of Chance Creek Series:

A SEAL's Oath

A SEAL's Vow

A SEAL's Pledge

A SEAL's Purpose

A SEAL's Resolve

A SEAL's Devotion

A SEAL's Desire

A SEAL's Struggle

A SEAL's Triumph

Read on for an excerpt of **Issued to the Bride One Navy SEAL**.

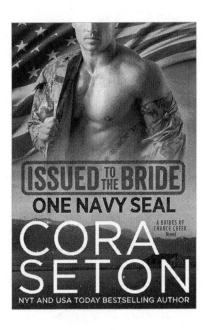

Read on for an excerpt of
Issued to the Bride One Navy SEAL.

Four months ago

ON THE FIRST of February, General Augustus Reed
entered his office at USSOCOM at MacDill Air
Force Base in Tampa, Florida, placed his battered
leather briefcase on the floor, sat down at his wide,
wooden desk and pulled a sealed envelope from a
drawer. It bore the date written in his wife's beautiful
script, and the General ran his thumb over the words
before turning it over and opening the flap.

He pulled out a single page and began to read.

Dear Augustus,

It's time to think of our daughters' future, beginning with Cass.

The General nodded. Spot on, as usual; he'd been thinking about Cass a lot these days. Thinking about all the girls. They'd run yet another of his overseers off Two Willows, his wife's Montana ranch, several months ago, and he'd been forced to replace him with a man he didn't know. There was a long-standing feud between him and the girls over who should run the place, and the truth was, they were wearing him down. Ten overseers in eleven years; that had to be some kind of a record, and no ranch could function well under those circumstances. Still, he'd be damned if he was going to put a passel of rebellious daughters in charge, even if they were adults now. It took a man's steady hand to run such a large spread.

Unfortunately, it was beginning to come clear that Bob Finchley didn't possess that steady hand. Winter in Chance Creek was always a tricky time, but in the months since Finchley had taken the helm, they'd lost far too many cattle. The General's spies in the area reported the ranch was looking run-down, and his daughters hadn't been seen much in town. The worst were the rumors about Cass and Finchley—that they were dating. The General didn't like that at all—not if the man couldn't run the ranch competently—and he'd asked for confirmation, but so far it hadn't come. Finchley always had a rational explanation for the loss of cattle, and he never said a word about Cass, but the General knew something wasn't right and he was already looking for the man's replacement.

Our daughter runs a tight ship, and I'm sure she's been invaluable on the ranch.

He had to admit what Amelia wrote was true. Cass was an organizational wizard. She kept her sisters, the house and the family accounts in line, and not for the first time he wondered if he should have encouraged Cass to join the Army back when she had expressed interest. She'd mentioned the possibility once or twice as a teenager, but he'd discouraged her. Not that he didn't think she'd make a good soldier; she'd have made a fine one. It was the thought of his five daughters scattered to the wind that had guided his hand. He couldn't stomach that. He needed his family in one place, and he'd done what it took to keep her home. That wasn't much: a suggestion her sisters needed her to watch over them until they were of age, a mention of tasks undone on the ranch, a hint she and the others would inherit one day and shouldn't she watch over her inheritance? It had done the trick.

Maybe he'd been wrong.

But if Cass had gone, wouldn't the rest of them have followed her?

He'd been able to stop sending guardians for the girls when Cass turned twenty-one five years ago, much to everyone's relief. His daughters had liked those about as little as they liked the overseers. He'd hoped when he dispensed of the guardians, the girls would feel they had enough independence, but that wasn't the case; they still wanted control of the ranch.

Cass is a loving soul with a heart as big as Montana, but she's cautious, too. I'll wager she's beginning to think there isn't a man alive she can trust with it.

The General sighed. His girls hadn't confided in him in years—especially about matters of the heart—something he was glad Amelia couldn't know. The truth was his daughters had spent far too much time as teenagers hatching plots to cast off guardians and overseers to have much of a social life. They'd been obsessed with being independent, and there were stretches of time when they'd managed it—and managed to run the show with no one the wiser for months. In order to pull that off, they'd kept to themselves as much as possible. He'd only recently begun to hear rumblings about men and boyfriends. Unfortunately, none of the girls were picking hardworking men who might make a future at Two Willows; they were picking flashy, fly-by-night troublemakers.

Like Bob Finchley.

He couldn't understand it. He wanted that man out of there. Now. Trouble was, when your daughters ran off so many overseers it made it hard to get a new one to sign on. He had yet to find a suitable replacement.

Without a career off the ranch, Cass won't get out much. She might not ever meet the man who's right for her. I want you to step in. Send her a man, Augustus. A good man.

A good man. Those weren't easy to come by in this world. The right man for Cass would need to be strong to hold his own in a relationship with her. He'd need to be fair and true, or he wouldn't be worthy of her. He'd need some experience ranching.

A lot of experience ranching.

The General stopped to ponder that. He'd read something recently about a man with a lot of experience ranching. A good man who'd gotten into a spot of trouble. He remembered thinking he ought to get a second chance—with a stern warning not to screw up again. A Navy SEAL, wasn't it? He'd look up the document when he was done.

He returned to the letter.

> *Now here's the hard part, darling. You can't order him to marry Cass any more than you can order Cass to marry him. You're a cunning old codger when you want to be, and it'll take all your deviousness to pull this off. Set the stage. Introduce the players.*
>
> *Let fate do the rest.*
>
> *I love you and I always will,*
> *Amelia*

Set the stage. Introduce the players.

The General read through the letter a second time, folded it carefully, slid it back into the envelope and added it to the stack in his deep, right-hand bottom drawer. He steepled his hands and considered his options. Amelia was right; he needed to do something to make sure his daughters married well. But they'd rebelled against him for years, so he couldn't simply assign them husbands, as much as he'd like to. They'd never allow the interference.

But if he made them think they'd chosen the right men themselves...

He nodded. That was the way to go about it.

In fact...

The General chuckled. Sometime in the next six months, his daughters would stage another rebellion and evict Bob Finchley from the ranch. He could just about guarantee it, even if Cass was currently dating the man. Sooner or later he'd go too far trying to boss them around, and Cass and the others would flip their lids.

When they did, he'd be ready for them with a replacement they'd never be able to shake. One trained to combat enemy forces by good ol' Uncle Sam himself. A soldier in the Special Forces might do it. Or maybe even a Navy SEAL...

This wasn't the work of a moment, though. He'd need time to put the players in place. Cass wasn't the only one who'd need a man—a good man—to share her life.

Five daughters.

Five husbands.

Amelia would approve.

The General opened the bottom left-hand drawer of his desk, and mentally counted the remaining envelopes that sat unopened in another stack, all dated in his wife's beautiful script. Ten years ago, after Amelia passed away, Cass had forwarded him a plain brown box filled with envelopes she'd received from the family lawyer. The stack in this drawer had dwindled compared to the opened ones in the other drawer.

What on earth would he do when there were none left?

End of Excerpt

The Cowboys of Chance Creek Series:

The Cowboy Inherits a Bride (Volume 0)
The Cowboy's E-Mail Order Bride (Volume 1)
The Cowboy Wins a Bride (Volume 2)
The Cowboy Imports a Bride (Volume 3)
The Cowgirl Ropes a Billionaire (Volume 4)
The Sheriff Catches a Bride (Volume 5)
The Cowboy Lassos a Bride (Volume 6)
The Cowboy Rescues a Bride (Volume 7)
The Cowboy Earns a Bride (Volume 8)
The Cowboy's Christmas Bride (Volume 9)

The Heroes of Chance Creek Series:

The Navy SEAL's E-Mail Order Bride (Volume 1)
The Soldier's E-Mail Order Bride (Volume 2)
The Marine's E-Mail Order Bride (Volume 3)
The Navy SEAL's Christmas Bride (Volume 4)
The Airman's E-Mail Order Bride (Volume 5)

The SEALs of Chance Creek Series:

A SEAL's Oath
A SEAL's Vow
A SEAL's Pledge
A SEAL's Consent
A SEAL's Purpose
A SEAL's Resolve
A SEAL's Devotion
A SEAL's Desire
A SEAL's Struggle
A SEAL's Triumph

The Brides of Chance Creek Series:

Issued to the Bride One Navy SEAL
Issued to the Bride One Airman
Issued to the Bride One Marine
Issued to the Bride One Sniper
Issued to the Bride One Soldier

About the Author

NYT and USA Today bestselling author Cora Seton loves cowboys, hiking, gardening, bike-riding, and lazing around with a good book. Mother of four, wife to a computer programmer/backyard farmer, she recently moved to Victoria and looks forward to a brand new chapter in her life. Like the characters in her Chance Creek series, Cora enjoys old-fashioned pursuits and modern technology, spending mornings in her garden, and afternoons writing the latest Chance Creek romance novel. Visit **www.coraseton.com** to read about new releases, contests and other cool events!

Blog:

www.coraseton.com

Facebook:

www.facebook.com/coraseton

Twitter:

www.twitter.com/coraseton

Newsletter:

www.coraseton.com/sign-up-for-my-newsletter

Made in the USA
Middletown, DE
10 February 2017